STORMKINDLER

EMILY BARLOW

For my mom, who has always encouraged my hobbies, whatever they may be.

CHAPTER 1

Cold wind sliced across the gathered tribespeople, seeking any chink it could find in their sealskin clothing. They stood in a rough semicircle in the bare twilight that passed for night at the year's apex, their brown faces turned toward the shoreline and the smaller group standing beside it. The tide was neap and the time ripe for the start of their journey.

One figure stepped forward. A shock of white hair loosened in the wind and fluttered across her weathered features as she approached her kin. She raised her hands above the group and intoned a blessing in the ancient language, the one their ancestors spoke and few now remembered, then reached into her shirt and produced a jar of seal oil kept warm and soft by the heat of her own body. Working quickly, she anointed the foreheads of the ship's crew, speaking a soft benediction to each in turn. The young boy she saved for last; her eyes narrowed to slits buried in the folds of her wrinkles as she reversed the anointing motion, then spat into the snow. "You I will not bless," she explained, "for you will not return to the people after your job is done. Your kind have no home here." With that she turned and stalked back to the waiting assemblage.

The tallest of the crew, a lithe woman with black hair and olive skin, stepped forward and motioned for them to take their places aboard the vessel that waited in the harbor. The ice was thin this time of year and the seas free of its pincers, but the ship was built with a heavy enough keel to withstand a few impacts. Still, they could never chance returning in winter; no ship could navigate the northern waters during any time but the height of summer. It would be at least a year before they returned, if ever.

Taking one last look at her home, the woman boarded last of all the crew, a zealous fire in her dark eyes. They would return victorious–or not at all.

A week's travel lay before the crew as they cast off from the small pier. The northern seas were treacherous, even in summer, but their people had navigated these waters since the birth of their tribe; many of the water's mysteries were theirs to command. There was always the chance they might run afoul of other ships on their journey south. The shipping lanes–such as they were this far north–were plagued by pirates. The captain's eyes flicked involuntarily to the one crew member who'd waited for them aboard ship when they left. His red hair and pale skin marked him as an outsider, but it was his soul that made him an outcast, unworthy of a place with the people. *Unworthy, yes, but useful,* the captain thought, her boot heels clicking as she ascended the steps to the quarterdeck. The small band of sailors committed to their cause stood to attention and saluted. She gave the order for full sails and watched the craft leap away from the shore.

Captain Ordulla had sailed the northern seas most

of her life, but this trip was different. They would venture further south than she'd ever dared in the course of her fishing, hunting, and trading, and their purpose was far less commonplace. Too long had they allowed the cursed foreigners free reign to attack their vessels and steal their goods. Her people, though pure, were vulnerable on the seas, and they lost ships, cargo, and souls each year to the grasping, greedy outlanders. It was time to fight back, to stamp out the foreigners' advantage at its source and take control of their waters once again.

Whatever the cost.

Two days later

"You." Captain Ordulla's voice carried above the incessant wind to lash out at the figure languishing in the midday sun on the main deck. His pale skin blistered where it wasn't covered, showing his people's weakness to nature and the elements. Still, she had to admit his form was pleasing. He turned dulled eyes on the captain in response. Parched lips seeped pink blood into the stubble on his chin. "I am in need of your services." The man didn't respond, only gazed dumbly back at her.

She turned to the first mate, a middle-aged man with broad shoulders and a scar above his right eye bisecting his eyebrow. "Did we bring him along only to have to carry his dead weight?" she demanded.

"No, ma'am."

"Has he not been fed? Given shelter? Water?"

"None of the crew want anything to do with him, ma'am." The larger man looked sheepish in spite of the massive difference in their sizes.

"Then it falls to you, Sental." The captain regarded their prisoner with the same cold calculation she would turn upon a wrench or any other tool. "Clean him up, get some water in him, and give him something to eat, then bring him to my cabin. I have a use for him." She ignored the curled-lipped sneer on the first mate's face and turned on her heel. "You have one hour."

Sental was nothing if not efficient; three quarters of an hour later the pale-faced man was marched into the captain's quarters and shoved unceremoniously onto a hard wooden stool. His clothes were clean, but worn; his hair had been cut and his beard shaved, but his skin and lips still wore the ravages of the sun, and his wrists were chafed from the rope that bound them. Captain Ordulla circled him, waving for Sental to leave them. The first mate made no sound on his departure beyond that of the door clicking closed. Now to see how best to tame this foreign beast.

"What is your name?" the captain asked. A choked sound escaped his lips. When no discernible answer was forthcoming she tried again. "Your name, outlander. I grow tired of waiting." This time she was able to make out the word "water" in the garbled syllables, so she grabbed a waterskin from her desk and held it to the man's mouth. He drank freely until she deemed he'd had enough for his dehydrated state and replaced the cap. "Now, your name."

"Brizen," the man croaked.

"I would say 'well met,' but I think we both know pleasantries mean nothing between us." Captain Ordulla ceased her circling to pull up a chair, which she sat directly in front of the foreign devil so she could stare him in the eye as they spoke. "Let me be clear: you are alive because I have use for you. As your usefulness ends, so does your life." She waited five heartbeats to gauge the man's reaction. When his expression didn't shift from bleak apathy she moved on. "Your use to me is threefold. First, you will keep this vessel and its crew safe from high winds and other ships. I have seen your skill in this firsthand and know you to be capable. Second, there is a boy on this ship who is cursed, like you. You will teach him how to use his curse to help protect the crew and to carry out his mission. Do you understand?" The prisoner nodded warily; the water she'd given him was clearing his mind. She could see it on his face, in the small movements he hadn't made before.

"You said threefold," he half-whispered.

Captain Ordulla's eyes glinted as she stood from her chair. She trailed a finger across his shoulders as she strode around his stool, digging a nail in here and there where his blisters were the most raw, and stopped behind him. He went still, delicious fear running through his body as he did his best to lean away from his captor. Ordulla smiled and knew he could hear it in her voice as she leaned to whisper in his ear. "You are a beautiful man." Her tongue flicked out to caress his ear and she watched him shiver. "Keep me entertained and you may earn some freedom." Her teeth found the flesh of his earlobe and bit down on the blistered skin, puncturing it. "Disappoint me and your usefulness ends." Brizen went still and she pulled away to peer at his sunburned face. He refused to meet her gaze. *So easily conquered.* At least he would make the trip more entertaining.

The next morning Captain Ordulla awoke Brizen with the sun to begin training the young boy they'd brought along. He was small and thin and looked to have been ill treated; the crew gave him no breakfast, forcing him to pilfer what he could from the ship's stores when no one was looking. Brizen found him tucked between two barrels in the hold, trying his best to gnaw on the end of some hard tack.

"Best not to eat that without some tea," he hazarded. The boy looked up in alarm and clutched the biscuit to his chest. "Don't worry, I won't take it from you," Brizen explained. "I'm here to teach you."

"We're not supposed to listen to foreigners." Yet the boy boldly met his gaze.

"And you always do what you're told?"

"If I don't, I'm beaten." No rancor sounded in the boy's words, only a statement of fact. *What kind of life has he led?* Brizen wasn't good with children, having had none himself–at least, none of which he was aware–and he felt adrift in uncharted waters. *How am I supposed to teach him anything?* On the heels of that came remembrances of how he'd learned his own trade. The grizzled face of the old man who'd taught him to tame the winds and make them do his bidding floated across his mind's eye, bringing with it an involuntary shiver. He'd been a hard taskmaster, but fair.

"What if I'll do the same if you don't listen to me?"

Brizen warned. A part of him disliked hearing his own master's sentiments echo through his own mouth, but he shoved it aside. *He was hard for a reason. Life is hard. So must I be.* A lid of stone locked down on Brizen's emotions. In the last day he had gone from being a prisoner left out for the seagulls to becoming the captain's plaything in a way he hadn't been used since he was a cabin boy, and now he was expected to make something useful out of this cowering, abused scrape of a child. Anger suffused him with a wild energy and he snatched the young one's shabby, filthy shirt, pulling them face to face. "I've been tasked by the captain with making something of you before we get to port," he growled. "If I fail, she'll take my hide, bit by bit. So I will do whatever it takes to get you up to speed and trained up sharp like." He let go and watched the boy's feet slam onto the floor of the hold. "You and I are both unwanted creatures on this ship. What that means is that I can beat you within an inch of your life and no one–*no one* on this ship will care. Work with me and I can teach you how to use your abilities and turn them to your advantage; fight me and you'll regret you were ever born. Understood?" The boy nodded mutely at him, his hard tack forgotten on the floor beside him. "Good. Now pick up that tack and come with me." The boy scrambled to follow as Brizen climbed the stairs to the main deck.

The sun stared at them from just above the horizon. It was a clear day above them, but clouds threatened to the far east, just above where the sun sat perched. Brizen pointed them out. "See those clouds? I give them an hour before they bring us rain."

"But they're so far away," the boy answered.

"View distance is treacherous on the seas, boy. If

you can see it, it's within an hour of reaching your ship, and that's if you're lucky." He squinted, the blisters on his face heating in the sun and crinkling painfully. "Doesn't look like a thunderhead, though; just a squall."

"How can you tell? They just look like clouds to me."

"They're thin and gray, not thick and gray-blue," Brizen explained. His patience for questions and explanations already wore thin and they'd only just begun. "Think about the clouds you've seen at home when it's stormed. These are different."

"I remember snow clouds," the boy volunteered.

"Like snow clouds, but darker and heavier." Brizen pushed his sweat-dampened hair from his face lest the sweat sting his wounds. "Now, close your eyes and feel the breeze coming off the water." He demonstrated, holding onto the railing to keep his balance in the sea's light chop. The boy did the same, facing into the wind as soon as he found it. "See if you can find where it's coming from." He felt the working nearby as the boy reached out with his senses to find the wind's origin. It was an exercise Brizen used regularly to ground himself and stretch his limits. "Good; now find the exact thread that's running toward the ship and see if you can split it in half." Immediately the breeze fanning the ship from the starboard side died. Brizen could see the pennant hanging from the stern flapping in the wind, but on the main deck there was not even a whisper. "Let it go," he ordered, and the wind filled the sheets once again.

He rounded on the boy. "Who's been teaching you? Someone must have taught you the basics for you to be able to do that first try."

"N-no one," the boy stuttered. "I just...knew how

to do it. I've practiced on my own when no one was around, but no one has ever taught me anything." He winced and shied away as Brizen raised a hand, then lowered it without striking.

"They probably told you not to tell, didn't they? Or you'd both get in trouble?"

"No, sir; there really is no one–" The boy's words died as Brizen's hand flew across his face, leaving a cut on his lip.

"Lie to me one more time and both hands fly." Brizen wiped the blood from his knuckle on the boy's shirt. "What else can you do? Can you call a wind where none exists?" In response the boy woke a small breeze that lifted his hair in the opposite direction of the wind off the sea. "What about winds that are farther away? Can you push the clouds?" The boy's face screwed up in concentration and his cheeks turned beet red as he held his breath, exerting all his will to reach his senses into the sky and move the clouds with his windwaking. Brizen couldn't help but laugh; it was a trick his teacher had played on him early in his lessons. It wasn't possible for any one windwaker to do alone.

The laughter died on his tongue, leaving a bitter aftertaste in its wake. The closest of the rain clouds shifted direction until they sat to the south of the boat instead of the east. Beside him the boy blew out the breath he'd been holding and panted, dropping to one knee on the deck. Brizen stared down at him, this reed-thin youngling who'd lived his life tucked away in some nowhere part of the world, who could do weatherworking Brizen's own teacher couldn't equal.

And they were both stuck on this gods-forsaken voyage, the end of which held only their deaths.

He turned on his heel and marched back down into the hold to think.

CHAPTER 2

The next three days at sea put the ship past the danger of migrating icebergs and into the shipping lanes. Captain Ordulla trusted her crew to keep a sharp eye for any problems on the horizon and spent most of her time either in her cabin, enjoying the pleasures of her arrangement with Brizen, or watching him attempt to teach the boy they'd brought aboard. She didn't even know his name. She wasn't sure he had one, seeing as how his parents had left him with the elders at a young age with the expectation they would send him out to sea on the ice and let the ocean take him. But the elders had chosen to keep him with the knowledge that this mission–her mission–would require a sacrifice. And he was the perfect candidate.

"Ship off the port bow!" The call came from the crow's nest. Captain Ordulla pulled her spyglass from her belt and peered through it, scanning the horizon until she found it. They flew the colors of Zhedaba, but that meant little; most pirate vessels picked colors to fly and either changed them at the last minute or not at all.

"Beat to quarters!" she ordered. A sealskin drum sounded the alarm and the small crew rushed to man the few guns and single cannon they carried. "Brizen!" she barked. "Now's the time to earn your keep. You and the boy." The man nodded in response and took up a spot on the prow, dragging the boy with him. "See if you can give us enough speed to outrun them," she ordered, and the wind that had only touched the sails made them billow as the craft surged ahead. The captain took pleasure in the widening gap between her vessel and the closest pirates. *It's child's play when the field is even.*

A few minutes of full sail put them beyond the view of their pursuer. The captain asked for an extra ten minutes or so of full speed, then gave the cursed ones a break. They had earned their keep for the day; she would leave them to their own devices.

Besides, she had penance to do. Using the cursed souls came at a cost to her own; she had to purify herself each time she ordered them to use their curse in the name of their cause, holy as it was, or risk tainting the sanctity of their mission. Nodding to Sental, she retired to her quarters alone, locking the door as she passed through. By the time she reached the wall beside her bed she'd removed her clothing from the waist up. She knelt over a wooden frame at the foot of her bed and leaned her torso on its upper bar to support it. From beneath her bed she drew a stained scourge with knotted ends. *With this, the mortification of my flesh, I ask the ancients for forgiveness.* With all the strength her arm could produce she flung the weapon over her shoulder and rent her own skin, every knot on the flail ripping its own burning path. *May I succeed in my mission to rid the world of the cursed ones.* Another strike; she could feel the tender flesh peel further. *I give my body and soul to this*

cause, and I pray it is enough to see the ancients' will done.
A third hit and the blood trickled down her back. Satisfied, she returned the scourge to its place beneath her
bed and re-donned the white shirt she'd worn previously, heedless of the stains seeping into the cloth. They
let the crew know she took the burden of carrying the
cursed ones on herself.

Another few days saw them safely to Fisherman's
Watch, the northernmost port in Midlands. Captain
Ordulla had no more occasion to perform the purifying
rites; they avoided most of the regular shipping lanes
and were too small a craft to tempt the larger pirate
vessels plying the more southern waters. When they arrived she met with their contact in the red light district,
as planned. By sunrise the next day their boat cast off
to head north once again with full supplies and some
extra crew, but minus one young boy. Captain Ordulla trusted that Brizen had taught him enough to enact
their plan once he was in place. He was the lynch pin
in their grand scheme. Given what she'd seen, she was
sure it would be sufficient.

Headmaster Thayer,

Thank you for your letter notifying me of the death of Sunchaser Keross. He was a great mentor and friend, and shall be dearly missed by many of his former colleagues and pupils, myself included. I am honored to have studied with him during my time at Weatherwatch.

I will admit the second part of your letter took me quite by surprise. You will of course understand that I have many diverse obligations here, in Joveru, which I will need to discharge personally on occasion, and that I will need a few weeks to set my affairs in order and travel to Weatherwatch, but I will be honored to take up the mantle which my predecessor has laid down after so many successful years. I will, of course, need to use his cottage during my tenure, and I'm sure you will notify me as to any other subjects for which he was responsible so that I may endeavor to fill his shoes as seamlessly as possible. I would also like to request a briefing upon my arrival on the current affairs and state of the school so as to lessen the burden on my fellow teachers in getting me up to speed on school policies and expectations. We may speak about compensation after I arrive, as you seem to have omitted that information in your original request (a mere oversight, I'm sure).

It has been many years since I set foot in Weatherwatch Valley, but I shall be proud to once again call it home.

Sincerely,
Sunchaser Glorya, 5th Rank

CHAPTER 3

Glorya stepped out of the *Serpent's* guest quarters and onto the main deck, squinting into the brilliance that met her as she emerged. That the ship had been in port in Joveru close to her departure date was a lucky happenstance, especially once she found out they were headed for her final port of call. She waved to the captain up on the quarterdeck and smiled as he nodded in return. Captain Henrick was far more serious than he'd been the first time she sailed with the *Serpent* all those years ago, but Glorya supposed he had reason to be; with a merchant vessel and her crew under his command he carried a greater responsibility.

A young boy of about twelve scooted past her and up to the quarterdeck to stand beside his father. They were two peas in a pod, both broadly built and brown-haired with open countenances and quick minds. Glorya wondered what the boy's mother had been like; there must be something of her in him, though she knew not what to look for to find it. Henrick's wife had died a few years after their child was born. A moment's reverie made her wonder what life would've been like had she stayed with the Serpent and courted Henrick all those years past. He'd seemed willing, but was too good a man to hold her back when she decided to leave. *You could try again,* she mused, then immediately dismissed the idea. Her business was elsewhere, with the school that needed her–and with her niece, who had just come of age to leave home and study at Weatherwatch. *You promised Marya you'd take her. Time to make good on your word.*

She climbed the steps to the quarterdeck to watch alongside the captain as the ship pulled into Fisherman's Watch, confident her life was still on the right track despite–or perhaps because of–the opportunities she left in her wake.

That morning, in Farmer's Bend

Zayira had known for years this day would come. It had dawned like any other; the cock had crowed at first light, starting a chain of auditory events that culminated in the waking of the house, Zayira included. She'd pulled on her breeches–another hand-me-down set from her brother, Danil–found a work shirt, and headed straight for the barn. On her way she met a sleepy Maks, the oldest of the three siblings, on his way to let the cows out to pasture. He didn't even recognize that she was there, which wasn't unusual; it took breakfast and some coffee to get him going, and neither was available before chores were done.

For once, Zayira had trouble dragging her consciousness into the present moment. It normally snapped into place shortly after she awoke, but she had been up later than usual to finish packing the night before, so it was taking some time to catch up. Or it was protesting. She wasn't sure which. Either way, the cows were milked before she managed any coherent, productive thought.

Danil met her on the way back to the house. "Today's the day, isn't it?" he asked with a sunny smile. Danil had always been a morning person. "You packed?"

"Yeah." Zayira opened the door for her brother, then followed him into the house.

"Just wait, Mom's going to ask if you've packed enough underwear. She always asks that when we leave to hunt." Danil arrived at the kitchen and beamed a smile at their parents. "Morning, Ma. Morning, Pa. What's for breakfast?" He leaned around his mother and over the frying pan on the stove in an attempt to discern its contents.

"Zayira's favorite: oat cakes with molasses," their mother replied. Danil slumped a bit, then flopped into a chair. Zayira still wasn't sure how he could be so bony, yet look so boneless when he slouched.

"Are you packed yet, Zayira?" their mother asked.

"Yes ma'am. Finished last night. Just need to wash up and I'll be ready to leave." Zayira cast about the kitchen absently. "When did you say Aunt Glorya would be here?"

"Last note I had from her said midmorning. She's coming on foot, so I wouldn't expect her any sooner than that." Zayira's mother flipped over an oat cake, inspected it, then turned it out onto an earthenware plate to indicate that it passed muster. "Come get something to eat, honey. You'll need energy today."

Zayira obeyed mechanically, taking the plate, a fork, and the jar of molasses back to the spot she'd occupied at the large table near the kitchen. She poured a slightly more liberal measure of molasses than usual, justifying it by telling herself that it was likely the last she'd get for some time. Her mother made the best molasses.

A few moments later her oldest brother, Maks, joined them in the kitchen, grunting a brief greeting to all and heading straight for the coffee pot. "You'll have to make some," their mother interjected from the stove. "Your father had the last of what I made." A slow smile spread across the broad features of their father's face as he read his almanac. Maks growled an unintelligible response, grabbed the percolator and the beans, and proceeded to make another pot.

While he waited, Maks turned to Zayira, who was slowly chewing on an oat cake. "Leaving day, huh? You packed?"

She swallowed hurriedly. "Yes! Does nobody else have anything to do but check up on my preparedness this morning?" Zayira shoved another large bite into her mouth as if daring anyone else to ask a question.

"I hope you packed plenty of underthings," her mother replied, heedless of the darkening of the room. Danil looked sideways at his sister, who replied by sticking out her tongue, half-chewed breakfast included. He smothered a chuckle, covering it with a barely-credible cough.

After breakfast they all went separate ways. Maks, now fully aware of his surroundings, made his way back outside to help their father repair the cattle shed while Danil disappeared conveniently just as someone started looking for him. Instead of helping her mother start churning their butter for the week, Zayira returned to her room to recheck her bag. Conscientious to a fault, she wanted to be sure she'd stowed everything securely and included everything on the list her aunt had sent last month. There were her spare clothes; the few basic toilet items she kept; the small sketch Danil had made for her of the farm in spring; and yes, there were all the underthings she owned, right where she'd packed them late the night before. Rolling her eyes, she reclosed the oiled canvas bag and shouldered it, stopping briefly by her dressing mirror on her way out.

The sight of herself still in her dirty work breeches and milk-stained shirt stopped her mid-stride. Setting her pack hurriedly on her bed, she stripped off her filthy clothes, a fleeting guilt crossing her mind for leaving her mother more laundry as she washed herself as quickly and thoroughly as possible using the basin on her dresser, all the while expecting to hear her aunt's firm knock announce her arrival.

It came just as she threw on her clean linen shirt. The door opened almost immediately, and Zayira recognized her mother's voice. "Glorya!" A muffled greeting followed, barely intelligible against her mother's expansive shoulder. She was a tall, stoutly-built woman, and her hugs tended to be all-encompassing.

"Good to see you, Marya." Extricating herself from her sister's warm embrace, Glorya glanced down the hall just as Zayira appeared out of her tiny room. Her aunt nodded to her as she approached. "Zayira. I see you're packed. Ready to head out?" Zayira nodded, not quite trusting her voice. Aunt Glorya had always been a favorite with her, especially since they shared a close family resemblance; both had their family's trademark thick, coppery hair and stout build, along with a liberal scattering of freckles. Regardless, she was still appre-hensive about their imminent journey–especially since she knew it was likely to change a lot about their rela-tionship.

"Good. We've a long way to go." Aunt Glorya turned back toward the door.

"Can I convince you to stay for lunch?" Marya pleaded as Zayira followed her aunt. "We don't get much time to catch up, and that would give Zayira a chance to say goodbye to her brothers and Pa."

Glorya shook her head, her hair swinging around her round chin. "We have half a day's walk ahead of us, and I'd like to be back at the inn in Market by dinner-time." She gestured to Zayira. "Go say your goodbyes–I see Pa and Maks over by the cattle shed. I'll wait here."

Zayira spotted her father and brother engaged in fixing the roof, which had fallen in earlier that week during a storm. Danil was nowhere to be seen. She approached with her pack on her back, waving to her father to get his attention. He waved back, spoke to his son briefly, and the two of them descended the ladder set to one side of the structure. "It's that time, eh?" her father asked, clapping her heartily on the back. His hands were weather-worn and large, matching the rest of his broad, tanned figure. He stood a head taller than his oldest son, though Maks–a younger version of his father–was fast catching up. Both had dun-brown hair with eyes to match and plain, but pleasant countenanc-es.

"It's that time," Zayira confirmed. She hugged her father about the waist as tight as she could since it was the highest point on his form she could still get her arms around. He squeezed her in turn, then released her to the embrace of her brother, who knuckled the top of her head good-naturedly.

"What, no cloud?" he asked after letting her go. "Not even a parting drizzle?"

An angry look crossed Zayira's face, and a tiny peal of thunder rang out overhead. Maks smiled. "There's my Zay-Zay." She smiled impishly as a miniature storm cloud appeared over Maks's head, dumping a light rain on his sun-drenched form. He chuckled as the rain tickled his exposed skin.

Zayira looked toward the porch where her mother and aunt waited in casual conversation. "Where's Dani? I need to get going, but I haven't seen him since this morning."

"You know he doesn't like goodbyes," Pa reminded her gently. "I bet he's up a tree somewhere close by. Wave and he'll see you." She did, turning a circle, then waved to her Pa and Maks and jogged back to where her aunt waited.

"Ready?" Aunt Glorya asked. Zayira nodded, then ran over to hug her mother, heedless of the butter on her apron. Marya deftly redirected Zayira to her side to avoid soiling the new linen shirt she'd just donned. "We'll see you soon enough, dearest," she said as she kissed the top of her daughter's head. "You listen to your aunt; she'll help you get settled and know what to expect. And be extra careful on your trip!" she called as her sister and her only daughter started toward the road. Sniffing once, she stayed on the porch long enough to watch them disappear into the distance.

CHAPTER 4

Zayira looked back twice before they passed out of sight of the porch. Both times she smiled and waved at her mother, who waved the towel in her hand in return. It seemed like hours before they passed over the gentle swell that led down to the closest road and out of sight of everything she had ever known.

She'd been to town before, of course. Everyone pitched in on market days to help get the beef cows to sale and carry the eggs and produce, plus the butter and other baking items she and her mother sold every tenth-day. Her aunt had even been with them a few times when she came to visit. She seemed to take a simple joy in helping out around the farm. But today was different. They wouldn't return at sundown with seed or money or flour or any of the things they usually bought at the market. It would be months before she saw her home again.

Aunt Glorya chuckled. "You would think I was taking you off to the slaughter," she said, smiling at Zayira. "What are you thinking about?"

"Nothing." That wasn't true, of course.

Aunt Glorya looked skyward, her eyes unfocusing a little. "What a nice day for travel," she mused. "I remember walking out of my house on a day just like this, hitting the road, and never once looking back." She sighed heavily. "That was probably the hardest thing I've ever done."

Zayira stared at her independent, successful aunt as if she'd grown a second head. "Why?"

"Because I wanted so badly to turn around and run right back to Mother. But I couldn't let her see that. She was already worried enough, sending me off to a new school miles away to be taught the goddesses only knew what. Our mother wasn't as strong as your mother is; she worried about the smallest things, but never seemed bothered by the big ones, except my leaving…" She trailed off, lost in memory, and they passed under the trees at the edge of the property in silence.

"I'm not scared," Zayira said after a while. "I'm worried, and curious, but I think I'm too excited to be scared. After all, you made it through school there and did so well for yourself, and we're a lot alike."

Glorya chuckled. "I never said it was easy, though I suppose if you look at it from the outside in you might think that." She absently fingered the golden sun brooch pinning her cloak at the shoulder. "I worked very hard for this. Not as hard as some, but harder than others, and more than I needed to in order to make my way in life without becoming a burden to my family."

"What was it like? What sorts of things did they make you do? And learn? Did you make friends?" Questions spilled from Zayira as she finally started to consider the new situation she approached with each footfall.

"Slow down," her aunt laughed. "I can't answer all your questions at once, but I can give you an overview of the school and how things work–or at least how they used to work." She considered a moment. "Where to start...I suppose I can give you an idea of what the school looks like first; that was the biggest point of curiosity for me when I left home." She stopped walking for a moment, casting about for a stick, then returned to the dusty highway and began to draw. "The school consists of three main buildings for classrooms and another for meals. They're laid out so–" she indicated three parallel rectangles in her drawing with a fourth, shorter and wider, across the bottom. As she spoke, she continued to draw, sketching lines in a ragged U-shape around the rectangles. "The dormitories are cut into the sides of the valley along all three sides." She pointed to the left side. "You will be in these dormitories, with the rest of the stormkindlers. The windwakers live here, at the base of the valley, and the students who are sunchasers live on the opposite side from you." A line appeared on the left side of the valley, bisecting the left-hand wall. "The only entrance is here, in between the wings of the stormkindler dorms. Otherwise you have to approach the valley by sea–and good luck getting in if you're not wanted." Glorya scratched out the drawing with her foot once Zayira had a chance to view it.

"Why's that, Aunt Glorya?" she queried.

Her aunt chuckled. "Boats are powered by sails. With the windwaker dormitories at the back of the valley, they can easily put up enough force to keep out even the biggest ships. Plus there's a great boom chain across the mouth of the bay to stop them if no one knows they're coming."

"Oh. That seems smart," Zayira mused. "Why are the stormkindlers close to the entrance, then?"

"Why do you think?" her aunt asked.

Zayira pondered for a moment. "Because we have an ability that helps defend against ground-based invasion. Heavy rain can create a lot of mud, and lightning can start fires."

"Exactly!" Aunt Glorya cried.

Zayira fell silent for a bit. "Has the school ever been invaded?"

Glorya gave her niece a sidelong glance before answering. "Yes," she replied. "Once. It was before I was a student. You may learn more about it in class." She picked up the pace a bit. "What else would you like to know?"

"Hmm…I guess I'd like to hear more about the classes. What sorts of things will I be studying? I haven't had much in the way of schooling…" She trailed off self-consciously.

"You'll have classes based on your strengths and weaknesses. Chances are you'll have basic figuring, geography, and history to start with. You can read and write already, so you'll start with slightly more advanced topics than the average lower-class first year student." She paused to gauge Zayira's reaction. "Of course, there will be students who come in already knowing the basics. Children of wealthier families have already been tutored in them and begin with things like second languages and higher-level maths."

Zayira's cheeks reddened. "I suppose that gives them an advantage." Her tone was carefully neutral, but the sky above her head darkened.

"Yes, it does," Glorya answered, her words clipped and matter-of-fact. "Some will have also received instruction on how to control their abilities from other graduates who tutor for a fee, so they'll have an advantage there, too. Lucky for you, you've had an aunt for a teacher, and a better one than most of the tutors you'll find." She winked conspiratorially, and the cloud that had formed dissipated. "Besides, the high-borns may have book learning and manners, but they never last a day without someone to do things for them. You'll have the advantage there."

They walked in silence for a while as Zayira digested what she'd learned so far. Scrub trees and scraggly bushes lined their path, directing them inexorably onward toward town and the inn.

"How far of a ride is the school on horseback from town?"

"About another half day."

"Will we have to ride through the night, then?"

"Good havens, no!" Glorya exclaimed. "The ostler only comes in twice a tenday, so if we want to hire mounts we have to be there by sundown. We'll stay at the inn and leave in the morning."

"How much will it cost? I didn't bring much coin."

"Not to worry; I'll pay for the rooms and the mounts, and happy to do so." Glorya smiled fondly at her charge, who beamed back at her aunt gratefully.

The rest of the trip was filled with questions, answers, stories, and the sharing of memories, all of which sped them along until they arrived in the town of Market. The inn–if it could be called such–was first and foremost a public house, with a couple of rooms attached for the few overnight guests who came for market days. Zayira had seen it many times, but had never been inside.

The interior of the building was clean and comfortable. A few men and women sat at the close, sturdy

tables, enjoying a meal they didn't have to cook and sa-
voring the dark, house-brewed ale. Zayira and her aunt
took a table by the door and were soon in possession
of their own meal, complete with dark beer for Glorya
and a thin, heavily watered wine for Zayira. The fare
was simple and filling, and when they'd finished their
dinner Glorya approached the woman behind the bar to
secure their room for the night. The proprietress showed
them upstairs to a small space just big enough for two
single beds and a table, told them where the privy was
in case they needed it in the night, then closed the door
behind her, leaving aunt and niece to settle themselves
in. The beds held a light settling of dust on the head-
boards and the wooden frames creaked as Glorya sat
on hers. "Ah, this should do nicely," she sighed, laying
back on top of the well-used quilt.

Zayira cast her aunt a dubious look.

Glorya chuckled. "When you sleep in your first
ship's berth you'll understand," she explained. "I've
spent years traveling by sea, and compared with the
accommodations I've had on most vessels this is a
luxury." She stripped off her dusty travel clothes and
changed into a shift to sleep. "You'd best get comfortable; we have a good ride ahead of us tomorrow that
will end in a sore backside for us both. I haven't ridden
much in recent years. At least, not horses," she amended.

"What have you been riding instead? Oxen? Don-
keys?"

"Camels." Zayira's eyes went wide. "You don't ride
them astride like a horse," her aunt explained. "They
have a saddle with a sort of chair you sit in at the top.
It's awkward at first, but once you get the hang of it it's

wonderful." Zayira's jaw dropped open, eliciting another chuckle from her aunt. "Go ahead and change," she admonished, shoving Zayira toward her pack. The girl shook her head to clear it and reached for her things.

They spent the rest of the evening trading tales, one of home, the other of her exploits across the sea and beyond. Once night fell Zayira began to nod despite her desperate desire to stay up and hear more of her aunt's stories. The last thing she remembered before slumber overtook her was the feel of her aunt's warm hand tucking her into the blankets as a strange, but beautiful song drifted over the room. She'd heard her aunt hum it before and wanted to stay awake to hear the words, but couldn't bring herself to open her eyes any longer. So she let the sound set her adrift on the tides of slumber, uncertain of what the morrow would bring, but optimistic about its prospects.

CHAPTER 5

The next morning after breakfast Glorya spoke to the serving boy, who pointed to a table containing a single, middle-aged man before ducking off to continue his rounds.

Zayira followed her aunt to the man's table. "Pardon, but are you the ostler, by chance?"

The man looked up from his ale. "Luck favors thee; I be'est. What canst do for thee?" His voice was scratchy and deep, with a rumble like the wheels of a loaded wagon.

"We seek to hire mounts," Glorya replied, seemingly unaffected by the man's thick accent. Zayira did her best to remember her manners and not stare, which constituted all she could manage in the face of such a strange way of speech.

The ostler grunted. "I mayhap can help thee. Whereabouts art thee headed?" He squinted at Glorya for a moment, then answered his own question. "The school? Aye, ye've both the look about thee, and you with the broach, ma'am. Two I can spare, for thy trip. Wouldst tha like to see 'em?" He drained his mug before they could answer and stood. "Be'est they at the stables. C'mon." Without a backward glance he pushed in his chair and started toward the door. Glorya looked at Zayira and tossed her head in his direction, then followed briskly.

They followed the ostler across the street to a long, low building that served as stables for both the inn and the ostler. Of the seven stalls in the building, the last three were occupied, and the ostler paused by the first to await the ladies. "This be'est the first," he began, gesturing toward a dun-colored mare placidly chewing the hay baled in the corner of her stall. "I call'st her Honey, an' she answers to't sharp-like." To illustrate the point the mare's ears pricked as he uttered her name. "She's a smooth seat an' fair tolerant of beginners." He moved to the second occupied stall, which held a roan gelding much taller than the mare. "This be'est Cinnabar." The horse barely registered his name spoken aloud, choosing instead to remain staring across the stall toward his compatriot one door down, a bay-colored mount. "He be'est a bit stubborn, but mayhap'll get along with thee," the ostler gestured toward Glorya. "He bain't afraid o' red-heads, if ye'll pardon my saying, as they look a bit like hisself, and I'll wager thee'll know how to keep 'im in line." At this the horse turned his head to take in his visitors and, noticing Glorya, was so forward as to shove his muzzle toward her neck. The ostler smiled. "See? He likes thee a'ready." Glorya smiled and gave the beast a scratch on his forehead. He leaned into her hand and closed his eyes in bliss.

Zayira looked back at the mare she was to ride. It looked back at her with a placid expression while chewing its cud, then leaned down for more hay, unconcerned by the newcomers to her stall. At least it was calm. She wasn't anywhere near what could be called an accomplished rider, having only ridden a horse a handful of times in her life, so her disappointment at her mount's plainness was tempered by her knowledge that she'd rather not be thrown. Arriving at a new school with broken bones and bruises would definitely put a damper on her first few weeks.

Glorya and the ostler haggled for a bit over the price for the use of the mounts and someone to fetch them, but not nearly as much as Zayira felt they should have. In the end they reached an agreement that seemed to satisfy everyone, and the ostler even offered to help saddle the mounts for them.

Fifteen minutes and a few carrots later Zayira and her aunt were mounted and waving their goodbyes to the town of Market. The road was dusty, but their mounts didn't seem to mind; Honey plodded along behind Cinnabar, who trotted ahead with his tail held high. He'd tried once or twice to misdirect them, but each time Aunt Glorya had given him a smart rap on the top of the head and he'd fallen in line. They were making good time north across the dry, rolling grasslands.

Zayira noted to her aunt that they were heading into the hills. Glorya chuckled. "Yes, these are the outer foothills of the Wall Mountains. The road follows the only pass through them north of Market." They crested a hill and she pointed ahead of them. "You can just make it out between those peaks."

For the first time on their trip Zayira stretched her gaze across the horizon. Ahead she could easily make out the silhouette of a mountain range barring their path. A tiny sliver ran between two of the taller shapes–

the pass her aunt had indicated. The range extended as far as she could see to the east, disappearing into the distance. Glorya reined in Cinnabar to ride beside Zayira for a bit. "Do you remember your geography?"

Zayira nodded. "I think. That–" she pointed to the northwest horizon "–is the Razor's Edge. It's the end of the mountain range, where it meets the sea." She'd never seen the ocean, and was having trouble picturing anything that vast. "East of us, the Wall Mountains continue all the way to the eastern plains, running roughly parallel to the Galahan River."

Her aunt nodded and clucked at her mount to continue. "Very good. Where is the closest city of any decent size?"

"Riverbranch, nearly twenty miles southeast," Zayira replied. It was a source of mystery to her almost as compelling as the sea. Traders had brought tales of the country's capital and its wonders to Market, fueling her nascent imagination as she listened to stories of wondrous machines and libraries so vast no one could explore them in a single day. Books were few and far between outside the city, which made the national library even more exotic. Zayira vowed to herself that she would visit it one day.

The pair continued on in silence for some time, each contemplating where they were headed for different reasons. For Glorya this was a homecoming of sorts; she supposed it should feel warmer, but all she could muster was detached interest. The outside world was so much bigger than what she'd learned in her years of schooling, and she was afraid she would no longer fit within the confines of the valley. She glanced at her niece riding along beside her and felt her resolve strengthen. The headmaster's letter to her sprang to mind as well, goading her with its obsequiousness and barely-veiled condescension. She figured it was time to return to her roots, if for no other reason than to make certain they could still help others grow.

Zayira, on the other hand, spent the trip entranced by the scenery. The way the horizon changed from flat and open to jagged and obscured fascinated her in the way only liminal spaces could. Puffy clouds skidded right up to the edges of the range before them only to slide along its length before dissipating. Some few made it across to deliver their moisture to the valley beyond, and Zayira could feel an effect at work drawing the precipitation northward. She decided it was worth interrupting her aunt's thoughts to ask about it.

"It's part of your required schoolwork," Glorya explained. "Once you reach a certain point in your studies you'll be added to the rotation to help manage the weather over the valley so the growing season goes as well as possible. Much of the food we'll eat there is grown on site." Zayira focused her attention even harder on the stranger weather pattern, trying to figure out how it worked as they rode on.

They stopped for lunch in the scant foothills just south of the Razor's Edge. Glorya declared they were making good time and that they'd likely make the evening meal at Weatherwatch if it was still served when it used to be. Zayira continued to ask rapid-fire questions about everything she saw, from their stout ponies to the scrub bushes dotting the hillside and the terns circling above it. Her aunt took the opportunity to shift her mind into a teaching mentality in preparation for her new role. She pointed out bits of flora and fauna by the sides of the road and explained what she knew about the lives of each creature and plant. Their stories fascinated Zayira, who collected small bits of nature and tucked them into her pockets before re-mounting her mare. Their horses spent the short lunch break grazing on the spiky, brown grass nearby and snorted their displeasure at being made to bear riders again. Cinnabar shied sideways as Glorya mounted, earning him another smart rap on the skull. He quieted and they set off for the last leg of the journey.

The foothills terminated in sheer cliffs at the edge of the mountain range. Zayira stared up at the bare rock looming hundreds of meters above them and felt smaller and more insignificant than she ever had. A single stone could break free from that wall and drop straight onto her head and that would be that. She shuddered as they entered the pass that loomed before them. The afternoon sun that had warmed them on the way through the hills now hid behind great stone behemoths and withheld both light and warmth. Thanks to Glorya the wind that threatened to chill them despite the warmth of the season died down with a thought, but there was a pall over the single-cart path that gave Zayira chills. For the first time since leaving home she wondered what she'd gotten herself into.

Nonsense, she told herself. *Your aunt wouldn't bring you here if it wasn't safe. You're just not used to anything besides the farm. That's all.* Sitting up straighter in the saddle, she clucked at her pony to catch up with Cinnabar and rode on, head held high.

A half hour's ride brought them over the apex of the pass and provided their first glimpse of the valley below. Glorya thought back to her days at Weatherwatch and her own first journey to the school and was surprised by the sight of wooden pipes suspended in midair. They must be a new addition; the only plumbing she recalled were the pit latrines they'd dug and filled in and moved a few times a year. The pipes were connected to the valley's various school buildings through holes in the roofs, but otherwise the buildings were the same squat stonework she recalled from her days within their halls. At least the fundamentals were the same. Moss still grew on the sides and tops of many of the buildings, dotting their unrelieved gray with tufts of greens and reds. The road before them continued to drop as they rounded the crest of the pass and revealed the rest of the valley below. Four rectangular buildings, each a single story, dominated the center of the valley and stood amidst verdant gardens filled with vegetables and herbs. A stream that began as a trickle at the valley's apex watered the growing plots, widening as it traversed the length of the valley to spill into the bay at its western edge. Three foot bridges just big enough for a donkey cart crossed the flow and allowed passage between the near and far sides of the valley. In the distance sat two offset rows of cottages facing the river and one large, two-story house that sat at the edge of the beach, overlooking all the goings-on nearby.

Between the two travelers and their final destination sat a large, muddy field with an even stockier building to their left as they emerged from the pass. A breeze brought the familiar smell of livestock across Zayira's nose and her head whipped around to locate its source. The near portion of the closest building contained a stable with five stalls, only two of them occupied. One held a medium-sized draft horse that looked more eager to eat than to work, while the second restrained a donkey that began braying as soon as the riders came into view. The hoarse cacophony brought a hulking, dark-haired man out of the other half of the building. From thirty yards away Zayira felt his stare from beneath bushy brows, inspecting her, assessing her as a threat as they approached. His expression hid behind a thick, glossy mustache and short beard, giving her no indication of his intent as he walked toward them. His gait held no menace, but was measured and balanced as he approached.

"Hail, sir," Glorya called out, breaking the spell that kept the tension high. "I come bearing a new student, and to take over for my late mentor, Sunchaser Keross. We wish no trouble." Her hand sat on the hilt of the short sword she carried, relaxed, but ready.

"Glorya?" The man's voice held more questions than a simple name allowed. "No, it can't be…how did Headmaster Thayer convince you to come?"

"Rylen? Is that you?" Glorya squinted at the figure before them.

"In the flesh!" The man before them relaxed, jogging the last few yards to stand before them. "And that's *Armsmaster* Rylen, thank you very much." He bowed with a flourish as Glorya slid out of her saddle, careful to keep a hand on Cinnabar's reins to avoid an incident. Up close Zayira saw that the armsmaster and her aunt were roughly of an age. Hard-lined muscles ran across the sleeveless expanse of his arms and into a simple linen shirt spotted with sweat and belted at the waist. The barest hint of softness showed above his linen breeches, his physique's only nod to his age outside the smile lines around his eyes. These last were in full evidence as Glorya clasped arms with the larger figure, grinning wider than Zayira had seen her smile in long years.

"You handsome devil, how'd you manage to convince the headmaster you have half a brain and can teach younglings?" Glorya chuckled as she leaned on Cinnabar's saddle. "Last I knew you were still just another mercenary looking for work."

"It was Antonus, actually." Rylen shifted from foot to foot for all the world like an embarrassed schoolboy.

"Antonus, the shy, bookish kid?" Glorya's brows knitted in confusion.

"The same. You see, my last job was an escort mission for his employer. He was working on some sort of historical dig far to the east that kept getting attacked by wandering nomads out of the desert. A few folk from my old company hired on to keep them safe as they transported some of the artifacts they found back to the city for further research." Rylen's eyes flicked to Zayira. "I'll spare you the details, but Antonus and I were the only ones who made it out. Thrown together as we were and trying to survive…well, we–ahem–formed something of a bond, and as soon as we got back to the city he told his employer in no uncertain terms what he thought of his job, his research, the university's purpose, and the role of the headmaster and his dog in alleged illicit activities, and we marched straight out of there." He ran a hand through the side of his close-cropped hair. "Before long there was a posting for a history teacher at the school, and he leaped at the chance. We've been here ever since."

"Well, I'm glad to see a friendly face, that's for certain," Glorya said as she glanced at the sky. "I'm afraid we must get on–oh, where are my manners? Rylen, this is my niece, Zayira. She's here to learn more about stormkindling…and about the rest of the world, as well." The girl waved and nodded from atop her mount. "Zayira, this is *Armsmaster* Rylen." Her emphasis on his title came with a glint in her eye.

"Pleased to make your acquaintance," Rylen replied, nodding back. "I'll be teaching you self-defense and control of your abilities." A small cloud formed over her head and she traced the line of force behind it to the armsmaster, who grinned out of one side of his mouth. Without thinking she shoved the cloud back in his direction, then dissipated it with a thought.

Rylen's eyes shot to Glorya, eyebrows raised. "Was that you?" he asked, pointing at the space left by the disappearing cloud.

"We'll…need to talk about that another time," Glorya prevaricated without meeting Rylen's eyes. "For now, is there a place we might keep the horses until they're sought after?"

"Of course," the armsmaster rumbled as he led them toward the stables. "You'll want to put them in the far stalls, though; Zinnia is awfully temperamental." To illustrate his point the jennie in question continued the braying she'd put on hold as they'd neared the stable. Zayira, for one, was glad to climb down from the saddle. Her legs hadn't been so sore since the last time her brothers challenged her to a contest to see who could lift the biggest log in the wood pile a few years back. At least she wouldn't have to ride again for a while, from the look of things. She handed Rylen the reins of her pliable mare and patted her neck as he settled the tired creature into her stall to chew on fresh hay. The look her aunt had shared with the armsmaster bothered her. She hadn't done anything strange, had she? It seemed like a kind of test to see what she was capable of, so she'd responded the way she always would with her aunt when they practiced. Her aunt had said they'd talk about "it" later, but they really meant they'd talk about her. Zayira's nerves jangled around her already-slipping confidence. It must have shown on her face, because the armsmaster clapped her on the shoulder after fastening the gate for the stall. "You look like you're used to a day's honest work," he said as he sized her up on foot. "If you're half as able as your aunt we'll have you in the intermediate weapons form in no time. The farm kids tend to do well there."

Zayira found her voice somewhere in the bottom of her stomach where it had gone to ground. "I've a little training, sir, and my brothers say I have fast hands. My aunt has taught me a bit of swordplay." She stopped, not wishing to ramble in front of what might be an important ally at her new school.

Glorya beamed. "She's quicker than she looks, that's for sure." She settled Cinnabar in his own stall–of which he took up far more than Zayira's modest mount did of hers–and removed her saddlebags, slinging them over her shoulder. "For now we should get Zayira settled, and I'm in need of a bit of the headmaster's time. Where do you suggest we start?"

Rylen looked at the darkening sky to the west, where the setting sun dyed the water line brilliant colors. "I'd say everyone's at the dining hall given the hour, and if you're in need of a meal before anything else I'd suggest making it there before they finish. Cook doesn't take kindly to latecomers, but she'll make an exception for travelers, methinks."

Thanking Rylen, the two set off across the soggy expanse of the training field toward the four low-slung buildings ahead. It was easy going with a mild down-hill grade, and Zayira realized as they reached the first set of buildings that the stream in the middle of the valley was flanked on both sides by kitchen gardens full of vegetables and the few fruits that would grow this far north. The beds were well weeded and metic-ulously laid out; every section was marked as to what grew there. Since it was midsummer Zayira picked out squash, corn, potatoes, tomatoes, carrots, and some kind of melon just in the sections they passed as they crossed the stream by its middle bridge.

"The plumbing's new." Glorya's voice against the sound of the waves crashing downstream startled them both. She pointed at the pipes jutting from the valley walls ahead of them. "That will be wonderful, especially if they can heat some water for bathing." Baths remind-ed her of her home in Joveru, where she'd discovered a way to both distill clean water from seawater and heat the water at the same time using a contraption on the roof of her house. The tang of salt was dulled enough to become an afterthought, and the water was pleasantly warm as long as she got to it before the chill of the night took over. If she was lucky the school would be willing to let her build a heater onto her cottage, but that would have to wait until after she discovered what the school planned on paying her. Somehow she knew it wouldn't be enough to cover the supplies she'd need.

Soon they faced a set of large, wooden double doors set into the long side of a rectangular building. They looked heavy, but Glorya was able to tug one open with ease once she put down her saddlebags so they could pass into the room beyond. The clanking of silverware on wooden plates played a staccato counterpoint to the ebb and flow of many conversations. The closest discussions stopped as they entered, starting a ripple of pregnant silence that traversed the spacious room faster than Zayira would have thought possible. Forty or fifty students of varying ages and dispositions stopped their meals to study the newcomers. All of them wore some variation on the same clothing: a simple cream-colored linen shirt belted at the waist with matching linen pants. Each also bore a silver pin shaped as either a storm cloud, a whirlwind, or a blazing sun. Thanks to her aunt's habit of wearing her own sunchaser pin Zayira guessed the other two marked their bearers as stormkindlers or windwakers. She wondered which pin she'd get–probably the storm cloud, as her kindling was her strongest talent.

A few teachers had scattered themselves at tables around the room, differentiated from their students by their age, their attire, and the gold color of their pins. One noticed the pair enter and stood, smoothing her ankle-length gray skirt and matching top. The gold whirlwind pin displayed meticulously on her shirt declared her a windwaker. "Good evening, travelers," she called through the silence without raising her voice. "Welcome to Weatherwatch. I am Mira, professor of languages and etiquette." She curtseyed without taking her eyes off the newcomers.

Glorya bowed at the waist, meeting the woman's brown-eyed gaze from halfway across the room. "Sunchaser Glorya, at your service. I am here to replace Sunchaser Keross, though I'm afraid I may be a much poorer substitute. This is Zayira, a new student I agreed to escort on my way here." She rested a hand on her charge's shoulder to forestall any introductions Zayira might wish to give. It would be best if the students found out slowly that the two of them were related instead of thinking Zayira enjoyed any sort of preferential treatment.

"Welcome, Sunchaser Glorya and Zayira. I assume you are in need of refreshment." Mira extended a pale, graceful hand toward a set of double doors in the far short wall. "If you will follow me I will show you where you may wash up while I arrange for your meals." She turned without waiting for an answer and glided across the room on soft-slippered feet, giving them a better view of her immaculately-coiffed light brown hair. Both marked her as noble-born, and Glorya wondered what in the havens a high-ranked woman was doing all the way out at Weatherwatch. Her salary would surely be less than her family could provide in the way of means.

The rest of the diners resumed their cacophony as the group strode toward the doors. Zayira noted every head that turned her way as they passed. Some looked friendly, others neutral, but a few wore openly hostile countenances. These last studied Zayira's plain attire and sturdy build and looked down their noses at her from two tables away. She wasn't sure how they could look down their noses when she stood higher than they sat, but they managed it. Just then she passed a table with a single occupant, a boy not much older than she with jet-black hair tied back from his round, tanned face. He was thinner than most of the other students and regarded her with sunken brown eyes that widened as he took in her coppery hair. As soon as Zayira met his gaze he looked away, turning his back to her and hunching over his empty plate. Zayira wondered why he was sitting by himself.

"Are you coming?" Glorya asked. Zayira realized she'd slowed down to study a *boy*, of all things, and hurried to catch up with her aunt, cheeks burning. She felt eyes follow her until the double doors swung shut behind them and cut off their view.

Mira waited in the short hallway beyond, her plain face fixed in a polite expression. "This is the lavatory," she explained, indicating a door to their right. "We have running water for our sinks, but we ask that you always follow the instructions posted over each latrine, as their misuse can cause a great deal of work and consternation." Before either of them could work out a question for clarification Mira bobbed another curtsey and disappeared through a set of swinging half doors. The clanging of pots and cookware confirmed the next room as the kitchen.

"After you," Glorya directed, gesturing at the open latrine room door. Zayira entered first, her footsteps ringing across the flagstones as she explored the small rectangular room. It contained six latrines, each with wooden seats and dividers between. Wooden doors hung open on all six boxes with simple latches on the back for enforcement of privacy. On the long wall across from the latrine boxes a trough was mounted flush with the stone, ready to catch and drain the runoff from the three taps set above it. Small cakes of lye soap sat on little shelves built into the trough by each tap.

Zayira poked her head into one of the boxes. The smell was far from pleasant, but she'd expected worse, and she wondered how they kept the whole building from reeking of sewage. A piece of paper hung over the back of the latrine caught her eye and she read aloud around the graffiti scrawled in the margins. "'This latrine is for liquid waste only. Anyone caught putting solid waste of any sort down this latrine will be responsible for clearing it and will be on latrine duty for a full month.'" She leaned out of the box to look at her aunt. "Do they mean you're only supposed to pee in this latrine?"

"I believe that is the intent, yes," Glorya mused as she read the instructions in the next stall. "'This latrine is for solid waste. Please refrain from putting non-compostable items down the latrine as you will be responsible for fishing them out.'"

"So they mean poo?"

"Yes, Zayira, they mean you're meant to defecate in these and urinate in the others." Glorya indicated the last three boxes as solid waste only.

"But what if you have to do both?" Zayira wondered.

"You would use the solid waste latrine," her aunt answered as she stepped into one of the liquid waste boxes and latched the door. "Now I suggest you use the facilities while you have the chance."

A short time later both ladies had made use of the strange new latrines and washed themselves up at the sinks. The water from the taps was cool, almost cold, despite the warmth of the fading day, and Zayira wondered where it came from. It felt wonderful on her face. She asked her aunt how they managed to get cool water in the summertime, and Glorya thought back on the trip into the valley, when she'd seen the wooden pipes jutting from the cliffs. "They have to have cut cisterns into the cliffsides around the valley," she concluded.

"What's a cistern?" asked Zayira as she dried her hands as best she could on her dust-covered breeches.

"It's a big container meant to hold rainwater," Glorya explained as they ventured back out into the hallway. She turned away from the conversation and almost bumped into Mira, who waited by the kitchen doors with a large tray laden with food. "May I assist?" Glorya asked, gesturing at the heavy serving platter.

Mira shook her head with a small smile. "Thank you, but no; you are new here, and as such are guests until properly settled. Please follow me." She swept past them and Zayira smelled beef with rich broth. Fresh bread underscored the rest of the scents coming from the tray, along with a hint of lavender she thought must be from the professor herself. They made their way back into the dining room and found a seat, trailing in Mira's wake. Something told Zayira she would never see this teacher looking any less put-together than she was at that very moment, and it made her wonder if the woman slept that way.

Her aunt's words floated into her realm of reverie and pulled her out of it. "...was wondering who would be responsible for getting Zayira settled into her dormitory."

"She's a stormkindler, you say? That would be Annalia, their senior student." Mira inclined her head toward the table filled with snooty rich kids. "I'll speak with her directly. Please, enjoy your meal." Professor Mira rose, curtseyed, and floated over to Annalia's table, where Zayira noticed she was welcomed with every polite grace. She realized they must all be rich; their manners matched perfectly, and they all simpered to gain their teacher's favor. It was sickening. Zayira decided then and there that the penalty of wealth was living with the rich and swore off fame and fortune forever.

Glorya slid one of the plates in front of Zayira and commanded her to eat. The girl had a hearty appetite and needed no second bidding; before Glorya had finished a third of her meal Zayira was done. Glorya noticed that her charge spent the rest of her time studying the students and teachers around her who would be her primary companions in the days to come. Zayira was canny; she'd do all right, perhaps even better than her aunt, depending on the situation she'd been dropped into. She recognized none of the other teachers present. It had been her hope that at least one of her old schoolmates or professors would still be around, but outside of Rylen she was out of luck. It was time to make some friends, and fast.

Just as they wiped the last crumbs of the delicious meal from their lips Mira rejoined them with Annalia in tow. She was the first one who had turned her nose up as Zayira passed on the way to the latrines earlier, and her perfectly-arranged, golden locks barely swayed as she approached on silent, slippered feet. "Sunchaser, Zayira, meet Annalia, the senior stormkindler student. Annalia, this is Sunchaser Glorya, here to replace Sunchaser Keross."

"So pleased to make your acquaintance," Annalia simpered, her curtsey a mirror image of Mira's. Glorya nodded her acknowledgment.

"And this is our new stormkindler student, Zayira." Mira's outstretched hand moved to encompass Zayira, who was glad she'd followed her aunt's lead and stood as the pair approached.

"A pleasure," Annalia replied in a more neutral tone. Zayira ducked her head in an awkward bow and mumbled something unintelligible in reply. By the time she straightened Annalia was already turning to leave. "Come," she cast over her narrow shoulder. "I will show you to your room." Zayira threw a nervous glance her aunt's way and was rewarded with an encouraging smile and nod. Squaring her shoulders, she followed the older girl out the front doors and into the deepening night.

CHAPTER 6

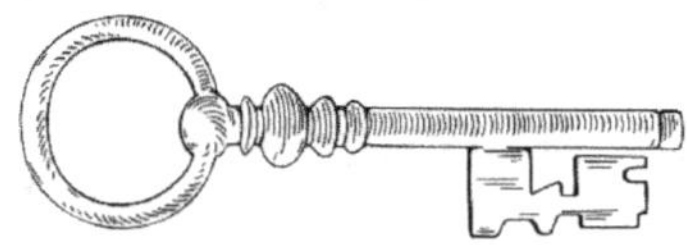

Glorya watched her only niece disappear through the double doors they'd entered earlier, the smile sliding off her features. *That noble girl will be trouble. Time to do some digging.* "Professor Mira, would you be so kind as to help me reacquaint myself with the school a bit?" she inquired. "I'm afraid much has changed since I last spent time here and I'm a bit adrift, as it were."

"Of course," Mira replied. "And please, call me Mira. I only stand on ceremony with the students." Glorya doubted that, but maintained a neutral expression.

"Then you must call me Glorya. I was hoping you could tell me a bit about what it is you teach and how my instruction on sunchasing fits in with it."

"I teach etiquette and languages, as I said in my introduction," Mira answered, a patient look on her plain features. "Of course, much of what we teach is Midlands culture, as that's our home country, but the students also learn bits of the older forms of our language, along with those of our trading partners. At the moment that includes only Zhedaba, I'm afraid, as I am lamentably ignorant of all concerning the language of Temalingar. I do wish to learn it, but have found no references or assistance in doing so."

"You speak Zhedaban?" Glorya's eyebrows raised in surprise. "Few in Midlands do."

Mira made a small gesture of polite deferral. "*I am competent, but in need of practice,*" she replied in Zhedaban.

"*I can most certainly help you there,*" Glorya replied in kind, gesturing her support for the woman's attempt. "*I have made it my home.*"

"Thank goodness for that." Mira sighed as if a weight had lifted from her shoulders. "We're expecting a group of new students from Zhedaba in a fortnight and I'm not entirely sure what to do with them–or with the regular students. I would be most grateful if you could assist me with the preparations."

Glorya signed the Zhedaban equivalent of "I'd be happy to" before remembering to also speak aloud. "You have only to let me know how I may be of service." She stood, deciding that was enough alliance building for one meal. Mira rose with her. "Would you be so kind as to point me to my accommodations? I requested my predecessor's quarters for my use, but received no reply from the headmaster."

"He is…absentminded on occasion," Mira admitted. "I'm certain it will be no issue. Allow me." She indicated a single door directly opposed from the one they'd entered and ushered them both through into the twilight.

Glorya's eyes adjusted quickly to the lower illumination provided by the limited number of stars above. That was one thing about living in the valley she hadn't noticed as a student: how little of the horizon was visible. At sea one could view countless constellations in every direction unobscured by hill or tree. It pricked at her spacial awareness, making her feel as though the cliffs were closing in on her despite their comfortable distance. *I don't know how long I can do this,* she thought as she considered the looming blackness beyond.

As long as you have to, said another voice in her mind. She remembered her purpose in coming to Weatherwatch: to watch over her niece and to help fill the void left behind by her teacher. *I do wonder what he was up to before he passed; he had some fascinating theories on weather patterns across the world.*

"Here is Sunchaser Keross's cottage," Mira announced at the stoop of a single-room building set a short distance away from the cliffside. "I'm afraid the accommodations for our teachers are not spacious, but I do find them comfortable." Producing a key from a pocket in her skirt she unlocked the door and stepped inside. "Apologies for the mess; it seems no one has cleaned up in some time." Mira coughed as dust puffed out from a nearby table covered with books and paperwork. Glorya walked through the cloud it left behind with no adverse effects; the dust in Joveru was persistent, and she'd long since grown accustomed to it in her home.

"On the contrary, I'm glad all is as he left it," Glorya replied as Mira lit a candle stuck to the short mantel with its own melted wax. The meager light revealed a one-room cabin with a small fireplace and a loft for sleeping, though the mattress had been moved onto the ground floor in acknowledgment of its geriatric prior owner. The narrow door across from the main entrance barely had enough room to open properly due to the overflow of vellum sheets from atop the desk and the side table next to it. Some sort of rug occupied the center of the room, but it was impossible to tell if it was orange or faded red in the current lighting. A threadbare easy chair sat at one edge of the rug with a crooked end table beside it piled high with books. Glorya thought the faded upholstery looked green through the multiple coffee and tea stains on its surface.

She picked her way through the intellectual debris until she reached the mattress. "Where might I find clean linens?" she asked. It appeared they hadn't been changed in some time, and while she'd certainly slept in worse conditions, she preferred not to when she had the choice.

"Oh, there's a linen closet right over here." Mira lifted the hem of her skirts just enough to pick her way across the room next to Glorya. She opened a small cabinet at the foot of the mattress and revealed a single clean sheet folded haphazardly and stuffed into the cubby. Pulling it out, she reached over and removed the bottom sheet from the mattress with a single tug. "Here, let me assist you. We will have the washing crew come take these away on the morrow." Glorya took hold of the top half of the clean sheet and helped tuck it around the mattress, which was stuffed with some sort of feathers and another cushioning substance, perhaps straw. It gave off a musty scent tinged with lavender. They must've added some dried herbs when they made it. *Thank goodness for that.*

"Do you think I could also have it moved back into the loft?" Glorya wondered, inspecting the ceiling above her head as if she could discern what was there through the wooden boards.

"Armsmaster Rylen should be able to help you move it," Mira replied, dusting her hands on her skirt.

"It was he who moved it down for Sunchaser Keross. And you look quite able enough to assist him." A measuring look crossed the etiquette teacher's face as she regarded her new colleague. "In fact, I have a feeling you will adjust to life here far more quickly than some of our number. We shift for ourselves in most things, with the exception of laundry and cooking, and that has been a difficult transition for some of the staff." Her eyes slid away from Glorya's before she could get a better read on what Mira had said. "But I digress. I'm certain the headmaster will wish to see you tomorrow. If you would like to bathe after your journey you may use the running water available in the attached washroom." She indicated the narrow door that now sat to their right as they looked out from the alcove in which the mattress lay. "I'm afraid it's cold unless you build a fire, but it's clean and abundant thanks to the work of the students and staff."

"Thank you for helping me settle in," Glorya replied, feeling the conversation winding down and exhaustion from her journey setting in. "I think I'll build up the fire a bit and see if I can manage a hot bath tonight in anticipation of tomorrow's business." She shifted her saddlebags from where she'd dropped them to closer to the mattress for ease of access, figuring she'd be living out of them until she could organize the disaster that was her predecessor's home.

"You're most welcome," Mira replied. Her expression wavered for the first time since she'd taken up her hostess duties before she schooled it once again into the bland countenance she'd worn all evening. The words she was about to utter turned into a placid "please let me know if there is anything else you require, as I reside next door" before she curtseyed and retreated through the open door.

I wonder what that was about, Glorya mused as she pulled the door to and dropped the simple wooden latch. Something was definitely afoot at the school; she could feel it in her bones. *But can I trust her? She's noble, which means she may have an agenda outside of her school responsibilities, and I know nothing about her whatsoever.* She picked over the items on the bedside table in an attempt to make room for a few of her own things. Most of it was run-of-the-mill academic detritus: a grease pencil, a ragged quill, some shells from the beach below, a tooth from one of the large fish that swam in the deeps off the coast, and a few smooth rocks polished by the stream made the squat surface their home. *It seems he missed the sea, too.* She'd met few sunchasers who weren't called to the wild weather patterns only found on the water. Not having known Sunchaser Keross before his time as her teacher she had no idea whether or not he'd had another life elsewhere, but she bet he'd spent some time abroad and on the ocean.

Smiling, Glorya swept the trinkets off the table into a rush basket she found sitting by the door and heard a metallic *clink.* Curious, she dug through the bits and bobs until she found an iron key the length of her hand. It was old and coated in a thin layer of rust that gave off a metallic smell when she picked it up. Deciding it might be important, she placed it in her bag, away from prying eyes, and cast about for a kettle to heat some water for a warm bath. After ten minutes of searching she gave up, deciding a cold bath was better than no bath at all. It was getting late, and she'd had a long few days.

Half an hour later she slid onto her freshly-made

bed, thankful the night was warm enough she didn't need her extra blanket.

CHAPTER 7

Zayira had a hard time keeping pace with the older, taller girl before her without jogging. She was certain Annalia set out so quickly out of contempt, but Zayira was determined not to let any of the noble-born students at Weatherwatch get the best of her. So she half-jogged across the muddy path back toward where they'd entered the canyon before turning right partway across the open field she'd seen before. In the darkness it looked much less expansive, but she could feel the open distance in the breeze that drifted across the space; it told her of open terrain and wet grass, of mud and tiny insects fleeing from the night's predators. She inhaled it as her last moment of comfort before they entered an opening she hadn't noticed in the cliff face across from the armory building. At night it was a gaping hole ready to swallow them, and Zayira fought the urge to slow down. She refused to show fear on her first night at the school. So great was her determination that she almost trod over Annalia as the girl stopped just shy of the doorway, half a sentence out of her mouth.

"Now, don't be afraid of the–oof!" The two collided, Zayira's shorter-but-bulkier form winning the force contest and knocking the smaller girl into the wall. It was too dark to see Annalia's expression, but Zayira felt the girl's stare as she helped her back to her feet. "Well," Annalia began, dusting off her linen skirts. "I can see you have no fear of the dark."

"Not since I was little," Zayira replied from a safer distance. "Apologies for running into you like that; you were going so fast, and then you just…stopped."

"Yes, well, I thought it prudent given your age–" she glanced down her nose at her charge–"to warn you of the frightening entryway, but it appears you are quite certain of yourself despite your youth." Composure regained, she led the way around a corner and into a hallway lit with guttering braziers that hung from small hooks in the stone ceiling. The passage itself was roughly hewn from the mountain above and contained enough space for three to walk comfortably abreast. Heavy wooden doors zigzagged back and forth across the walls at regular intervals as far as Zayira could see before the passageway curved to the left toward the point of the valley.

Annalia stopped at the third door on the right. "This will be your room," she announced as she dragged on the iron ring serving as a handle. The door screeched open, carving a path in the dust on the floor as it passed over it. Inside was a room that held a single bed on a wooden frame a bit larger than the one she slept in at home, a bedside table with three legs, a rough wooden desk, and a rickety chair that didn't look like it would hold more than a book. "I'm sure you'll be most comfortable with our humble accommodations," Annalia declared as she gestured for Zayira to enter. "Latrines for both waste and bathing are down the hall to your right. They're shared among the students in the dormitory, so bring everything you need if you plan on bathing. Classes start at second bells sharp. Someone will be along to get you first thing in the morning. And if there's anything you need, please don't hesitate to ask." Before Zayira could reply Annalia swept from the room, closing the door behind her with a final thump.

The silence in her room rang with the echoes of every loud noise she'd ever heard. A smaller version of the hallway lamps sat in a little sconce next to the door and lit the small space enough for Zayira to maneuver around the sparse furniture. The corners were left in forbidding shadow. Determined not to be afraid of her new home, she peered into every nook and cranny of the space, committing it to memory and dispelling any mystery the shadows held so her rational mind could hold sway once more. Turning toward the door, she reached for her bags–and realized she'd left them on her pony when they'd arrived. *Great work, Zayira. Now you have to go out in the dark without a light and hope you don't end up in the stall with the angry jennie.* Heaving a sigh, she shoved the door open once again, finding it easier to open than Annalia had made it look. *Bet I can make it quieter.* She remembered her da asking her mother for some rendered fat to grease the hinges on the barn door so it wouldn't wake the house every morning when he opened it. He'd also straightened it somehow so it hung more evenly, but Zayira was afraid that was beyond her current level of skill. *Maybe I can find someone to help.* She slipped out the door and started down the hallway to her left toward the opening they'd entered after dinner.

A figure loomed in the doorway ahead of her. Zayira stepped back, her fists coming up out of habit as she felt behind her for the wall. Her brothers had always liked to sneak up on her in the early morning dark, and more than once in recent memory she'd boxed them on the ears for it.

The figure stopped and hunched over long enough to drop its burden, which she realized had made it look far larger than it was. "Have no fear, young one," reassured a now-familiar voice. "It's Armsmaster Rylen, come to bring you your saddlebags. Why on earth were you heading outside without a light?"

"No candles in my room, sir," Zayira answered. "The lamp's attached to the wall. 'Sides, I'm used to going out in the dark without a light."

"No candles in your…did no one show you where the supply closet is?" The armsmaster's thick brows–the only feature she could make out in the darkness–furrowed in concern. "Here, let me take you there. It's not far. Which room did they put you in?"

Zayira pointed as they passed her door. "This one."

Armsmaster Rylen stopped. "All the way out here? When there are plenty of rooms closer to the privy? And it's so drafty at the edges of the halls; you'll freeze come winter." As he talked he hauled open the door, wincing as it scraped the stone beneath. "Would you like to choose another one? I'll be happy to arrange it if you'd like."

"This is fine, sir," Zayira answered as she took her bags from the armsmaster, setting them by the door. "I'd rather have some space, and I sleep hot, so colder in winter is just fine. Do you know where I might get some rendered fat or grease?" The shift in topic further confused the already bewildered Rylen.

"Whatever for?" His puzzled expression further clouded his features in the dim light.

"The hinges," Zayira explained, and understanding dawned on the armsmaster's face. "To make them quieter. Da used rendered cow fat, but I'm sure anything similar would work."

Rylen's expression softened to one of fatherly affection. "I'll do a sight better than that. We'll have someone come check on the hinges tomorrow and straighten up this door. It's a right pain to open."

"I'd be thankful," Zayira answered, ducking her head in gratitude.

"In the meantime, let's get you some candles, young lady." Rylen showed his young charge out the door and down the hall a short ways. Most of the doors on either side of the hall were of similar make, some older, some newer, but one was labeled "SUPPLIES" in bold, chiseled script across the middle. Rylen tugged on the iron ring to one side and the door lumbered open to reveal a plethora of candles, bed linens, towels, and spare sets of clothing to match what Zayira had seen everyone else wearing at dinner. The armsmaster sized her up, then dug through the clothing until he produced two sets of pants and two shirts that looked like they would fit. "You already have a belt, yes?" Zayira nodded. "Good. And socks, and small clothes, I'd wager." She nodded again and recalled her mother's last question about her packing. A wash of homesickness splashed against her soul as she took the uniform from the armsmaster, and she swallowed it down in time to thank him. He dug around in the back of the closet for a moment and produced a silver pin in the shape of a storm cloud with lightning stamped across it. "This goes on the left side of your tunic in the morning," he explained, pointing to his own golden version winking in the firelight.

Guess that answers that question. Zayira was a little disappointed there was no pomp and circumstance around getting one's weatherworking pin and uniform. She wasn't sure what she'd expected in the first place, but was discontent nonetheless. *What did you expect, farm girl? Honey and biscuits and tea all day with nobles treating you like equals? Come off it. Make the best of what you get.* She straightened her spine, found her sense of pride, and stood still as a stork as Rylen loaded her down with her uniforms, a towel, three candles, some vellum, and a quill and stoppered ink pot. This last puzzled Zayira. It must have shown on her face, because the armsmaster chuckled. "To write letters home if you'd like," he explained. Zayira's mouth formed a little O of comprehension as she balanced the head-high stack of goods. "I think that will do for now, seeing as you already have bed linens, but if you need aught else, now you know where to find it." He pointed two doors down on the same side of the hall. "Latrines are just there and work the same as the ones in the dining hall. Just follow the instructions and you'll be fine." Zayira peered over the stack of goods at a door marked "LATRINES" and nodded, almost tipping the ink pot off the stack. "Baths are weekly and on rotation except in extenuating circumstances," Rylen continued. "I'll make sure Annalia adds you to the rotation tomorrow. Any questions?" Zayira shook her head. "Good, then let's get you settled and to bed! You must be exhausted." The armsmaster clapped her on the back solidly enough to make her stumble, but she managed to keep hold of the items he'd handed her. Some brief mental math told Zayira she held more than a month's worth of market pay from back home in her arms. *Can't afford to drop anything.*

Miraculously she made it back down the hall and into her new room without incident. Rylen entered just long enough to help her set things down properly, bade her clean up down the hall before bed, and wished her a good night. Zayira thanked him for all his help as he closed the door as gently as possible, which meant only disturbing the next two rooms down instead of the entire hall. *I wonder who lives in the next room over.* She'd likely find out on the morrow. For now it was time to settle down for the night, which meant washing off the dust of her journey and falling into bed. *Just 'cause I've come from a farm doesn't mean I need to smell like one.* She grabbed her towel and a clean set of clothes and headed back down the hall, stopping by the supply closet for a cake of soap that smelled like lye on her way.

The dorm latrines were similar to the ones in the dining hall, with marked toilets for solids and liquids. The main difference was the set of narrow windows cut into the outer wall. They bore neither coverings nor shutters, but were thick and angled such that rain would have a hard time getting in. Another door stood opposite the toilets, flanked by sinks with wooden taps. It was marked "BATH." *Guess that's where I'm headed– certainly this counts as "extenuating circumstances," and the armsmaster himself did tell me to bathe.* She pushed inward on the door.

A muffled grunt stopped her before she opened the door. "Almost done," called a male voice much older than she. It reminded her of her brother Danil, which brought on another pang of homesickness. "Just let me get dry and clothed and it's all yours."

"S-sorry," Zayira stammered as she pulled the door

closed once again. "I didn't know anyone was in here."

"'S all right," the voice answered. "Though I don't know who's up next; not supposed to be anyone else on bath rotation tonight. You'll have to hurry." The door opened and Zayira realized she'd stayed in front of it throughout the brief conversation as a young man in his late teens flung the door open, nearly running her over as he exited. "Oh. Sorry about that," he said as he reached out to keep her from falling over. "Didn't see you there." He peered at her face and she blinked owlishly at him, taking his measure just as he took hers. "You're new," he announced.

"First day," Zayira confirmed without breaking her gaze. "Got in this afternoon."

"Welcome," the boy said, extending a damp hand. Zayira took it and felt the grip of a boy who was no stranger to hard work. "Name's Jase."

"Zayira." They shook hands and nodded. Jase stepped back to allow her access to the bath.

"Well met," Jase stated as he glanced out the closest window. "Anybody told you how the bath works?"

Zayira leaned into the next room, which contained a tub with a water tap resembling the ones on the sinks, but larger. She shook her head. "No, but it looks simple enough. Like the sinks?" She mimicked turning the tap and Jase nodded.

"No hot water, so I don't recommend soaking. Just in, clean, and out is best. I see you found the soap and the supply closet–good. If you need anything else I'm down the hall two doors on the inside." Zayira mentally counted the space between their rooms, then nodded.

"Thank you," she called after him as he headed out the door. Jase waved, then was gone.

He didn't seem too bad. Bet he's another farm kid, though he's been here a lot longer. Zayira laid out her clothes on the small bench within easy reach of the tub and closed the door. The tap for the bath did indeed work much like the sinks, only the larger faucet sprayed water much faster into the round wooden tub. Before long the water was ankle deep and frigid. Deciding that was plenty to get clean with, Zayira stripped off her filthy clothing, stepped into the tub, and applied the soap vigorously to her person. She could hear her mother in her mind as she cleaned behind her ears and washed her hair. *"Now Zayira, you must put your best foot forward. Don't go to your first day of classes looking like the potatoes we dig up out of the yard, all covered in dirt."* Don't worry, Mother, she thought back. *At least they won't have that to tease me about. There's plenty elsewise.* Exhaustion washed over Zayira as she ran the tap long enough to rinse off, then grabbed the towel she'd brought and stepped out of the tub.

A heavy thump shook the door. "Hey in there!" called a high-pitched male voice. "It's my turn! Hurry up! Didn't you read the rotation?"

"One moment," Zayira called, pulling on her school-crest-emblazoned pants and tunic while only half dry. "I'm almost done."

"Who is that? Annalia, is that you?"

Zayira pulled the door open, supplies in hand, and stared at the red-faced boy standing in front of her. "No," she answered in flat tones as she pushed past the young man. He was average height for someone about her age and had glossy black hair pulled back in a fashionable knot at the back of his neck. As she passed him she caught the scent of lilac and lavender. *What on earth does he need a bath for? So impatient, too. And didn't Jase say there was no one else on rotation tonight?*

"Hey!" The boy's tone stopped Zayira before she made it out the door to the latrines. Turning, she almost dropped her soap from atop the hastily-stacked pile of belongings in her arms. It fanned the flames of annoyance kindled by the upstart in front of her.

"What?" Zayira snarled, her anger at the mortifications of the day getting the best of her. She could feel the warning bells in her mind telling her to calm down, but she ignored them. *He looks like an absolute prat. I bet he has whatever I'm about to say coming.*

The look on her face set the boy back a pace before he regained his composure and tilted his head back in an attempt to look down his nose at Zayira, who was almost as tall as he. "Watch where you're going," he demanded coolly from across the room.

"I will if you will," Zayira snapped back, a tiny cloud forming over her head and drifting toward the boy. *Uh oh…nice work, Zayira.* His eyes narrowed as he watched the bit of indoor weather inch closer and he sneered.

"Look at you–you can't even control when you kindle," he taunted. "You must be new. And not very well off, else you'd know what you're doing." This last he tossed over his shoulder as he disappeared through the door to the bath and closed it behind him, trapping the cloud in the latrines with Zayira.

"Oooooh," she fumed. He was right; she knew better than to lose control of her weatherworking like that, even when she was mad. With a thought she woke a light breeze and sent the cloud scudding out the narrow window and into the night.

On the way back to her room she realized how lucky she was no one else was in the latrine as she left. Her aunt had seemed very secretive about her weather-working earlier in the day, which gave her the impression she shouldn't do much of it around others. But she was there to learn about it; how could she learn if she couldn't practice? She resolved to ask her aunt about it the next chance she got. But who knew when that might be?

Zayira took out her frustration by yanking open her bedroom door with more force than was necessary. She knew it was too heavy for her to slam, so it seemed like a safe option for dispelling some of her anger. Once it was closed behind her and she'd hung up her towel to dry, the absolute silence in the rock-hewn room took over. It was odd to a girl raised on a farm, where the environs were never quiet unless something was wrong, and it set her teeth on edge. But she was too tired to consider it deeply, and the bed looked so inviting.

Before she knew it she was fast asleep beneath the blankets.

CHAPTER 8

Off the coast in the North Midlands Sea

Brizen almost missed the sniveling boy they'd left in Fisherman's Watch. Ever since he'd left there was nothing for Brizen to do but watch the weather and find any occupation he could around the ship. He was forbidden from practicing arms with the mercenaries lest he get any ideas, but he found ways to be helpful elsewhere on the ship. As long as his hands were busy there was a better chance the captain would leave him alone.

The galley was Brizen's favorite place to avoid detection. The cook always needed someone to peel potatoes or stir something, and she was one of the only crew members who didn't seem to care much about his abilities. She was a middle-aged woman who spoke none of the Midlander tongue, nor Zhedaban, but they communicated easily enough through pantomime for Brizen to know what she required. She hid him anytime the rest of the crew came by, which made him wonder what they would say if they found out their food was prepared by someone who was cursed.

Brizen knew it was only a matter of time before

his safe haven was discovered, but when the time came he still felt a deep disappointment and sense of loss. Captain Ordulla herself happened to stop by the galley one afternoon and caught Brizen peeling a wrinkled, wizened apple. Before he could hand it to the cook she slapped it out of his hand. "Infidel! How dare you touch my crew's food supplies?" She backhanded him across the face and wheeled around to face the cook. Brizen had no idea what she said to the woman, as they spoke their strange native tongue, but all color drained from the cook's face and she fell to the floor, prostrate, before her captain. Ordulla sneered at her and walked away. Just when Brizen thought he was safe she called to him from across the room. "Your punishment awaits you in my quarters, cur. Presently."

He didn't dare make her wait.

The deck of the ship swayed with the swells. Some days it made Stiven sick; today it was gentle enough to keep him from casting his breakfast back out to sea before it did his body any good. He'd always hated traveling by sea and avoided it whenever possible. *So why'd you take this job, old man?* The answer was simple, of course: he had to eat, and for someone who earned their coin fighting for the highest bidder, that meant doing whatever was necessary to be in the proper position for battle. They'd been given no time frame for the assignment. All the captain had told them was that they'd be at sea for weeks before they were needed. She'd paid her steel up front, so he and his men were happy to oblige.

Still, something didn't sit right. Stiven had been around long enough to know when to trust his gut, and his gut said there was something off about this job. He was used to operating under the least amount of information possible to protect his employer, so that couldn't be it; they'd worked with less intelligence before and come through just fine. Mostly. So what had his hackles up?

It was that captain, if he was honest with himself. She and that brute who followed her like a whipped dog unsettled Stiven. His men weren't too fond of them, either, though he heard the whispers when they thought he wasn't listening. *She's a pretty face, isn't she? Aye, but she'd as soon cut you as look at you. Sure, sure. I'd still take the chance.* He shook his head. Young and dumb, the lot of them. It was a shame he had none of the old guard. Young Rylen would've figured her out before a tenday was out and had the crew eating out of his hand.

"Sir?" One of the younger mercenaries in the company sidled up to Stiven. "You feeling all right?"

"I ain't feeding the fish back my breakfast, am I?" The young man shook his head. "I'm fine. What do you need?"

The lad shifted his weight from foot to foot. "It's just…we was listening to some of the crew earlier, and Trin, he speaks a bit o' their tongue, and he's not sure, but he thinks…" He leaned closer. "He thinks we're headed for the weatherworking school."

"Whatever for?" Stiven tried to come up with a reason they would need mercenaries at Weatherwatch and came up blank.

"They hate them that work the weather. Trin heard 'em say that much." The lad tugged at his hat and nodded a polite good day to Stiven in time to not look suspicious as one of the regular crew swept past on some errand. Stiven stood rooted to his spot, realization dawning blood red in his mind.

He'd killed many men and women in his lifetime. All of them had the misfortune of being on the opposite side of a conflict from his company. None of them had been innocent, or unarmed, or helpless. And none of them had been children.

What did this woman–this formidable captain–expect them to do? Were they simply security against pirates, or did she plan on asking them to fight the inmates of a boarding school? Stiven believed Captain Ordulla was capable of whatever heinous acts she deemed necessary, so he wouldn't put it past her.

It was time to do a little more digging.

CHAPTER 9

Sunlight in Weatherwatch Valley never filtered down to the bottom of it until later in the morning than Glorya was accustomed to. Her home in Joveru saw the sunrise from its topmost point, waking her early enough with its first rays that she never had to rely on anything else to wake her. This morning it was her bladder that awoke her sometime after dawn. She stumbled to the indoor latrine and back, contemplating a lie-in before deciding that starting late on her first day as a teacher would set a poor example for her students. So instead she cleaned up as best she could, donned one of her nicer pairs of breeches and a new shirt, and went to seek out the headmaster.

Headmaster Thayer resided in the only two-story building on the grounds, built as both an administrative office and a domicile for the school's highest official some thirty years prior. Glorya remembered it being in better repair, but for the most part it still looked just as imposing as it had when she was a student. *Except it looks smaller now,* she mentally amended before striding up to the door and knocking three times. There was a scurry behind the door and a strident "One moment!"

from a high-pitched male voice before the door cracked just enough to show a single brown eye. "Who is it?" the disembodied voice asked.

"Sunchaser Glorya, here to speak with the headmaster about my new position." At the mention of her name the eye widened. The sound of multiple locks releasing in sequence followed a set of bony fingers upward until the door swung open on creaking hinges to reveal half of the young man who admitted her; the rest remained behind the open door.

"Please, do come in!" he exclaimed. "You're here just in time for breakfast." He shuffled off toward the smell of sausage cooking down the hall, trusting his guest would follow. Glorya took the time to study her surroundings as she moved through the building after her guide. She'd only been in the headmaster's house once while she was a student. She'd gotten in trouble for fighting with one of the other students her very first year of school, and the headmaster–not the current incumbent, but his predecessor–had asked to speak with them both. He'd been stern, but kind as he explained that fighting was not acceptable behavior at school, then quizzed them on various topics to see how much they knew. In the end he'd spoken with the teachers and had both moved up one form in two of their subjects. She remembered the man fondly. Bits of his influence remained in the pictures on both walls down the front hall and the trinkets on shelves in the sitting room beyond, which sat dusty and unoccupied.

Continuing down the hall the smell of frying sausage thickened. She turned a corner and was hit by a wave of smoke. "Oh bother, please excuse me; I seem to have let my pan get too hot." The young man who'd let her in fussed over a smoking skillet. *At least he caught it in time.*

"How can I help?" Glorya asked. "Here, let me open these windows." She reached toward the openings set equidistant from the door on the wall next to her.

"Oh, good idea. Let me get them." The erstwhile chef gestured toward the runny glass windows and a breeze sprung up, strong enough to turn a set of small fan-shaped cranks attached to each window. The panes and their frames tilted outward to allow an egress for the smoke thickening around the ceiling. An extra push from the young man corralled the fumes and shoved them outside.

"Very neat work," Glorya applauded as she down-graded the winds the young man had called, leaving just enough to draw air through the room and keep it cool and clear.

"Lots of practice, I'm afraid." The young man finished flipping over each piece to inspect it before pulling them all out of the pan and onto a plate to cool. "If you would follow me, I'll show you upstairs to the study, where Headmaster Thayer takes his breakfast." He picked up the plate of sausages and a spatula, then cast about for something. "Ah, if you would be so kind as to bring those two plates and some utensils…" He nodded toward the only two clean plates Glorya could see and started up the narrow, winding staircase at the back of the kitchen. She grabbed the plates and two forks and followed, careful not to crowd the young man, but following closely enough to try to catch him if he fell. His steps were precarious on the smooth wood-en treads.

Two turns of the stairs later they emerged at the

end of a hallway with equally worn wood flooring. The walls were whitewashed and sprouted shelves every so often that held plaques commemorating the various achievements of the school and its occupants, both past and present. Glorya barely had time to glance at them as she strode to keep up with the young man before her. He made a beeline for the open door at the end of the hall, through which they could see what appeared to be a desk; it was difficult to tell with all the mounded documents, books, and academic detritus piled atop its surface. Behind it sat a man in his mid- to late-60's who was bent over a tome of considerable size.

"You had better have a damned good reason for being late," the man grumbled without looking up from his study of the material before him

"I–I do, sir," the young man stammered. The sausage bounced dangerously close to the edge of the plate he carried as his hands began to shake. "W–we have a–a–a guest this morning for b–b–breakfast." He almost dropped the plate of sausages gesturing toward Glorya, who ducked around him and bowed at the waist to introduce herself.

"Sunchaser Glorya, at your service," she said, managing to keep her embarrassment for the young man next to her out of her voice and expression. *Hopefully I can keep him from punishment.* "I'm afraid my arrival interrupted his cooking."

The older man looked up for the first time. "Good havens, Brint, why didn't you lead with that?" He motioned toward the single uncluttered chair in the room. "Please, Sunchaser, do sit down." Glorya scooted around the young man–*Brint,* she reminded herself–and sat, still carrying the plates and forks. "I see he's already put you to work, guest or no."

Glorya glanced at the dinnerware in her lap. "Oh, no, I insisted," she explained. "He appeared to have his hands full enough as it was."

"Quite right," Headmaster Thayer mumbled. "Here, hand me one of those plates, would you?" He extended a delicate hand over a pile of what looked to be jars full of various substances. Glorya half stood to make sure her burden reached its destination without disrupting anything below as it passed. "So, Sunchaser, I hear you are the best of the best," began the headmaster as he waved Brint forward to serve.

"I have yet to meet a storm I couldn't handle," Glorya ventured, "but I will admit to a lack of direct classroom experience–hence my surprise at your request." She slid two sausages from Brint's serving plate to her own and waited for the headmaster to begin his own meal. She didn't have to wait long; the man speared three of the remaining links with the precision and speed of a frog catching flies, leaving one sausage on the plate. Brint frowned, but took the plate and turned to leave.

"Bring up some scones and jam as well," the headmaster called after him. A muffled "Very well, sir" bounced down the hall from the direction of the stairs. Headmaster Thayer eyed Glorya over a forkful of sausage. "You are a bit younger than I had thought," he admitted, "but Sunchaser Keross spoke very highly of you."

"I am honored, sir," Glorya replied, uncertain of the conversation's direction. *Time to take the tiller myself.* "If you don't mind, I had wondered–"

"Of course, despite your lack of years you have

accomplished much," the headmaster continued as if she hadn't spoken. Glorya stabbed a piece of sausage and pasted a bland smile on her face. "It seems you are responsible for–" he consulted a list to the side of his plate, onto which he dripped grease from the sausage suspended over it–"strengthening trade with Temalingar, starting your own highly successful business in Zhedaba, and establishing the weatherworker ranking system used by every port on the Western Ocean." His eyebrows raised at this last point. Glorya chewed on her sausage, awaiting an actual question before speaking again. She knew the headmaster's type; pompous and self-aggrandizing to a fault. *I'm certain he'll find some way to list my accomplishments as his own assets.* It was disgusting, but as long as the pay was worth it–and she was able to keep an eye on Zayira–she could stick it out. Speaking of which…

"Correct on all counts, sir." When no further comments were forthcoming she continued. "As you can see, I am a busy woman, and I've agreed to help while you find a suitable replacement for Sunchaser Keross, but I'd like to discuss the terms of my employment."

"Yes, of course," the headmaster agreed. "I'm certain you found them adequate."

"I did not find them at all," Glorya countered. She extended the rolled-up letter she'd received requesting her aid as evidence. "My own letter of acceptance and inquiry may not have preceded me by long, so I'm sure you've missed it. In it I asked for permission to use Sunchaser Keross's cottage and for particulars on remuneration."

Headmaster Thayer unrolled the vellum and skimmed the contents. "Brint!" he yelled. "Blast it, where is that boy?"

"Coming, sir!" The tinkle of fine crockery announced the return of Brint with refreshments. A plate piled with scones wobbled atop one forearm as he struggled to keep hold of the teapot and cups beneath it. A pile of saucers for the teacups occupied his other hand, and on entering he stared at the cluttered table, at a loss as to where to place any of it. Glorya saved him the trouble by lifting the plate of scones and placing it on top of the most stable pile of books she could find. Brint deflated as he found a rolling side table to use as a tea service and poured the tea. He threw her a grateful look as he handed her a cup of steaming liquid much like the tea she was used to, but her nose told her it was much more bitter. *I've had worse. As long as there's sugar...* "I'm afraid we're out of sugar," he apologized as if answering her unspoken question. "But I can fetch some cream from the cellar if you'd like."

"No need," Glorya answered, then amended, "at least, not for me. Headmaster?"

"No, no, you know I like mine strong and black," the headmaster replied, sitting back in his chair with his cup. "Young Brint, before you go, what did you do with the employment contract you were to copy and send to Sunchaser Glorya here?"

Brint's face paled. "I–I sent it to her, sir...?"

"You most certainly did not," Headmaster Thayer chided. "Where is the original? We will let her peruse it now." He slurped at his tea and it took everything Glorya had not to cringe.

"It's filed under–let me get it for you, sir." Brint rushed to prove his usefulness under the hawk-like gaze of his employer, pawing through piles of paperwork and stirring up dust until he produced a rolled-up vel-lum. He sneezed as he handed it to Glorya. "Abologies," he sniffled as he wiped off the vellum before releasing it. "Hay fever." Glorya smiled wanly as she unrolled the vellum and devoured its contents. *Monthly stipend, room and board, holiday and leave days unpaid…standard fare, really. But what's this?*

"I have a question about the contract," she an-nounced. At the headmaster's nod she continued. "It says here that I shall be required to furnish my class-room with supplies out of my stipend, which is not nearly generous enough to cover much of what I might need. Is that standard?"

"Indeed," Headmaster Thayer assured her. "In fact, we've extended you an offer that is above the usual beginning stipend given your ample real-world experience. We believe it will be of great benefit to our students." He smiled his encouragement, though Glorya noticed it didn't quite reach his eyes. *I'll have to watch this one,* she thought.

"And I have the use of Sunchaser Keross's cottage while I'm here?"

"Of course, but certainly you'll allow for it to be tidied up first; I understand it's in quite a state." The headmaster's concern seemed genuine, but Glorya sensed an ulterior motive beneath it.

Let's see what he does with this. "Actually I've found it very helpful to go through some of my predecessor's things. It's been good to see some of what he was work-ing on with the students and read some of his notes on same. After all, they'll soon be my own charges."

Headmaster Thayer leaned forward in his seat. "And…did you find anything of particular use?" He asked the question as nonchalantly as possible, but it was obvious he had a vested interest in the answer. In the corner Brint choked, turning it into a cough and mumbling an apology at a glare from the headmaster.

"Not yet." It was all Glorya could do to keep her expression neutral. "But I'll be sure to let you know if I find anything of use to the school." *And just like that, I have leverage.*

The headmaster deflated back into his seat. "Yes, yes, very good," he said as he waved a hand dismissively in the air. "Did you have any other concerns about the contract?" He looked weary and a few years older than when she'd entered the room, and Glorya took pity on her erstwhile opponent.

"I do not," she reassured. "Where do I sign?" Brint unstuck himself from the wall long enough to indicate a blank at the bottom of the document and she scrawled her no-nonsense signature in a fair, legible hand. Headmaster Thayer melted a bit of red wax onto the corner of the document and produced a small metal seal, pressing it into the warm, malleable substance. It took on the impression of a lighthouse much like the one that Glorya knew sat at the mouth of the bay outside.

"All done," the headmaster announced as he set the vellum aside to dry and cool. "Now, if you will excuse me, Sunchaser, I must get on with my studies. I'm sure you have many things to attend to, and if there is anything we can do for you, please don't hesitate to ask Brint." He bent once again over his stack of books in clear dismissal of both Glorya and Brint.

"It was nice to meet you, Headmaster," Glorya ventured as she rose from her seat. She was rewarded with a muttered "You as well" before she withdrew, smiling.

Brint followed her like a curious shade. Neither of them spoke until they were back below the second floor, at which point Brint burst into a flurry of apologies. "I am so sorry, Sunchaser–I could have sworn I included the contract with the letter! Please forgive my oversight. I–"

"Brint," Glorya interrupted, holding a hand out in supplication. "It's fine, I promise. All's well that ends well, and I planned on taking the contract no matter the terms." Brint's narrow eyebrows shot up at her admission. "Though if I had found them *too* unfair I would certainly have negotiated for better to the best of my ability–which I've honed over a long career haggling in the markets of Zhedaba." She winked at the young man as his eyes widened in awe. "Now, I could use a bit of assistance acquiring some cleaning supplies, if there are any on hand."

"Of course," Brint agreed, scrambling around the kitchen for a moment before getting his bearings and sailing toward a small closet. "Our cook makes the best lye soap," he called from the depths of the tiny space, which was filled with brooms, mops, washcloths, and the like. *It takes someone that skinny just to fit in there,* Glorya thought as a wooden handle clattered to the floor, the first casualty of Brint's war with the cupboard. "I know we have some extras–ah ha!" A cake of cream-colored soap appeared in the bony hand protruding from the doorway. Glorya took it before it disappeared again, then liberated a cleaning cloth and bucket as they tumbled out onto the floor at her feet.

"I believe this is all I need," she called over the din. A muffled cry answered her as another bucket fell directly onto the young man's foot. Glorya removed the offending pail to clear a path for him to escape, which he took with alacrity. "Are you all right?"

"Yes, absolutely," Brint ground out between bared teeth. "I've had much worse, trust me. And it's high time I did something about the state of that cupboard anyway!" He shouted this last at the pile of cleaning supplies on the floor at his feet.

"Do you need any help?"

Brint stared at her as if she'd sprouted a tail. "The headmaster would have my hide if he found anyone else cleaning in here! I wouldn't be able to sit down for a week! No, no, it's best if you go. But I thank you for the offer." He turned toward the mess and bent down to start cleaning. "Let me know if there's anything else you require," he cast over his shoulder at her.

"Many thanks," Glorya replied, saluting him with the soap before seeing herself out. *Poor kid,* she thought as she carried her supplies back to her cottage. *I'll have to keep an eye out for him; seems like he doesn't have many allies.*

A short walk later Glorya stood in the open door of her cottage, watching the dust motes dance in the morning sun all through the interior. They were plentiful. *Looks like I have my work cut out for me,* she thought as she eased inside and set to work tidying up her new space.

CHAPTER 10

The same morning, just before sunrise

Zayira awoke at her usual time from a surprisingly deep sleep. She thought it might take some time before she found it comfortable falling asleep in near silence, but if all of her days were as tiring as the prior day, she'd learn quickly. No sound reached her ears from the hallway beyond. *Guess I'm up early.* She threw her feet over the side of her bed–much shorter than the one she was used to at home, but wider–and let the cool floor on her soles finish waking her up. The harsh scrape of her door made her wince when she opened it, but she slipped down the hall barefoot to use the latrine without seeing another soul.

About the time she donned her new uniform a quiet knock startled her. "One moment," she called, straightening her tunic before cracking the door. Jase stood a polite distance away in the hall beyond. "What can I do for you?" she asked, widening the crack with effort.

"Heading to arms practice and thought you might be up and in need of occupation. Us farm kids tend to be up early anyway. Want to join?"

"Yes!" Zayira exclaimed, then hushed her tone and repeated, "Yes, I'd love to! What should I bring?"

"Just yourself." Jase motioned for her to follow. Zayira slipped out the door, closing it behind her, and followed the older boy down the hall and out onto the grounds. In the dawn light she could clearly see his curly brown hair and solid build, so much like her own brother's. But his gait was less uncertain, more graceful and sure, and she wondered as they walked what exactly she was getting herself into. Still, he seemed friendly, and she was in sore need of friends and allies. So she dug around in her manners for some polite questions to ask while they walked.

"How long have you been at Weatherwatch?" she asked, glancing sidelong at her companion as they strode across the dew-laden lawn.

"Five years now. I expect I'll be asked to test soon."

"Asked to test?" No one had mentioned anything to Zayira about tests, and the thought made her nervous.

"For my golden pin. You've seen the ones the teachers wear, right?" Zayira nodded. "Those pins mean they've passed evaluation in their field of work and are certified. It's the last step in studying here, and it's different for everyone; the teachers base the test off of each student's strengths and weaknesses, so it changes every time." He slowed as they approached the first building Zayira and her aunt had encountered the day before and turned to face her. "Now, don't let the early morning training crew scare you off. They act tough, but they're good folks. Mostly. You'll sort out the ones who aren't quick enough." With a nod he led them both through the door to the armory.

The interior of the building looked just as utilitarian as the outside. Cream-colored plaster covered the walls, which bore racks of various types of weaponry, both for practice and for use. Zayira recognized the swords and bows, but wasn't sure of the rest; some were short and blunt, while others resembled the harvesters they used on the fields in the fall. A group of youth bunched in the center of the room, staring at her as she entered. *I guess I stick out as the new kid,* she thought as she met every gaze pointed her way. *Just gotta earn their respect.* She nodded politely at the group.

"Everyone, this is Zayira." Though he didn't raise his voice, the group hushed its banter as Jase spoke. "It's her first day, so let's make her feel welcome." His eyes settled on a few boys at the edge of the group and she could feel the warning in his glance. *Guess those are the ones I need to look out for.* She silently thanked him for the hint.

"Heya." Zayira greeted the group with a small wave. Most of the students nodded, but a few waved back, and one–a brown-haired girl a few years her senior–even smiled. Hope that she might find support with this group flared in Zayira's chest as she wandered over to the younger folks to await whatever might happen next.

She didn't wait long; before anyone could strike up a conversation Armsmaster Rylen appeared in the doorway. "Good morning!" he bellowed cheerfully. A few half-hearted greetings floated up from the students. "Everyone grab a weapon and head outside; we'll get our practice in before it gets too hot." As the rest of her peers ambled over to the racks, the armsmaster's eyes lit on Zayira. "Good to see you here!" he exclaimed as he wove through the crowd to where she stood. "You said your aunt taught you some swordplay?" Zayira nodded, her voice eluding her. "Then grab one of those wooden practice swords from the left rack over there and follow the others. We'll pair you with…" He cast about for a moment until his eyes lit on a boy about Zayira's height. "Kristus!" he called, and to Zayira's horror the dark-haired boy from the bathroom the night prior split off from the group. She hadn't noticed him when she'd entered.

"You called, Armsmaster?" he answered without looking at Zayira. *Not him, not him, anyone but him…*

"Yes," Armsmaster Rylen replied. "I'd like you to put our new student, Zayira, through her paces, if you would, and let me know how she does. She's had a bit of training and looks sturdy enough." He smiled to reassure her.

"Of course, Armsmaster." Kristus regarded Zayira from atop the full length of his sharp nose. It took some effort, as he wasn't much taller than she, and it almost made her giggle. "Come with me," he ordered, picking up another wooden blade and striding out the door. Zayira followed, head held high.

They joined the rest of the students on the verdant, dew-laden pitch that ran half the length of the valley. Zayira recognized the entrance to the pass she and her aunt had used to enter the grounds the day before and wondered how long it would be before she'd travel it again. Her woolgathering earned her an abrupt stop as she almost ran into her partner for the morning, who had stopped in line with the next pair of students. He indicated a space across from him for Zayira to stand and they awaited further orders.

"On your guard!" The armsmaster's voice rang out across the pitch and all the students took up a fighting stance. Zayira balanced her weight between both feet like her aunt had shown her and raised her wooden practice weapon, feeling the heft of it in her hand. It was lighter than the one she'd learned with. *Maybe that'll give me an advantage…or maybe it'll make things harder.* "Begin!" As soon as the command came Kristus launched himself at Zayira weapon-first. She barely had time to get her weapon up and step aside before he'd scored a hit on her upper arm. It stung, but not enough to slow her down. She reset her stance and waited for the next attack, which came in the form of a feint to the outside of her guard. It tricked her just long enough for him to slip his weapon under her arm and stab the point into her ribcage. *All right, so that's how it is.* Her brother's perpetual advice rang out in her mind as her anger flared to life: don't get mad–get even. It was time to try something different.

Feigning slow footwork, Zayira inched closer to her opponent until she was inside his reach. Just as he realized his mistake she lunged and batted away his weapon hard enough to create an opening. Before he could bring it back to bear she'd left a nice bruise just above his breastbone and earned the same fiery stare she'd seen from him the night prior. Zayira grinned and pressed her advantage, sidestepping to his open side and parrying his next wild thrust. He managed to recover just in time to deflect her counterattack, but lost his balance in the process, landing with a squelch in the wet grass.

Zayira offered him a hand up. Kristus stared at it, then took it and yanked, pulling Zayira to the ground. She abandoned her practice weapon in favor of a second free hand as she let her momentum carry her forward and onto her opponent. His eyes narrowed as he tried to regain the upper hand without success. *Bet he's not used to girls who can wrestle.* Zayira pulled out one of her brother's finishing moves, pinning Kristus's arms with her knees and laying her forearm across his throat.

"Do you yield?" she asked, inches from his face.

"I will never yield to you, you low-born mud wallower!" he snarled in return, bucking wildly to dislodge her.

"Kristus! Zayira!" Armsmaster Rylen's voice popped the bubble that surrounded the two and sound flooded Zayira's consciousness. She realized to her dismay that everyone else had stopped their practice to watch them. Armsmaster Rylen strode toward them with purpose, his face cloudier than the sky before a storm. "What do you two think you're about?"

Zayira shifted off her erstwhile opponent as quickly as she could. "Having a friendly match, sir," she answered, hoping she could save the both of them some trouble.

"Friendly my arse!" exclaimed Kristus as he picked himself up off the ground. The back of his uniform was covered in grass and mud stains. "She was trying to kill me!"

"I was not!" Zayira protested.

"You choked me!"

"I didn't even put any pressure on it! You could yell plenty loud."

"That's enough," interjected the armsmaster as he reached the pair. He turned toward Kristus. "I saw most of what happened, and it looked to me like Zayira bested you. You, on the other hand, took it upon yourself to exceed my request and evaluate her ground fighting skills along with her sword skills. I hope you learned your lesson today on following instructions."

"But she–" Kristus began.

"Ah ahh," the armsmaster replied, holding up a hand to forestall further commentary. "Go pair up with Jase and practice your parries. They were wide and off balance." Grumbling, the boy shuffled over to his next partner, dragging his practice weapon behind him.

"As for you," Armsmaster Rylen continued, facing Zayira, "don't let him bait you like that. And make sure you follow instructions out here; they're for your own safety and the safety of your opponents. I expect full and immediate compliance at all times. Do you understand?"

"Yes, sir," Zayira answered smartly, all the while doing her best to keep a self-satisfied grin off her face. It must've shown anyway since the armsmaster's next whispered comment took her by surprise.

"Be careful of the enemies you make. A snake will only strike when it's guaranteed to get a meal." The comment left her blood cold. "Everyone else find a new partner and continue!" A chorus of "Yes, sir!" answered him as the students shuffled around and paired back up. This time Zayira found herself facing off against the tall, thin, brown-haired girl who'd waved at her earlier. She looked graceful and settled easily into a ready stance that left little of her body available to hit. She was left handed, too, which threw Zayira for a loop; she'd never had to fight anyone whose best targets were on the opposite side. "On your guard!" The girl's half smile disappeared as she focused on her opponent. "Begin!"

The older girl's weapon snaked around Zayira's wrist and stuck her squarely under the arm before she could blink. *So fast!* A follow-up attack flicked toward her leg, which she managed to parry in time, but it left her out of position when her partner deflected her attack upward at the last moment. It poked Zayira's stomach before she could move out of the way. *I can't even get my weapon up in time! How can I hope to hit her?* The air above Zayira cooled as a tiny cloud began to form above her head. *No no no no no, I can't make another scene! Not now!* Just when she thought she might lose control of her kindling her partner lowered her weapon.

"Your parries are powerful, but too large," she explained in a musical voice tinged with an unfamiliar accent. "Small parries are fast parries. And don't just step backwards–go around to avoid hits." She demonstrated by stepping a quarter turn with her back foot. She made it look like a dance, but Zayira could see how it could help her make openings where previously there were none.

"Oh," was all Zayira could think to say. "Can you show me? You're really good at this," she blurted, blushing as she realized how awkward she sounded. *Get it together or they'll all think you're strange.*

"Of course! Attack me straight on." Zayira did as the girl asked and watched as she made the tiniest parry, stepping a quarter turn to the inside as she did so. "See how much target I have open now?" She indicated all of Zayira's torso. "Now you try it." Without warning she lunged at Zayira head on, watching as she controlled her parry and stepped a little more than a quarter turn to the inside. "Just make sure you don't step too wide or you'll be off balance." The girl kicked at Zayira's lead foot to illustrate her point.

"Halt!" Armsmaster Rylen's voice stopped everyone with a single word. Zayira realized she hadn't even heard him shout it during her first match and felt shame wash over her once again. "Rack weapons and head out for laps," he instructed. Zayira followed the rest of the students as they hung up their practice weapons and trotted back out to the pitch.

The next half hour consisted of various exercises Zayira was sure were designed as torture. They ran around the field three times, flipped rectangular bales of hay from one end of the field to the other, dragged a rope with a heavy stone attached back across, and generally were made to do things even more strenuous than she was used to back on the farm. By the time the sun cleared the horizon they were all moving slower. "All right, back to your dormitories and clean up for classes!" The armsmaster dismissed them, stopping to speak to each student as they left the armory. Some drifted across the closest bridge; others headed straight toward the point of the valley. Zayira attempted to squeak past unnoticed with the small group bound for her own dorm and felt a tap on her shoulder. "A moment, Zayira." She hung her head and stood aside to let the last few students past. Kristus made such a point of ignoring her that it drew her attention, but said nothing. Zayira snorted as his grass- and mud-stained back came into view and he stiffened, but kept walking.

"That one's going to be trouble." The armsmaster shook his head. "Best watch your back; he has a nasty habit of trying to sabotage people in any way he can. It's a shame his parents contribute so much to the school; if they didn't we could kick him out and have done with it." He looked sheepish for a moment and winced. "Forget I said that–I don't normally speak so freely around students, but you have so much of the look of your aunt about you. It's like being in school with her again."

"You went to school with Aunt Glorya?" Zayira's eyes went wide. *He knew my aunt when she was my age! I wonder what she was like...are we that similar?*

Armsmaster Rylen chuckled. "I did, when we were no older than you. But that's a story for another day, and you need to get changed before your first day of classes! Did anyone give you a schedule?"

"No."

The armsmaster grumbled. "I am going to have a talk with a few of our fifth-formers. So much has already been mishandled and it's only your first day." He pushed himself off the door frame at his back and started toward the stormkindler dormitories. "Come along," he added when he realized Zayira had stayed in the doorway to the armory.

"Sorry, sir!" She jogged to catch up.

Armsmaster Rylen dropped Zayira off at her room with instructions to clean up and change into the spare uniform he'd found for her the night prior before joining the rest of her classmates in the dining hall. Her soiled clothes from the morning's exercise went into a basket in her room she hadn't noticed before. It was marked "LAUNDRY" in large, block letters across the front. *I suppose they come pick this up,* she mused as she tossed her dirty uniform into the basket before slipping down the hall to the latrines wrapped in a towel with a washcloth in her hand. Five minutes and a minor amount of scrubbing saw her much more presentable as she joined the flow of students heading to breakfast.

CHAPTER 11

Midmorning, between first and second block

Glorya plopped her cleaning cloth back into the bucket of water at her side. She'd had to empty and refill the bucket twice just cleaning the indoor latrine, which made her thankful the building had running water; carrying it back and forth to and from a well would've taken twice as long. *I suppose it's a good thing the old wells dried up and they figured out the cisterns.*

Her knees complained as she stood up for the first time in half an hour to survey her handiwork from above. The latrine no longer reeked of human waste, though she was sure it would never smell pleasant, and she'd managed to dust, sweep, and mop the floor beneath her bedding. The mattress she'd inherited hung halfway out one of the windows in the main room where she could use her broom to beat the dust out of it. She was sure it would take more than one round of beating for it to reach her standards of cleanliness, but there was plenty of time left in the day to finish it up.

Someone rapped a short succession of knocks on her door. It reminded Glorya of a woodpecker, and for a moment she wondered if it had, indeed, been a bird. Just when she'd decided it was nothing, a voice floated in through the window.

"S-s-s-sunch-ch-aser G-glorya, ma'am?" A timid girl a year or so older than Zayira peeked over the
windowsill. Her platinum blond hair was pulled back
into pigtails on either side of her head, accentuating her
sharp features.

"I am," Glorya responded. "And to whom am I
speaking?"

"L-l-livia," the girl replied, her pigtails bobbing as
she curtseyed.

"It's nice to meet you, Livia. Now, what can I do for
you this morning?"

"It's H-h-hulvai," Livia stammered. "We n-need
you to c-c-c-come help him–he's b-being b-b-bullied
by the bigger k-k-kids and n-n-nobody can g-get near
him."

And that's where I come in. Glorya opened the door
and slipped outside. "Take me to him." Livia nodded,
seeming not to trust her voice to answer properly.
Glorya wondered if the girl always stuttered or if it got
worse when she was nervous. Either way, she followed
the girl around the teachers' cabins and toward the
point of the valley, which held the windwaker dormitories. She could feel the workings in play before
she could see any of the participants in the schoolyard
drama: three distinct sources waking northbound winds
and a fourth pushing back. *Shame to see some things don't
change,* Glorya thought as they cleared the last building
and surveyed the scene. Three boys stood facing the cliff
side just north of the languages building where they'd
pinned a smaller boy to the wall with the winds they'd
called. At least, that was how it looked–until Glorya
realized they were the ones doing their best not to fall

over against the smaller student's counterattack. *He's holding off all three of them single-handed?* Before either side could win the contest of skills she grabbed each of the lines of wind and snapped them simultaneously. All three of the larger boys pitched forward onto the ground, while their dark-haired target sagged against the stone behind him, clearly spent.

"What is going on here?" Glorya demanded of the group. Livia hovered at the edge of the building behind her, but she paid the child no mind. "Someone explain this, please. Now."

"He started it," replied the largest of the three apparent bullies.

"Only if by 'started it,' you mean 'walked away when you spoke to me,'" answered the smaller boy by the wall. *Hulvai,* Glorya recalled from Livia's initial report.

"Enough," Glorya interrupted before the argument could begin anew. "You three, what are your names?"

"Nic."

"Pavli."

"Zak, ma'am." The last to respond was the one who'd answered her in the beginning, a brown-haired boy with pale skin and freckles. The other two looked to be younger by a year or so, one with red hair and the other blond.

"Points for remembering your manners, Zak." The boy beamed. "Now, why on earth did you think it was a good idea to pin someone against a wall?" His face fell as Glorya's questions dug in.

"He threatened us," Zak declared, pointing at Hulvai.

Glorya paused for a moment, then laughed. "You

honestly expect me to believe you three–as big as you are–felt threatened by a *single first-year?*" All three hung their heads.

"They should feel threatened," Hulvai hissed. "I'm going to show them what bullying really means." A breeze stirred Glorya's loosely-tied hair and she sighed.

"No, you're not." She found the thread of the boy's working and crushed it with barely a thought, watching him as she did so. His eyebrows shot up, but he said nothing. "Now, seeing as how it's my first day and I'm not fully acquainted with all the new rules yet, I'm not certain what the punishment is for fighting these days." Circling the group, she gauged their wary reactions as she continued. "Back in my day, the penalty for mis-using your gifts with the intent to harm others was ten lashes–and that was for the first offense." The boys' eyes went wide and two of them began to blubber.

"Please, ma'am, don't give us lashes!"

"We didn't mean no harm! It was just a game!"

Hulvai, on the other hand, silently removed his shirt, turning his back on the group and bowing his head. The rest went silent as they surveyed the cross-hatched scars marring his young, tender skin. *Dear havens, what has happened to this boy?*

Glorya approached slowly, sure to make plenty of sound as she trod the wet grass so as not to scare him. "Don't worry," she reassured. "No one is getting lashes today." She set a hand atop Hulvai's shoulder as lightly as she could. He flinched anyway, but turned to glance at her hand. "Put your shirt back on and follow me to my cottage. It's the last one before the headmaster's house." Nodding, he re-donned his shirt and turned around to await her departure.

"As for the rest of you," Glorya announced to the three boys, who had turned to sneak off before she noticed they were gone, "you will report to your head teacher at once. Tell her what you have done and that you accept whatever punishment she finds suitable for such. If you do not do this, I will go directly to the headmaster and have you sent home. Are we clear?"

A dejected chorus of "yes, ma'am" answered her, and the sad group shuffled off to meet their fate. Glorya heard the ghost of a giggle follow them and realized Livia was no longer in sight. *I'll need to watch out for that one.* "Come," she said aloud, motioning for Hulvai to follow her. He kept pace exactly three steps behind her all the way to her cottage, where he rushed ahead to open the door. When he tugged at the iron handle and found it locked he froze. "Don't worry," Glorya reassured. "I brought the key." She smiled in what she hoped was a benign way and produced her key from the pocket of her trousers.

Once inside the boy seemed even more on edge. He stood against the wall between the door and the window, his eyes darting around the room. When Glorya noticed his hands shaking at his sides he shoved them into his sleeves to hide them. *This boy has seen ill treatment. Certainly not here...*The idea of someone at Weatherwatch abusing any of the children enough to cause these reactions was absurd, and Glorya did her best to discount it. *How do I put him at his ease?* "Your name is Hulvai, is it?" The boy nodded vigorously. "And you're a windwaker." Another nod, this one more subdued. *Something to that, with the way his eyes cut downward as he nodded.* "And you're still pretty new at Weatherwatch." The boy's head snapped up and he met her gaze for the first time, looking for all the world like a quizzical bird. *He's skinny enough to be one, that's for sure.* She chuckled. "Nobody's told me anything, if that's your worry. It was a lucky guess." The boy deflated, resuming his wary, tense posture and scanning the room. "So tell me, Hulvai, where are you from? Yours is not a name I recognize, and I've been all over most of the known world." His eyebrows rose at her last statement.

"Even to Zhedaba?" he asked. His voice was thin and sweet when he wasn't yelling, not at all how Glorya would've pictured it. She nodded.

"I live in Zhedaba," she answered, and Hulvai's eyes grew even larger. They were such a dark brown they were almost black. Set wide in his high-cheek-boned face, they opened a window into what the boy was truly thinking for a moment before he shuttered his expression again. "If you'd like I can tell you about it sometime," Glorya offered in an attempt to keep the boy from shutting down completely. He looked away, then shrugged.

This shell will take time to crack. "Think about it," Glorya advised. "In the meantime, I suggest you return to your studies. You can tell your teacher I kept you if you get in trouble for returning late."

"Thank you, ma'am," Hulvai replied automatically before slipping out the door. Glorya watched him scamper across the grass and into one of the instructional buildings by the stream that bisected the valley. *There's something going on with that one,* she thought. *I can feel it in my bones, but it'll be hard for me to get through to him. Maybe Zayira…*She hated to use her niece, even to help with a good cause, but she had a feeling the girl would be happy to help; she had a kind heart, and if she understood the reason behind the ask she figured Zayira would commit to helping. *But it's not something we'll sort out today, or even tomorrow, and I've got chores to do.* Heaving a sigh, she took up her cleaning cloth once again and turned her attention to the living area.

It was, in short, an absolute mess. Sunchaser Keross had at one point maintained some modicum of organization; some of his older documents were ordered and filed away in bins or folders made of larger pieces of vellum wrapped around bundles of texts, but the more recent additions were scattered across every surface in the room. It was as if he–or someone else–had been searching for something in the piles of folios and files. Glorya recalled the man as meticulously dressed and well prepared from her own time as a student, so this lack of care for his research and teaching materials felt out of character. Glorya let that simmer in the back of her mind as she gathered sheets of vellum covered with calculations and maps and figures and sorted them into stacks based on subject. Most dealt with geography and map making, with a smaller portion devoted to a study of tidal effects. She could feel there was a theme to the work, but tying it all together would have to wait until it was properly filed and easier to review. Besides, she didn't know how long she would have before her instructional duties would kick in and require most of her time.

It took the rest of the morning to clear enough space in her living area to use the desk hiding beneath the piles of vellum. The lunch bell rang, sounding just as she remembered it from her teenage years as it summoned her to the dining hall. Students thronged into the building ahead of her, and she craned her head as best she could to catch a glimpse of Zayira before joining the line to be served. It was no use; Glorya was of average height and many of the students stood a head taller than she. Sighing, she looked around for familiar faces, finding Hulvai alone at the back of the line and Livia toward the front with a group of other girls. Her stutter was still present, but was less pronounced while talking to her friends. Glorya made mental note of the group and tried to commit faces to memory as best she could without names to match.

The midday meal consisted of roasted root vegetables dried and rehydrated from the winter season with a thin stew that tasted like beef despite the dearth of meat within it. A thick slice of bread with a crisp, flaky crust sat on the side of her bowl, slathered with butter. It made up for the soup's deficiency, and Gloria found it a satisfactory way to refuel for her next endeavor: observation of classes. Since no one had let her know when and where she would have students–much less which subjects she must teach beyond sunchasing–she planned to take it upon herself to figure it out. *Better start with someone I know, then.* Perhaps Rylen would be amenable to some assistance to start things off. *Better yet, I could drop in on Mira and see if she still needs help with some Zhedaban.* Her course set, she finished her meal with purpose.

CHAPTER 12

Earlier that morning, after arms practice

Zayira finished a hearty breakfast of oatmeal and summer fruit with nuts sprinkled on top before the bell clanged for classes to start. Uncertain of where to go, she looked around for others wearing the storm-kindler pin, then found a group headed out the main door. Not having any better ideas, she deposited her dishes in the large basket at the end of her table and followed them out. Snatches of conversation drifted back to her on the light breeze.

"Wonder what awful things we'll have to learn today…those frogs we cut apart were *ghastly…*"

"I can't believe I didn't pass my maths exam last week…"

"…truly awful at kindling anything more than a tiny cloud…"

"Hear…new girl…Kristus this morning…" This last piqued her interest, but the speaker was too far ahead for her to make out anything more. *They're already talking about me, and I don't even know if it's anything good.* She supposed it was bound to happen with her being new and all, but it still stung to be spoken about instead of talked to.

The group of twenty or so stormkindling students crossed the central bridge over the swelling creek that bisected the valley and approached another squat building identical to the other three built around the stream. Vegetable and fruit gardens lined the pathways on each side, and Zayira could see ripening strawberries next to bushes covered in the late blueberries she'd added to her oatmeal a few minutes prior. The idea of helping grow the food they ate comforted her. *At least that's one thing I know how to do.* The thought bolstered her confidence as she entered her first classroom of the day.

The interior, though well lit by open windows around the room, was dim enough compared to the bright sunlight outside that it took a few seconds for Zayira's sight to adjust. She paused inside the doorway to avoid bumping into anything and was rewarded with a jostle from behind as another student shouldered past. He settled at a group of desks in the middle of the room that held three other occupants who turned to each other and began to gossip. Many of the older students peeled off and headed for the far side of the room to chat with each other, while most of the younger ones took up the seats closest to the door they'd entered. All total there looked to be about twenty students in the class, equally distributed among the groups.

Zayira shifted from foot to foot as she considered what to do. A few of her classmates sat watching her like vultures contemplating a prospective meal. She wiped her sweaty palms on her tunic and pulled her chin up higher to return their looks with a fierce self-assurance she didn't feel, but hoped she could fake until she did.

Her expression broke as the door to the classroom opened behind her, admitting a late-middle-aged woman of ample proportions. She wore a simple blue split skirt with a tucked-in cream-colored blouse and had contrived to get her mass of silvering brunette hair into a no-nonsense bun atop her head. Flint gray eyes scanned the room as she swept past Zayira, cutting off conversations as they met the students' stares. By the time she arrived at her teacher's desk the room was silent except for the occasional shuffle or cough. "Good morning, class," the woman announced in a strong, warm alto voice.

"Good morning, Ms. Sylene," the class chorused in return.

"I see they've once again given us a new student without forewarning," she observed as she nodded toward Zayira. "We're glad to have you, Miss…"

"Zayira." She curtsied as she said it, just the way her mother had taught her, in hopes it was the respectful thing to do here as well as at home.

"Well met, Zayira," replied Ms. Sylene. "And bonus points for manners, something a few of your better established classmates would do well to remember." Her voice rose as she uttered her last statement. Many of the students refused to meet her stern gaze. "Now, if you please, have a seat over here with me so I can evaluate you and get you situated." Zayira crossed the room as Ms. Sylene completed her instructions. "As for the rest of you, your tablets are inscribed with your morning work. Solve what's on them and check your work with your group. I'll be with the fifth formers shortly." Nodding to herself, she settled into the cushioned chair behind her desk and gestured for Zayira to be seated opposite on a spare stool. Zayira perched on the edge of it, eager to be out of the scrutiny of her peers.

Ms. Sylene raised a pair of spectacles to her face. "So, Zayira, from whence do you come to us? You've the look of the Midlands about you, but it never hurts to ask before making assumptions."

"I'm from Farmer's Bend," Zayira replied.

"A beautiful area. I'd love to retire there one day, in fact–have a little house on some land, keep chickens..." The teacher shook herself out of her reverie. "So, Farmer's Bend–that probably means figures are no stranger to you."

"Aye, ma'am," Zayira replied.

"You'll want to use 'yes' here instead of 'aye,'" Ms. Sylene warned. "We've enough highborn students you'll risk sounding like a country bumpkin." Zayira raised her eyebrows and nodded. "Now, where was I... oh, yes! Figures." She leaned forward, forearms on the desk, and peered at Zayira. "What is three plus fifteen?"

"Eighteen, ma'am," Zayira answered promptly.

"And what is three thrice?"

"Nine, ma'am."

Her teacher nodded, but Zayira wasn't sure if she was pleased or the opposite. "What would you say if I asked you to find ten percent of fifty?"

"Ten percent of fifty..." Zayira's mind froze. She knew what a percentage was, didn't she? "Um..." she heard herself say to cover the fact that she was floundering.

"How about I put it this way: you've taken a sow to market to sell. You know the auctioneer will take a cut of the profits from the sow in payment for running the auction. If his cut is one tenth the selling price and you sell the sow for one steel, how much must you pay the auctioneer?"

"Five copper," Zayira answered promptly.

Ms. Sylene nodded. "Very good. I think you'll benefit from a challenge. Are you up for it if I give you one?" Zayira nodded enthusiastically. "Wonderful! Then go have a seat at the second table there, the one in the middle, and pick up a slate and grease pencil on your way there." She nodded to indicate a small pile of same at the edge of her desk. Zayira curtseyed once more, took the top slate and pencil from the stack, and found a seat at the second table.

Most of the students in her group were older than she, but one looked more out of place than the rest; he was at least sixteen, where the rest of the group was closer to thirteen or fourteen. His long, freckled face was screwed up in concentration as he tried to work out the second problem on his slate. Zayira noticed the other students were already on their third or fourth problems and one had already finished. She leaned toward the boy who was having trouble and whispered, "May I copy your problems down? I'm new, and Ms. Sylene didn't have a chance to give me the work before I got here. Everyone else has answers, and I don't want to copy those."

"I just can't figure it out!" he exploded in return. Few heads turned, but eyes rolled all around the room. *This must be a regular occurrence,* Zayira thought. "What does tax rate have to do with how much pocket money I have?"

Zayira craned her head to read the problem herself. "Because you won't have enough to buy the herbs you're supposed to get unless you haggle down the price first," Zayira answered, scoffing at the words on the slate. "That's highway robbery for a bit of sage, that is. Shouldn't be charging that much anyway. But if you have to pay five percent in taxes on a silver's worth of herbs and you only have ten copper, you're a ha'penny short." Looking down at the third question on the slate, she began to copy it down, gears turning in her mind to solve it before she'd finished the last word.

"How can you do that?!?" the boy beside her demanded. Zayira started, having already forgotten about their brief exchange. She blinked at him.

"Do what?" she asked.

"Figure that out so easily!"

"I had to know it back home. My mam only sent me to market with so much money each tenthday, and I had a list of things I had to get with that money." Not wishing to babble any more or sound like even more of a country bumpkin, she turned back to her own work, solving the third problem as easily as the second. They were situational questions, such as the market question, and she found they made more sense than she'd worried they would.

The boy beside her shook his head, blonde hair falling across his eyes. "I'll never make anything of myself at this rate. I'll be here forever," he moaned.

Zayira didn't look up from her work to answer. "My Da always told me that can't never could," she told him in her best adult tone of voice. "Maybe most of it's in your own head. What do you want to do for a living?"

The boy stared at her. "My father wants me to take over his business. He's a merchant based out of Fisherman's Watch."

"Yeah, but what do *you* want to do?" Zayira stared back from beneath raised eyebrows. She wondered how someone could have gotten so old with so little sense, and she was sure it showed on her face as she waited for his answer.

His jaw went slack. "I dunno," he said. "Never really thought anything else was an option."

"Well, what're you good at?" Zayira pressed, her annoyance at the interruption in her classwork taking over her voice and coloring it with exasperation.

The boy scratched his head. "Well…Old Grom says I'm good at knowing when the plants need water," he said. "And I've got good control of my kindling to make sure I don't overdo it. In fact, he trusts me over anyone else to make sure the fall crops get watered in properly." Puffing out what little chest he had, he sat up straighter.

"Good money in that over Market way," Zayira answered as she turned back to copying down her morning work. "Loads of people around Farmer's Bend looking for someone to make sure their crops get the right amount of water." She sized the boy up like she'd seen her da do when he'd hired hands to help with harvest. *He's skinny, but if all he needs to do is make it rain…* "Might could make you some introductions if you don't know anyone 'round there." She continued on to the next problem on the slate, ignorant of the existential crisis going on to her right as the boy's face metamorphosed from confusion to hope.

"I'm Deen." A hand slid into Zayira's field of vision. She shook it without glancing up from her work.

"Zayira. Pleased to make your acquaintance."

"Likewise," Deen replied. He shifted in his seat for

a moment. "Do you think you could help me with my maths?" he asked sheepishly.

Zayira fought the urge to roll her eyes. *You need friends, remember?* "Yeah, sure," she answered, and the light that filled his expression told her she'd made the right choice.

The rest of Zayira's morning consisted of more maths practice, then stormkindling lessons. The latter were held on the pitch outside the armory, where Arms-master Rylen lined up the students by rank. Zayira, who stood at the far end of the line, learned that weather-workers were categorized by the extent to which they could use their powers. The scale ranged from first rank to fifth rank, but details on the classification system were scarce; the students around her all had conjectures, but none matched. Some said you had to be able to conjure and control a hurricane to make fifth rank while others said it was more about finesse and understand-ing. Zayira wondered why on earth someone would want to call a storm that big, then decided she didn't want to know the answer. *At least, not yet,* she thought. *Better to get through today without any more incidents.*

The armsmaster called the class's attention to an older student who stood at his side. "Everyone, this is Bree," he introduced, and the girl smiled and bobbed a curtsey to the assembled group. "She's a fifth year sun-chaser, and she's going to help us with lessons today."

"I heard she's having trouble getting past second rank," a voice near Zayira whispered. "Wonder if this is remedial practice for her." Zayira scowled at the gos-sip, but decided to keep an eye out just the same. Bree's smile looked more and more brittle as the whispers continued. *I know Aunt Glorya probably didn't want me to use anything but my stormkindling just yet, but if I have to…*

"…summoning small, *controlled* clouds," Armsmaster Rylen continued, either unaware of or uncaring of the muttering going on around him. "No thunder, no lightning, preferably no rain–just clouds. Now spread out and direct them in front of you, no more than five paces away. And if you can use them to shade yourself from the sun, more's the better." He nodded, then stepped back so that the closer students could work.

All around her Zayira felt threads of weatherworking spring to life. She'd never been this close to a group working before, and it drew her attention like a bottle fly to a carcass. To her right clouds popped up in all shapes and sizes, mostly pearl white, but some ripening dark. A few at the end of the line took peculiar shapes; a diaphanous butterfly winged its way skyward above a trim little boat that floated on a non-existent sea. These last made Zayira's jaw flop open. She'd never seen their like–never even thought to try making shapes with her own clouds.

A calloused finger pressed her jaw closed with gentle precision. "Best get to practicing if you want to be able to do that," Armsmaster Rylen reminded her, winking. He'd appeared in front of her without a sound, and she jumped, her teeth clacking together. "Let's see what you can do."

Zayira nodded, then took a deep breath and concentrated the way her aunt had taught her. She could feel the moisture in the air rising up from the damp earth at her feet, and she drew from it, drying the dew from the grass as she formed it into a spherical cloud in front of her face. It grew to the size of an orange before fizzling out and drifting away on the slight breeze coming off the water.

"Very good!" the armsmaster congratulated as he clapped her on the shoulder. "You've obviously been practicing. Next work on controlling it past when it forms–see if you can change it into something else without re-forming it." To illustrate his point he kindled a similar cloud, then turned it into a box. From there he rotated the box faster and faster until it broke apart into a million wisps. Zayira watched in wonder as they played across the breeze. "It has very little practical application outside of entertainment, but it's very good practice for control." Nodding, he turned to continue down the line of students.

Zayira spent the next quarter hour doing her best to shift her sphere into a box with varying success. She'd almost managed a pointy rectangle when a feeling of wrongness invaded her weather senses, shattering both her focus and her cloud. She looked down the line to see one of the middle students staring at what looked like a miniature thunderhead floating above their head. A line of force ran from the student to the cloud, but Zayira could feel another force at work, tickling along the edge of the stronger working. *Bree,* she remembered, and she watched the girl work to see what she could learn.

Within seconds she could tell the older sunchasing student was out of her depth. She tugged at a few bits of the cloud's structure and only managed to change its shape, not weaken it. The student who'd called it started to panic, which fed the storm's power, increasing its strength and sending jolts of electricity between it and the ground below. They narrowly missed the student who'd inadvertently called them, and he ducked out from beneath the oncoming squall. Bree kept picking at the edges of the cloud, but Zayira could tell it would never be enough to dismantle it. *Maybe if I just nudge her a little…*Reaching out with her own senses, she poked at the main updraft in the center of the cloud. It jiggled at her touch, and she felt Bree move her own working closer. *Come on, figure it out…*She tickled the thunderhead again and watched Bree grab ahold of the main line and pull. Sweat beaded her brow as she fought with the cloud, and Zayira could see her beginning to tire. *Fine, I'll help,* she thought, and she lent her own strength to the fifth year's efforts. Together they managed to break down the formation and scatter it to the wind.

Zayira wiped sweat from her own brow. *Must be the sun–it beats down on us so in this valley.* Certainly it had nothing to do with having spent the last half hour exercising her abilities in ways she'd never had to. The thought brought on instant fatigue, and Zayira's knees threatened to betray her. No, she thought, straightening her spine and drawing in a deep breath. *Can't let on I'm tired.* As soon as she'd steadied herself she looked up to find the armsmaster and his sunchaser helper glancing sidelong at her. Armsmaster Rylen was speaking, though she'd missed the first portion of his statement in her exhaustion.

"…think it's time for us to break for lunch," he finished. Bree sagged beside him, looking depleted. "Go ahead and get cleaned up, *but–*" he forestalled the group already starting toward the dorms–"make sure you wait for bells before you head to the dining hall. Cook will have my head if you arrive a moment early." A chorus of "yessir" wafted back across the lawn as the students shuffled off toward their rooms.

"Zayira." The armsmaster's voice stopped her in

her tracks. "A word, please. Bree, you may go–and make sure you have a good lunch today. Thank you for your help." The girl nodded, then trudged toward the closest bridge. Once she'd left earshot the armsmaster turned to Zayira, who stood alone on the pitch, shuffling her tired feet. "Thank you," he said simply. "I know you helped, and I know Bree could never have done that on her own. I'd like the details on what you did, if you don't mind; they might help with our lessons."

"You mean right now?" Zayira asked, glancing around the field. They were alone as best she could tell, but her aunt had acted so cagey about her abilities she wasn't sure what she should say or around whom. *But she did say she'd talk to the armsmaster about it later, which means she's planning on telling him eventually.* She swallowed, then nodded. "Can we go inside, though? My aunt didn't want me talking about it to just anyone." The armsmaster nodded and gestured for her to lead the way.

Once they were inside he closed the door to the practice pitch. The inside of the armory was warm without the breeze from outside, and Zayira felt prickles of heat dance across her skin as she started to sweat. Armsmaster Rylen settled himself on a block of hay set against one wall in an obvious effort to give her space. "Have a seat if you'd like," he suggested as he waved at a stack of boxes against another wall a comfortable distance away. "We won't be bothered for a while, so take your time if you need to." His easygoing nature and open countenance made Zayira feel that she could trust him, but she still didn't feel comfortable enough to sit, so she stood a few feet inside the closed door and closed her eyes.

"I showed Bree where to pull apart the cloud," she began.

"How do you mean?" The armsmaster's brow furrowed in puzzlement.

Zayira shrugged. "I pulled at the center of it, and that made it kind of vibrate. She eventually figured out that was where she needed to pull to take it down."

"Pulled?" His brows furrowed deeper, reminding Zayira of the furry caterpillars that sometimes left webs in the trees around her home. "I've never thought of any part of what we do as 'pulling.' Can you elaborate?"

Zayira considered, trying to think of another way to describe what she'd managed to do. "I don't just kindle," she explained. "I can also sunchase and windwake. Neither of those are as strong as my kindling, though." She paused to gauge Armsmaster Rylen's reaction. His expression went blank, so she continued. "Why does my aunt want me to keep that a secret? Can't lots of people do more than one thing?"

Armsmaster Rylen blinked at her for a moment before responding. "No, Zayira. That's very unusual–in fact, I don't know of another instance in the history of the school where we've had a student who could do more than one type of weatherworking." He wiped one hand down his face as he considered what to do. "I see why your aunt wouldn't want you to mention it, at least until the administration knows and can better advise you."

"So I'm not normal?" Realization hit Zayira as she said the words and threatened to bring tears to her eyes.

The armsmaster paused, considering his next words carefully before speaking. "Your abilities are different from what we've seen, but that doesn't mean there's anything wrong with you. In fact, you were able to use your knowledge to help people this morning without teachers stepping in. Differences can be a good thing."

"I guess so," Zayira grumbled. "Usually they just mean one more thing for people to pick on."

"A fact I know well," the armsmaster agreed with a sardonic grin that was more of a grimace than any expression of mirth. "For now, let's keep what we've talked about to ourselves. I'll speak with your aunt and see what her plan is for handling it, as I'm sure she has one." He stood and moved to open the armory door, pausing as he passed Zayira. "I know this is a lot for your first day; would you like to take the afternoon off? Start fresh tomorrow?"

She had to admit the idea was tempting, but it felt like running away from her problems, which was something she was never wont to do. "No thank you," she replied, bobbing a curtsey. "I'd rather have something to keep me busy." The armsmaster nodded and followed her out the door.

CHAPTER 13

After lunch, at the start of third block

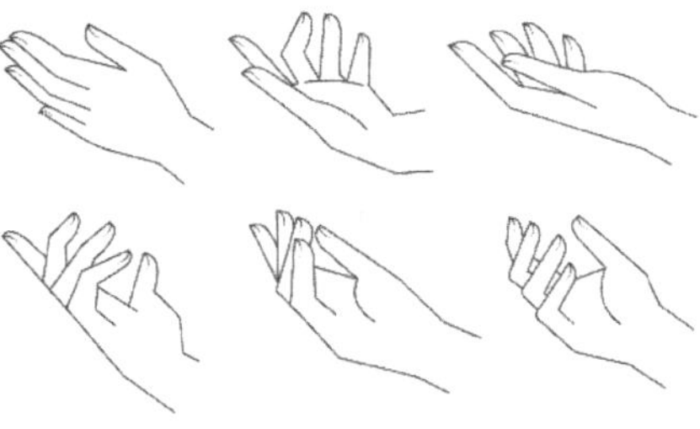

Glorya entered the language and etiquette building ahead of the next class by a few minutes. Mira floated from table to table with a grease pencil, adding to a few of the exercises already written on the slates set meticulously at each spot. She stopped to acknowledge Glorya with a shallow curtsey as soon as she entered. "Good noon, Sunchaser," she said as she continued about her work. "What brings you to the language and etiquette building?"

"Good noon, Mira. I recalled your desire for assistance with Zhedaban and Temalingari and thought I'd stop by to see how I might be of service, seeing as how I don't yet have a schedule for my own classes." Glorya glanced down at the slates closest to her, which were filled with writing exercises for basic Zhedaban letters. *"Do you start class with Zhedaban or manners?"* she asked in Zhedaban, ending the question with the usual head cocked to one side gesture that Zhedabans used to denote a request for an answer.

"I begin with Zhedaban," Mira answered in kind. *"I would be happy to have your assistance."* She gestured relieved acceptance a bit awkwardly.

"May I?" Glorya gestured for permission and reached toward the other woman's hand. She nodded and allowed Glorya to make a minor adjustment to the angle of her wrist that relieved the strain on it and allowed her hand to flow freely into the motion she'd just attempted. Mira practiced a few times, then signed her thanks as Glorya resumed her place by the door.

"I do my Zhedaban lessons with as full immersion as possible," Mira explained in Midlander, opting for the clarity of her native tongue. "I find it helps the students learn to think in another language. If you could help me with some dialogue I think it would better illustrate some of the nuances of the hand signals. Besides, the next class is sunchasers, which would give you a chance to meet the students to whom you'll be teaching weatherworking."

"How fortunate," Glorya replied, pleasantly surprised. "I've met a few of the windwaker students, but not many of the sunchasers yet. How long do you have them, and where do they go after this?"

"Half the afternoon," Mira answered. "Today they have weatherworking next. I assume since you have no schedule you also have no lesson plans?" Glorya winced and nodded. "Perhaps an evaluation of their knowledge would be best for the first day, then."

"I think that's a fine idea," Glorya answered, swallowing her annoyance at her peer's presumption. *She's been doing this longer than you have, woman. Take the advice and make use of it if you feel it's useful; the source matters not.* "Would you like me to return after weatherworking to assist with another class?"

"I appreciate the offer, but by then the school day will be over and the students will be free to socialize until dinner." Mira looked up as the first students trickled in from the dining hall. "*Sunchaser, if you please…*" She indicated the entering students and began to greet them in Zhedaban as they entered. Taking the hint, Glorya introduced herself to each one in the Zhedaban way, making sure they knew the correct words and gestures to use to denote polite greeting of someone older or higher in station. Many were confused, but caught on quickly as they watched their peers interact with the new teacher. One strode forward with confidence, signing the correct way and speaking the right words for polite greeting–for an outdoor setting, which meant he nearly knocked the next student in line over with a wide sweep of his arm. Glorya chuckled.

"*I see you have some knowledge of Zhedaban greetings,*" she said, testing the waters to see how much he knew.

"*My father is a sailor,*" he answered, again with the broader gestures reserved for outdoor use.

"*As am I,*" Glorya replied. "*But I'm afraid the hand signs he's taught you are for use on the deck of a ship, not in a classroom. It's like shouting.*" The boy's eyes went wide and his mouth made a little O. "*Watch and try again.*" She repeated the proper indoor greeting and walked through the correct hand signals. The boy mimicked her with deft attention to detail, his long, tanned fingers sliding through the signs like someone born to them. "*Good!*" Glorya praised as she turned to greet another student. The boy had almost slipped away before she tapped him on the shoulder. "*What is your name?*"

"*Els,*" he replied. "*It's short for Elsen, but that's my*

dad's name, so everyone calls me Els."

"*Well met, Els.*" Glorya nodded and kept half an eye on him as he drifted over to his seat. A few other students showed real promise with their Zhedaban, but many seemed not to grasp the concept of speaking with both their hands and their mouths at the same time. *It wasn't very intuitive for me in the beginning, either.* Glorya thought back on how she'd learned the language so long ago, deep in the heart of Zhedaba itself, and remembered her last visit there. She'd gone to mark the passing of the woman who'd taught her most of what she knew about the society she'd come to love not quite one year prior. The pain of her old mentor's loss on the heels of another who had shaped her life settled back into her soul. *Get it together, woman. You have work to do. There will be time to mourn later.*

The rest of the period passed quickly. Glorya committed as many names to memory as she could, but found herself struggling after about ten, which only covered half the class. She wondered if they could make name badges for everyone to wear until she learned what to call them.

Before she knew it language practice was over and the class looked to her with expectant faces. "I hear we still practice out on the pitch," Glorya announced. "Meet me there in five minutes. Use the latrines if necessary, but don't be late!" The group jostled their way out the door with enthusiasm. Glorya turned to Mira, who chuckled.

"They're always eager to practice with their gifts, but I think your reputation has preceded you," she said as she cleaned off the first set of slates using a bucket of water with soap at the back of the room. "Good luck taming *that* storm, Sunchaser."

Glorya grinned. "I've never met a storm I couldn't handle," she replied with a polite departure hand sign in Mira's direction. The woman returned it and went back to her cleaning, a small smile lingering on her plain features. *There's more to her than she lets on,* Glorya thought as she crossed the threshold and left the language building. Rolling her head around on her neck to loosen tight muscles she headed straight for the field by the armory, the walk from one side of the valley to the other still just as familiar as a well-worn shoe. By the time she got there the class had assembled and the younger ones were chasing one another with dandelions, blowing the seeds into each other's hair and faces. "Good afternoon!" Glorya called in her best deckhand voice to snatch the students' attention from their frolicking and conversations. It worked; they lined up shoulder to shoulder across the pitch. "As you all know, Sunchaser Keross has left us." Heads bowed as she paused in respect. "I recall him as a kind teacher, both patient and wise, and I'm sure his loss is felt keenly by the many lives he's touched. I will endeavor to do his memory justice." She stopped facing the center of the group to allow her voice to carry to both ends of the line. "My name, as many of you already know, is Sunchaser Glorya. I earned my golden pin some fifteen years back and have spent the subsequent time traveling the known world, from the Midlands to Zhedaba and even across the ocean to Temalingar. I've studied the weather patterns of our world in an attempt to better understand my role in regulating them–a role you all share." Here she paused again to read her audience. The majority of the class watched her with some combination of curiosity and awe, but there were still a few who didn't look convinced. *There are always a few.* "I will admit to a lack of experience teaching–" a few smirks emerged from the tough crowd–"but I believe my practical knowledge far outweighs my deficiency."

"Is it true you took apart a hurricane?" a young girl near the middle of the line blurted out. Her pale cheeks deepened into red as the rest of the class turned to look at her.

"I did," Glorya acknowledged, "though it was almost too much for me. I was unconscious for hours afterward."

"You've really crossed the ocean? What's it look like on the other side? Is it just desert or are there trees and plants?"

"Do you really live in Zhedaba?"

"Are you married? Do you have any kids?"

The questions streamed in from both sides until Glorya held up her hands in supplication. "I will answer your questions in time," she promised, "but for now we have work to do." Groaning accompanied her redirection, but the class quieted as she continued. "I was not able to prepare for today's class as well as I'd like, and given our lack of assistance on short notice I think it's best if we talk about some theory today and hold off on hands-on work until I can speak with the other teachers." The group as a whole groaned again. "I know, I know, but for safety's sake I need to understand where you all are in your practice and studies before we start on practical lessons.

"Imagine for a moment that I am completely unfamiliar with sunchasing. Who can explain to me what it is?"

Three or four hands shot into the air. Glorya dug around in her memory for names until she dredged one up and pointed at the tall girl whose hand she'd seen first–*Finya, that was it.* "Sunchasing is the ability to negate the effects of weather," she announced with a light accent. *Sounds like she's from the city.*

"And what kinds of effects can it negate?" Glorya inquired.

"Clouds, wind, rain, fog, and lightning," Finya answered promptly.

"Very good, Finya." Glorya's brief praise earned a flash of genuine smile from the girl. "Next question: if we can just turn off the weather whenever we want, what's preventing us from doing just that? Gireck?" She pointed at a short, spindly boy of about twelve whose hand looked like it might fall off if he kept waving it so hard.

"Because the plants and animals need the rain and the air currents and the fog and all of the things we can turn off," he rattled off with enthusiasm.

"Well done," Glorya acknowledged, nodding at her pupil. He beamed and looked as if he might continue his explanation, so Glorya plowed forward. "And that is the crux of our responsibility as sunchasers: we are stewards of the balance between the earth's needs and humanity's. Without us a single out-of-control storm-kindler or windwaker could set in motion events that would destroy civilization as we know it." She let that sink in for a moment, gauging her students' reactions to the bold statement. It was shocking, but true. "So the next time you feel like less of a weatherworker because you can't see what you've created, look around. See the flowers and trees and bushes and livestock and, yes, the people around you, and know that they are here because people like us exist." She met the gaze of every student before moving on. Most bore the fire of purpose in their eyes as they stared back at their new teacher, respect and interest forging a connection Glorya had only experienced from the other side. Pride swelled within her, not only in her students, but in her own ability to wake in them the same motivation that kept her going through difficult times.

"Now, who can tell me what those clouds mean?"

They spent the rest of the lecture with their eyes turned toward the skies, learning the types of clouds by both sight and feel. Before they knew it the rest of the classes were filtering out of the buildings nearby. "Class dismissed," called Glorya, "and I will see you all on the morrow." A few stopped to bid her farewell before running off to join friends.

"Sunchaser." Rylen's voice carried across the pitch from the armory door. "Do you have a few moments?" He stood in the doorway, leaning against the frame in a casual pose.

"Certainly," Glorya replied. She checked to make sure her students had all departed, then made her way to the armsmaster. "What can I do for you?"

He turned and motioned for her to follow him inside. "I'd like to ask you a few things, if you don't mind. About Zayira." He pushed the door closed and sat down on a bale of hay that had obviously been used for target practice, indicating another nearby for Glorya to use.

She sank onto the makeshift seat, finding it more comfortable than expected. *Well, I have been on my feet all day,* she realized. Aloud, she replied, "I'll answer whatever I can."

"You are aware of her…extra abilities, I assume," Rylen began.

Glorya blew out a breath she hadn't realized she was holding. "Yes, of course," she admitted, glad to have it out in the open where she could discuss it and strategize with someone she hoped she could trust. "I've known almost since she came into her powers some years ago. It struck her earlier than most, too."

"Why did you not tell her it was unusual?" Rylen queried, his thick brows beetling across his forehead. "She seemed to think it was commonplace to have many weatherworking abilities."

"Does the whole class know?" Glorya's blood ran cold as she contemplated what could happen if that was the case.

"No, thankfully," Rylen replied, shaking his head. "Though I think one of your sunchasers might have an inkling someone helped her defuse a situation in the stormkindler weatherworking class today. I don't think she'll put together who it was, so no harm done there."

Glorya closed her eyes, nodding. "That sounds like Zayira, all right." She leaned forward, her elbows on her knees, head sagging to look at the ground. "I promised when I brought her here I would make sure she was safe and well looked after," she began. "Her mother–my only sister among a passel of brothers–asked my advice when we learned she had more than one talent at weatherworking. I thought long and hard, agonized over it, and came to the conclusion that it was safer to keep it a secret until I figured out who to trust at the school. There are some who undoubtedly would want to pick her apart to figure it out." Her face darkened as she considered the possibility. *Not on my watch,* she vowed for the hundredth time.

Rylen abandoned his prior seat and flopped down next to her. She could see the gears turning in his head and recalled his brilliant mind for strategy, hoping it would help her navigate her current impasse. Minutes passed while he considered, theorized, rejected, and reworked, very little of his mental gymnastics visible on his face. Finally, he looked Glorya full in the face. "I concur," he stated. "You were right to bring her here for training, but there are people here I wouldn't trust not to try to take advantage of her situation or turn her into a test subject." He ran a hand through the dark hair atop his head, fingers just brushing the gray at his temples. "The headmaster, for sure, can't know about it. He'll have every possible source of revenue here to inspect her for a modest contribution to the school."

Glorya made a face. "Who else can we trust on the faculty? Anyone?"

"Sylene can be trusted to keep just about anything behind her teeth," Rylen offered, and Glorya smiled inwardly at the accuracy of her own instincts. She'd already pegged the woman as trustworthy with very little interaction. "Mira…could go either way," he continued. "She has some other agenda she's supporting, I can feel it, but I've gotten nowhere figuring it out."

"She's noble, yes?" Rylen nodded. "They always have more than one agenda, whether it's spying for their family or keeping an eye on business interests. She's very closed off, but I don't think she's malicious." The words rang true as she spoke them and Rylen nodded his continued assent. "Who else should I worry about?"

Rylen considered, his head falling to one side as he thought and a stray lock of dark hair flopping over one eye. Glorya remembered her disappointment when they were both students and she learned he wasn't interested in women. A wry smile fought its way to the surface. *Always finding men you can't have, for one reason or another. And more's the better; you need a friend more than anything right now.* "There are a fair number of students I wouldn't trust any further than I could throw them," Rylen continued, oblivious to Glorya's inner monologue. "Especially the snotty noble-born ones. My senior student has acted abysmally toward Zayira so far, and one of the boys has it out for her."

"On the first day?" Glorya exclaimed, dismayed. "I knew she'd ruffle some feathers, but that was a lot faster than I expected." She dropped her head into her hands.

Rylen chuckled. "Trust me, the feathers in question needed a good ruffling; in fact, I've been waiting for someone to come along and do just that. It'll be good for a commoner to give some of these spoiled rich kids a run for their money. But I do think she's better off not telling everyone she meets that she can do more than just stormkindling. They'll find out eventually, but maybe by then we can have enough boundaries in place that it won't be to her detriment."

Glorya nodded. "I'm glad I did the right thing," she admitted, pushing up from the bale of hay that had served so admirably as her seat. "Thank you for validating my thoughts–and for questioning them in the first place. You have no idea how often I've done the same thing." She stretched her aching back as she stood, wondering at how soft she'd gone. *Used to be able to stand for hours with no rest; now I teach half a day and I'm done in.* Then she recalled she'd spent most of the morning cleaning and amended her self image by a few years.

Rylen stood and joined her as she headed for the door. "I'm glad I could help–and that you haven't changed too much over the years," he said, winking as they clasped arms in farewell. "It's good to have a familiar, trustworthy face around here."

"Don't you have a husband now?" Glorya couldn't help teasing as Rylen opened the door to let in the evening air as it relinquished the day's heat.

"Well, yes, but you know how that goes…" His face twisted into a wry smile. "He's a bit jealous sometimes, so it gets hard to manage some days."

"Then I shall work my hardest to win him over," Glorya announced as they stepped out into the waning sunlight. Rylen smiled, a genuine smile this time, and they parted ways for the day.

Glorya ambled across the nearest bridge toward her quarters, watching the students drift by in clumps on their way to the dormitories or the seashore. A few stopped by the kitchen gardens and plucked weeds where they found them. Between the buildings she caught glimpses of the windwaker students engaged in a game of float-the-ball. But nowhere did she see any sign of Zayira. *I hope she's all right.* Glorya cast about for the noble-born children in hopes they weren't off somewhere tormenting her niece. They appeared down the main path at the back of the valley, grouped around something Glorya couldn't see. *Certainly not a student…* Her feet drifted toward the knot of teenagers just as Zayira appeared at the edge of the group, leaning in to see what was going on, and Glorya sighed in relief. Some general shouting ensued and the group broke apart to reveal a singed frog hopping toward the stream for all it was worth. *Looks like the kids still practice lightning on the wildlife. Some things never change.*

A faint, musical sound caught her attention as she approached the door to her cottage. It reminded her of the glass flutes the Temalingari made and sold in the markets in Jogete, only with a more hollow tone. Before she could locate its source it was gone, carried off on the ever-changing wind in the valley. Remembering she hadn't yet eaten, she stopped by the dining hall to see what she could find and grabbed a hot roll filled with meat and vegetables to take back to her cottage; she didn't feel like socializing more than she already had that day.

She unlocked the door to her lodgings and ducked inside, ready for some peace and solitude to reflect. But the research her erstwhile teacher had left unfinished and disorganized called to her from the desk in the corner, and before she knew it she'd lit her second candle trying to make sense of it. There was a massive amount of information documented on sheet after sheet of vellum, and much like her study of the weather patterns that drove the monsoons in Temalingar, she felt her mind teetering on the edge of understanding before tumbling back off a cliff into darkness. She finally gave up long after dark, but left the records in better order than she'd found them. There was plenty of time to figure out what Keross had left her and make use of it.

She changed into her shift and slipped under her covers with images of storms and wind patterns floating through her head.

CHAPTER 14

Earlier in the day, at the beginning of third block

Zayira followed the rest of her classmates toward their first afternoon class, which was history and geography. Lunch had been a boisterous affair; after spending the morning on maths and weatherworking the class had a surfeit of energy. Groups split off after getting their food, which consisted of a few bits of cold meat left over from the night before with some sort of nut-studded biscuit and fresh summer greens, and sat in clumps among the tables. Jase had invited her to sit with his group, solidifying her standing as one of the farm kids and giving her a chance to meet more like-minded students. She'd found all of them warm and helpful. It bolstered her confidence to have a good meal in her stomach and the support of people she might soon call friends.

The class wedged themselves as a cluster through the doorway of the history and geography building, chatting as they went. A few had letters from home, though many had parents who couldn't read or write and had to rely on secondhand accounts of their well-being from families who could. One student–Peony was her name, Zayira recalled–spent the entire walk from the cafeteria to the classroom recounting a report on her entire town for a few of the younger students whose parents weren't literate, stopping only when someone cleared his throat behind her. She whirled around to find herself face to face with a spindly man of average height with mousey brown hair and hazel eyes. He looked down at her through a set of round glass lenses propped onto his face with two small posts that sat over the bridge of his sharp nose. "I presume the mail call can wait a while longer?" he asked in an imperious tone.

Peony dropped a curtsey. "Of course, Professor Antonus," she replied, eyes downcast. The rest of the group bowed or curtseyed as they passed their teacher and took up their respective seats. The tables were arranged similarly to the ones Ms. Sylene had used for maths, leading Zayira to conjecture that the one closest to the door was the first form table. *That would mean the second through fifth go clockwise around the room,* she deduced as she started toward the first form table.

"You." The professor's voice carried across the shuffle of the settling class to grab Zayira's attention, pulling her around to face him. "New girl. What is your name?"

All heads turned toward her and she felt her cheeks burn. "Zayira, sir," she answered with a curtsey.

"Interesting; a foreign name, yet you look to be Midlander," he mused. "No matter; if you're one of the farm crop, go ahead and be seated at the table by the door with the rest of the first formers."

"But sir, I–" Zayira began, but was cut off by a gesture from Professor Antonus.

"I'm sure you know plenty of local stories and

have seen a map of the county in which you live, but please do not mistake those for actual geographical and historical knowledge. Be seated." The last two words lashed out like a whip, cracking over Zayira's head as she turned on her heel to find a seat. The table was full almost to bursting, and every single student seated around it was part of the group of farm children with whom Zayira had eaten her lunch. *Guess he's one of those folks,* she fumed, sitting down harder than was necessary on the only sturdy wooden chair available.

"Don't let him get to you," whispered a girl next to Zayira. Her honey-brown hair and large, dark eyes accentuated her round face and small mouth in a way that Zayira thought was very pretty. It reminded her of one of the girls Maks and Danil both hoped to court back home. "He treats us all that way. It just gets worse if you try to fight it." She pushed her thick braid back over one shoulder to get it out of her way.

"Thanks," Zayira stuttered, not wanting to look ungrateful, but dazzled by the girl's beauty. *Will I ever look like that?*

"I'm Delia." The girl extended a hand for Zayira to shake. Zayira took it, finding the girl's grip strong and firm.

"Zayira," she responded in kind. "Pleased to make your acquaintance."

"Likewise," Delia replied. They both turned toward their slates to see what the day's lessons had in store.

Zayira had entered the history and geography building with high hopes; both subjects fascinated her, and information on them was hard to come by back home. She'd read as many books as her aunt could send her on the founding of the Midlands and inhaled books on their prehistory at a prodigious rate. She'd even begun translating texts from Zhedaban to learn more about their history and culture beyond what her aunt had taught her. What she found on the slate before her was an insult. A crude map of the known world stared back at her with the names of the countries written in and the note "quiz tomorrow" at the bottom. *The capitals aren't even labeled,* Zayira grumbled to herself. "Is this a joke?" she whispered to Delia.

"No." Delia looked at her with a quizzical brow. "This is the first form table. Many of us come here not knowing any of it. You're telling me you already know the names of all the countries and where their borders lie?"

"And their capitals, and how they were formed, and when," Zayira answered, exasperated. "How do I get out of the first form table and start actually learning things?"

"You move up when I say you can move up," a cracking tenor voice stated from across the table. Zayira whipped her head around to meet the speaker's stare. It belonged to a boy of about sixteen with carrot-colored hair atop a matchstick of a head. His brown eyes held contempt and superiority as he stared down at Zayira, who refused to flinch under his scrutiny. *You won't scare me. I have brothers.*

Out loud she said, "And how do I prove to you I know all this–" she waved a hand over her slate–"so you'll let me move up?"

"Pass your quiz tomorrow and we'll see," he sneered.

"I will," Zayira promised, her eyes narrowed. It took all the control she could muster not to summon a tiny rain cloud above the boy's head and zap him with a lightning bolt. *I probably know more geography than you do,* she thought in his direction as she went back over her geography in her mind.

"Is there a problem here?" Professor Antonus's smooth voice cut into Zayira's internal litany of places and names.

"No sir," she answered before the older boy could elaborate. "I was just explaining to this boy that I already know enough to pass tomorrow's geography quiz." All sound in the classroom stopped and Zayira knew her mouth had gotten her into trouble again. *Stupid girl! Let's see what punishment you get now.*

Her teacher's eyebrows rose. "Do you now?" he inquired. "Well then, please enlighten the rest of your table mates. What is the capital of the Midlands?"

"Riverbranch, sir," Zayira recited.

"And where might I find Riverbranch?" Professor Antonus quizzed.

"Where the two great rivers meet in the middle of the country, sir."

"And how far is that from Weatherwatch?"

"About five days' travel, sir."

Antonus nodded his head, though Zayira couldn't tell if he agreed or if he was simply sizing her up. "And what country is south of Midlands?" he continued, clasping his hands behind his back and pacing in front of Zayira's table.

The entire class watched in silence as Zayira gave her answer. "Zhedaba, sir." The professor nodded and turned in his pacing.

"And what is the capital of Zhedaba?"

"Joveru, sir."

"And its primary exports and imports?" A smirk crept onto the older man's face as he tightened the proverbial noose.

"Mostly metals and gemstones as exports, sir, but they import a good bit of grain and foodstuffs from Midlands. Wood is their primary import from Temalingar." Professor Antonus's expression slipped as Zayira dodged nimbly out of the trap he'd set. His cheeks pinked as he paced faster, considering his next question.

"And how far is Temalingar from this side of the world?"

"A full eight weeks of sailing–eighty days," Zayira answered, certain of her response. Her aunt's stories of crossing the great ocean to visit her students and friends rang out in her mind.

Antonus's pacing quickened further. "And its capital? Exports and imports?" he spat, sensing defeat, but giving no ground.

"Ma-Reku," Zayira answered promptly, "where they sell wood and intricate glasswork along with exotic seeds not found in the Midlands or Zhedaba in exchange for metal and grain and vellum." She felt herself teetering on the edge between proving her point and getting into trouble and added, "sir." She wasn't sure if it mollified her teacher, but he stopped pacing.

"Go sit over there." Professor Antonus pointed to a table two spots over from Zayira's current location. "But don't expect any help from your classmates in getting up to speed." He glared around the room, daring any of the students to contradict his decree. Eyes lowered around the room as they met the professor's cold fury. Zayira stood and crossed the room, keenly aware of the scrutiny of her peers as she took a seat at the third table.

It held two empty chairs, and she took the one closest to her direct path, uncaring as to who sat nearest to her. She caught a look of shock from Delia before the girl shuttered her expression and stared at the table in front of her. *Probably trying not to get in trouble. I'm no good at that. Can't judge her for it, though.*

Class continued about as Zayira expected. Professor Antonus lectured, they took notes on their slates, and the groups engaged in discussions about various historical topics regarding the Midlands, many of which had Zayira doing her best to keep up. The general flow of learning involved a combination of rote memorization and long-form discussion to show understanding. For all that the professor himself was disagreeable, Zayira found his methods useful and engaging.

Halfway through class a tiny peal of thunder broke through the rhythm of study. One of the younger students at the first form table stared up at the thundercloud he'd called in a moment of frustration, his eyes wide with trepidation. Rain drizzled onto the desks nearby, illustrating the reason for their use of slates and grease pencils.

"Get that cloud under control or sit out the rest of class!" Professor Antonus called from the fifth form table. The first former who'd called the rain looked at his table mates, horrified.

"I...I can't, Professor," he answered in a pitiful tone of voice. "I'm not good at directing what I've called."

"Then get another student to help you!" When no one spoke up, the professor stood in exasperation. "Fine, I'll do it." He strode over to the first form table and Zayira noticed his weatherworking pin for the first time—a silver whirlwind. *Silver? But Jase told me graduates* *wear gold…*He took a moment to gather his thoughts and sent the tiniest breeze toward the cloud over the first formers. It butted into the miniature weather system and deflected around the outside of the clouds. Narrowing his eyes, he tried again, only to be rebuffed in similar fashion. One of the students behind Zayira covered a snicker with a cough and the professor rounded on them, anger etched into his middle-aged features. "I'd like to see you do better!" he yelled, then turned back to his work.

He needs help, Zayira realized on Professor Antonus's third try to shove the weather out of the classroom. *And I don't think he wants to call any of the other teachers for it. I could do it, but what if he finds out it's me?* He'd be mad, she knew, but he wasn't likely to admit a student had assisted him, at least to the rest of the class. Besides, if she was sneaky enough he wouldn't even realize what she'd done. She reached out before she could second guess herself and added the tiniest bit of power to his working, just enough to start the cloud formation trundling toward the door. "See there?" he panted as the clouds finished their march across the last few feet of space. He rounded on the first form student who'd caused the ruckus. "Learn more control before you enter my classroom again." Sweat beaded his receding hairline and ran down his forehead as he resumed his seat with the fifth formers, never once glancing Zayira's way.

The rest of the period went by in a hushed blur. No one seemed interested in doing more than the minimum required to get through class after all that had happened, and the arrival of the windwakers at the period changeover was a relief to all. Zayira wiped her slate clean like the rest of the third formers, then filed out behind them. She bumped into someone passing through the door and looked up in time to meet a pair of eyes so dark they were almost black, pupils widened in surprise. The boy from the dining hall the prior night–the one who'd sat alone–mumbled an apology and shuffled away, but Zayira turned her head to watch him go. He sat down at the second form table as she lost sight of him in the crowd. There was something strange about him, a wildness not present in the other students, and it piqued her curiosity.

Zayira and the rest of the stormkindlers trundled across the northmost of the bridges across the creek bisecting the valley. They were once again flanked by plants–more fruits and vegetables–as they crossed the swiftly-running water, and Zayira leaned over the low railings on either side to see how deep it ran. To her surprise it looked about knee deep, just enough to pull someone off their footing if the rocks beneath were slippery. *Bet it's awfully cold, too.* She filed that away for later in case it got too hot and she needed a place to cool off.

"Our last period is languages and etiquette," Delia said as she passed Zayira, who hung half off the bridge. "Ms. Mira doesn't like us to be late." Taking the hint, Zayira caught up with her new acquaintance as she entered their last class of the day.

Ms. Mira's classroom was spotless. Each of her five tables contained a number written on an extra slate to make it clear which form sat where. Chairs were pushed in neatly around each table with equal spacing between, and every slate sat empty and pristine with a grease pencil just beside it. Even the stone flooring held no sign of dirt despite the unpaved path leading up to the building. Zayira was conscious of every speck of dirt or sweat on her outfit as she followed the example of her fellow students, brushing off her shoes on a rough mat just inside the door before entering. It reminded her of visiting her great aunt when she was younger; the woman had the largest house in the village and paid someone to keep it clean, a luxury that was foreign to Zayira.

"Welcome," their instructor greeted in a musical voice that carried despite its gentleness. Zayira recognized the woman who had met them at dinner the night prior. "Please have a seat." She repeated the same in Zhedaban and Zayira answered in kind, gesturing polite respect as she seated herself at the first form table. Ms. Mira nodded at her choice before turning to the third form table herself.

An older student sitting with the first formers rapped her knuckles on the table to get the students' attention. "*Hello,*" she said in Zhedaban, her hands forming the simple greeting in time with her mouth. The first form students responded in kind and she moved on through introducing herself. Zayira quickly bored with the rudiments of a language she already knew much of from her aunt and began copying down the phrases the older student spoke along with their translations after responding. Before long the other first formers started glancing over at her slate to check their own understanding as they learned the basic pleasantries of Zhedaban.

Ms. Mira glided over to check on her younger students' progress. "I see you already know some Zhedaban, Zayira," she remarked as she checked the girl's slate.

"Yes, ma'am. My aunt taught me a good bit of the

basics, including the writing." Zayira sat up as straight as possible.

"*How is the weather today?*" Ms. Mira asked in Zhedaban, tilting her head to one side to indicate a request for response.

"*Sunny with few clouds,*" Zayira replied, adding a gesture to the end her aunt had told her was the equivalent of "sir" or "ma'am" not spoken aloud. Her teacher nodded.

"Please go join the second formers," she requested, and Zayira stood, curtseying before scooting to the next table down.

The rest of the class posed more of a challenge; the second formers learned more vocabulary words and more complex sentences, but Zayira was familiar enough with the grammar involved to pick up the missing pieces quickly. By the end of class the whole table was writing notes to each other in Zhedaban and asking questions about their collective families and histories. Zayira learned that most of her table mates were about a year older than she and half came from merchant families closer to the coast; the rest were farm children like herself who had a penchant for learning. They made her feel welcome with the exception of one, who sat apart from the rest and gave only the most basic responses. The neatness of her hair and attire marked her as either noble or putting on airs as such, and while the rest of the students at the table were polite to her, none were what Zayira would consider warm or open. She resolved to find out the girl's name at the very least.

Before she could blink class was over and they were set loose for the evening. Zayira migrated toward the rest of the farm students and learned that the entire student body had free time after classes were over for the day. Dinner was served for the next two hours, so they could either eat directly after class or spend some time blowing off steam after sitting for half the day. She opted for the latter, joining her group for a game of chase the pirate across the pitch before stopping by the stream to cool off.

As they approached the creek a knot of students formed by the middle bridge. Zayira could hear shouting and noticed a small cloud kindling above the group, which piqued her interest. She shoved her way far enough forward to see what was going on and found a second or third year stormkindling student terrorizing a frog with the lightning from his cloud. He managed to catch it before it hopped into the creek, but Zayira was relieved to see it swim downstream as she turned to go find something to eat at the dining hall.

Dinner consisted of simple fare; there were rolls filled with meat and vegetables like her mother sometimes made sitting in baskets set around the tables. Most of the rolls were still warm. She grabbed one and ducked back out the door to dangle her feet in the brook's cold water as the sun sank below the seas to the west. As she chewed a musical sound drifted toward her on the wind. It reminded her of the flutes folks played in the tavern in Market on festival days, only there was more than one note playing at a time. The tones pulled at her, dragging her feet from the chilly waters to go investigate their source, and she ambled east along the path outside the languages and etiquette building in search of it. Notes swirled between the buildings and down the creekside, making it difficult to determine their direction, but they always seemed to follow the wind. So Zayira picked up the thread of the wind itself and traced it back to its source within the cliffs to the northeast. Before she knew it she faced the north door to the windwaker dormitories, which stood open and inviting. She took one step through the doorway and heard a door slam closed just down the hall, cutting off the music and breaking its spell. Waiting as long as she dared–for she wasn't sure if she was allowed in the other dormitories–Zayira craned her neck as far as she could to see down the hall, but the music never resumed. Her shoulders slumped as she wandered back down the greensward toward the creek to find some of her newfound friends before cleaning up for the night.

When she returned to her room she noticed her laundry had been picked up and replaced with clean clothes. *At least I won't have that to worry about.* Reflecting on her first day she had plenty else to worry about; she'd made some friends, but had made some staunch enemies, as well. But that thought wasn't enough to keep her awake after such a long day, and she found herself unable to stay awake long enough to dwell on it. So she doused her candle and climbed into bed, letting exhaustion carry her off into the land of sleep.

chapter 15

Off the coast of Midlands to the north

Swells tossed the heavy ship from side to side, pitching and rolling as the skies darkened. They'd turned to face the wind and dropped a sea anchor some hours before in hopes of maintaining their distance from the coast; it was crucial, not only for the safety of the ship and crew, but for their mission.

The tall woman with black hair and light brown skin narrowed her dark eyes, staring across the horizon. There was no telling how long they would have to remain where they were. At least until the onset of winter, she thought, as it would afford the greatest chance of success. "Brizen!" she barked, her deep voice carrying across the deck.

"Yes, Captain?" The pale-faced man answered from behind her on the poop deck. He scuttled to her side, averting his eyes from her cold gaze.

"Anything on the wind?" she asked.

"Nothing, ma'am," he answered. A lock of greasy hair fell in front of his eyes, but he dared not reach up to remove it.

"I'm expecting word soon," the captain announced. "Keep a weather eye out for a message. The last one went in the drink before we could read it."

"Aye, ma'am." The man nodded, bowed, and backed away to find a spot to sit and rest his head. He'd spent the last three nights tossed about the captain's cabin along with anything else not nailed down–though she'd done a good job keeping him tied to something the whole time.

A few minutes later his head jerked up from its place on his bruised arms. It was late in the day, and the sun peeked out from between the clouds behind him, making it easier to spot the small item drifting its way across the water toward the ship. The man blinked, then caught the thread of the wind on which the item floated. In a few short minutes he was able to guide the small piece of vellum aboard the ship and pass it to the captain for her perusal.

"Hmm," she mused as she read the message scrawled on the inside of the folded vellum scrap. *There's a boom chain that must be raised to get into the bay. Researching. Will update soon.* No signature accompanied the piece; none was necessary. It could only have come from one source. The captain nodded, prepared to bide her time for a while longer. Their gambit was already paying off and would soon give them what they needed to get past Weatherwatch's defenses.

It was only a matter of time.

CHAPTER 16

The next two weeks passed in a blur. Glorya fell into the rhythm of the school, setting aside her free periods to plan for the next few classes and spending much of her time in the evenings organizing her cottage. It didn't take long to get it back in good order; portions of the file storage were still intact, and the rest of the single room contained few enough possessions that it posed no difficulty. Before she knew it a fortnight had come and gone and the Zhedaban students Mira had spoken of were set to arrive any day. *They're going to have quite the culture shock,* she thought as she set down the slate she'd used to write out the next day's lesson plans. *I wonder what they'll send us–probably sunchasers, maybe a few stormkindlers. No chance they'll send windwakers, as important as they are.* She made a mental note to make sure the other head teachers knew what to expect.

The well-organized stacks of vellum next to her desk drew her attention like a moth to flame. She felt she was on the verge of a breakthrough with understanding Keross's research, and the information on the pages called to her, begging her to keep studying it.

A knock on her door interrupted her reverie. "Sunchaser?" Mira's voice floated through the wood.

"A moment," Glorya answered. She brushed dust off her shirt and answered the door, still dressed for the day. Mira waited with her hands folded in front of her, patient and demure as always. "What can I do for you?" Glorya asked.

"We would be most gratified if you could help welcome the Zhedaban students," Mira announced. "They have arrived at the mouth of the pass."

Glorya stepped through the door and closed it behind her, locking it. "Lead on," she answered, falling into step beside her colleague. She wouldn't quite consider the woman a friend; Rylen was accurate in his estimation of her motives, and she mistrusted Mira's reserve, but otherwise they got along well.

The late evening air washed over Glorya, cooling her skin as she strode across the bridge closest to her cottage. It was also the closest to the bay, and a hint of salt wafted past, bringing with it a pang of homesickness. *Having some Zhedaban students to talk to should help. Maybe they'll have news from Joveru.* Before the thought finished the breeze reversed, pushing the salt air back out to sea for a breath and filling her nostrils with tilled earth and fertilizer–reminiscent of an older reference for home, one from her childhood. It reminded Glorya of her reason for traveling so much. *I don't fit in anywhere. Not truly.* But she'd made her peace with that long ago.

A cluster of shapes stood at the mouth of the pass, shifting from foot to foot. It was just dark enough Glorya couldn't make out any of the newcomers' faces, but she caught snippets of signed conversation–*cold, humid, so much grass, strange sticks in the sky*–that gave her an overall impression of nervousness. Rylen stood before the assembly, doing his best to reassure them. His Zhedaban was rudimentary at best. *I really should teach him more, and fast,* Glorya noted as she shouldered up beside him. He looked at her, relief evident in the slumping of his posture. "Thank goodness you're here," he exclaimed. "I've never had to speak Zhedaban in the dark, and I'm afraid most of my knowledge of the language is of a…less than savory nature."

"Not to worry," Glorya answered, patting him on the shoulder. "I'll take it from here." She turned to the group and signed for quiet, using the outdoor signals due to the dim light. *"Welcome,"* she began as she approached, stopping close enough for them to see her hands, but far enough away not to make anyone nervous. *"We're glad to have you at Weatherwatch. Who is your leader?"* She cocked her head to the side and waited for someone to emerge.

A boy of about fifteen stepped forward. *"I am,"* he answered, signing boldly.

"They sent no adults with you?" Glorya knew her shock was evident in the slight tremble of her hands, but hoped they'd ignore it.

"We are strong enough on our own," the boy declared, tapping a fist to his chest.

"They didn't want us to start with." A small voice piped up from behind the boy and a girl's face appeared bedside him. It was thinner than Glorya liked. *"We can't call the winds like the great ones. We can only bring the sun."* She hung her head, her lank, black hair slipping in front of her face.

Glorya knelt down to put herself on eye level with the child. *"I'm a sunchaser, too,"* she said, pointing at the pin on her shirt. *"And I live in Zhedaba when I'm not teaching here."*

The girl's eyes went wide. *"You really are the flame hair?"* she asked, and every head in the group turned her direction. *"The one from Ruja's stories?"*

Glorya chuckled. *"He exaggerates, I'm sure, but yes. I saved Ruja's caravan once. He's been a great friend and business partner ever since."* An awed hush fell over the group as Glorya stood. *"Now, let's find you all places to stay and something to eat."* Turning to the other teachers, she raised a brow, then realized it was invisible in the deep twilight. "They're sunchasers, the lot of them," she explained. "I can get them settled in the dorms after we get them something to eat. They all look like they could use a good meal."

"Please, allow me to assist with their rooms," Mira insisted. *"I would like to be of service in making them comfortable."* A few of the children gasped at her use of both languages, but most of them shuffled their feet and waited.

"Then I will get them fed," Glorya agreed. "Rylen, I'm taking them to the dining hall. Cook's left sandwiches out the last few days in case they arrived after dinner. Do you want to come?"

"They look like you can handle them," Rylen replied, sizing them up. "If they step too far out of line or you need help, just yell; Zinnia or I will hear you." He nodded politely at the students, who didn't seem to understand the gesture, and returned to his office in the armory.

Glorya motioned for the new students to follow her, counting heads as they filled in behind. There were five total ranging from smaller than Zayira to a head and shoulders taller than Glorya, and she began to mentally sort through how to place them in classes as they walked to the dining hall. They likely knew little of the Midlander language, and since most of the teachers spoke no Zhedaban the language barrier would be a problem. *Perhaps they can shadow me and I can help them learn immersively.* Mira's class might also help if she could shift her lesson plans around to teach both ways.

Full dark settled around the group as they entered the dining hall. The cook had left a few candles burning, blazing a path to the table where she'd left the sandwiches, and it gave Glorya her first half-decent look at her new charges. The taller boy who'd answered for them–a skinny young man who looked like he'd known hard labor–led the line, followed by the smaller girl who'd answered before. Both had the same elfin features, with narrow chins and wide eyes. *Related, perhaps? Siblings?* Behind them stood a rounder boy about her niece's age whose hair was cut short despite the current fashion in Zhedaba. He looked unconcerned about his surroundings, as if he was already at home in this strange place. The taller girl beside him, however, was not. Her painfully erect posture and darting eyes told Glorya she might bolt at any moment. She held the hand of a small boy, perhaps ten years old, with downcast eyes and long hair draped over his face. *Not all of these children wanted to come here. Does the headmaster know about Zhedaban prejudices against sunchasers? Was he told anything about these children, or what to expect? Or did they just foist them off onto us since they weren't wanted?* She fumed silently, vowing not to let any prior mishandling of the situation make the children's lives any harder.

"*Please, eat,*" Glorya invited, pulling the light cloth off of the plate of sandwiches the cook had left out. The children looked at her with suspicion. "*The school provides food and lodging for all its students,*" she explained. "*It will cost you nothing if you stay here.*" She stepped away from the table to give them some space to consider. The tall girl narrowed her eyes at the spread and whispered to the small boy at her side, who peeked through his curtain of hair at the sandwiches. The middle boy sauntered over to the table and surveyed the options with a practiced eye, only to be pushed aside by the oldest, who snatched a sandwich from the top of the stack. A few hand signs were exchanged, some of a less than polite nature, and the middle boy took two sandwiches for himself before trundling to another table to sit and eat.

Their antics encouraged the rest of the group, and within seconds the plate of sandwiches was empty. All five students crowded around the end of one of the long trestle tables in the dining hall, scarfing down as much as they could eat. Glorya sat herself a short distance away. She trusted Mira to come up with sleeping arrangements for the students, but it looked like a few of them might not do well separated from their…friends? Family? Whichever they were, they were close, and a few were young enough not to thrive on their own. It wasn't surprising that they had banded together; sunchasers were considered the lowliest of weatherworkers in the better parts of Zhedaba and were shunned as cursed in the worse ones. Glorya resolved to find out from the headmaster where these students had come from so that she could make note of how they'd been treated. Perhaps it was something she could change once she returned to Joveru.

When full bellies made for sleepy children Glorya

scooted closer on the bench. *"What are your names?"* she asked. *"Mine you already know, so it's only fair for me to ask."*

"Ri." The oldest boy–their de facto leader–spoke up first. He made the hand symbol for polite introduction along with it. *Apparently he's decided I'm worthy of his respect.*

"Len," squeaked the smaller girl beside him.

"Bo," said the rounder boy in the middle.

"An," answered the taller of the girls. *"And this is Jei."* She gestured at the smaller boy falling asleep on her shoulder.

With each name Glorya's heart squeezed a little more. Names in Zhedaban denoted their owner's importance based on their length. Cities had three syllables; most towns had two, and the people who lived in them were given the same number, as there would be no town without its people. Only criminals and outcasts–and those who were thought of as less than human–were stripped of their full names. *I've always known sunchasers were considered cursed, but I've never seen them treated this poorly.* Out loud she said, *"If you'll come with me, we'll find you a place to sleep."* She rose from the table and blew out the candles nearby. The exhausted children stumbled to their feet and headed for the door, Glorya following to extinguish the rest of the flames.

Mira met them as they emerged, scaring the small girl–*Len*–half to death as she appeared like a wraith from the settling fog. *"I've arranged for their rooms,"* she announced, *"but some will have to double up; we're two rooms shy in the sunchaser wing."* Glorya translated, and Jei clung to An's tigi, his fists bunching the rough fabric draped over her too-thin form. Len took

Ri's hand and nodded. Mira frowned, presumably over the opposite-sex pairings, but nodded and led the way.

Fifteen minutes and some explanation later the newest additions to the sunchaser wing were settled into their new accommodations, their mistrust of their good fortune plain on their faces. But exhaustion took over before they could ask any more questions, and all but the oldest were asleep when Glorya and Mira left.

As soon as they crossed the threshold of the dorms Glorya's face twisted in anger. "Where did the head-master find those children?" she growled.

Mira's voice remained as placid as ever. "I'm not certain. He received a letter from a contact of his in Jove-ru who offered to send him Zhedaban students as a sort of test to see if the school could manage them. He never named the contact or their origin." Her brow furrowed, puckering her plain face in the starlight.

"I'll find out in the morning," Glorya sighed as her anger drained out of her, exhaustion taking its place. "For now they're at least settled. I'll come get them for breakfast and see what I can do about helping them assimilate. I don't think classes will go well for the first few days; this is all a bit of a culture shock for them, and they haven't even seen most of the school."

"I agree," Mira conceded. "If you'd like I'll write up the names of the students whose Zhedaban is best so that we can spread out the responsibility of translating until they learn our language."

"I would be most grateful," Glorya replied. "I can't teach and act as a translator all day." She stepped onto the stoop of her cottage and fished in her pocket for the key. "Many thanks for your help this evening," she called to Mira, who waved and moved off toward her own cottage nearby. Glorya could swear the woman almost smiled as she turned away. *She never smiles, outside of that infuriating look she gives when she's being polite.* Chalking it up to excitement over having Zhedaban students to help her practice her language skills, Glorya slipped inside her cottage to find her bed, knowing the following day would test her organizational skills–and her patience.

CHAPTER 17

The breakfast tables were abuzz with chatter about the new students who'd arrived mysteriously under the cover of darkness. Zayira plopped down next to the rest of the farm bunch to find out what she could; her eavesdropping on the path to their table had revealed only that there were anywhere from three to thirteen of them and that they each wore frightening masks meant to scare small children. *Such stupid rumors. I'm sure they're just kids, like us.*

"I'm not sure what to make of it," Jase replied to a comment from one of the other kids. "The load of it seems like absolute rot, but I've never been any further from home than Weatherwatch…"

"They ain't like us," one of the younger boys announced. "They've got dark hair and dark skin and they wear weird clothes. I bet they don't even know how to talk right."

"You've got dark hair," Zayira pointed out, pointing at his mop of dark brown curls. "And you're tan from working in the fields."

"Yeah…well…it's not the same, and you know it," the boy spluttered.

"It's exactly the same," Zayira asserted, narrowing her eyes. *Don't kindle a cloud…don't kindle a cloud…* Somehow she managed to keep control of her weatherworking despite her temper. It seemed the lessons and practice were helping after all.

"No it ain't!" The boy's raised voice caught the attention of students two tables over, who stopped talking to listen. A breeze lifted the collar of the shouting boy's shirt.

Zayira stood her ground, glaring at him from the opposite side of the table. "Well, I'm going to find out for myself before I listen to you about it," she snapped. His expression soured as she swept past him to deposit her dishes in the cleaning bin more roughly than was necessary, then stalked out the door, nearly running over her aunt. Both of them stumbled backwards in surprise; they hadn't seen much of each other since Zayira's first night at the school. She mumbled an apology, then looked up to find herself face to face with a set of curious, dark brown eyes instead of her aunt's bright green ones. These were framed in an elfin face with high, hollow cheekbones and a cascade of thick, black hair that reached the young girl's waist.

"*Hi.*" The girl signed her greeting as if they were indoors instead of on the stoop of the dining hall, and Zayira wondered if that was the same as whispering in Zhedaban.

"*Hello,*" Zayira answered, remembering to be polite. The girl giggled and smiled up at her in the most charming way. "*My name is Zayira,*" she continued, encouraged by the open expression on the young one's face.

"*My name is Len,*" the girl answered. "*I'm hungry. Is*

there breakfast somewhere? I smell food." She signed more than she spoke and the symbols tripped off her tiny fingers, forcing Zayira to focus her full attention on them to catch every word.

"In there." Zayira pointed through the door, where students sat and talked while they broke their fast. Len's face lit up when she caught sight of what the children were eating.

"Please pay attention, Len." Glorya's teacher voice, as Zayira had come to think of it, rounded up the group's attention. *"We're going inside the dining hall to get breakfast. Please keep your clothes on indoors while you are at Weatherwatch; customs here are very different from what you're used to."* Zayira wasn't completely sure she'd understood all the words and signs. Why would they take their clothes off? The days were starting to cool, and the sun hadn't yet cleared the mountains to warm the valley. *They do come from a hotter place. I suppose it helps there.* The group nodded their assent and followed Glorya inside.

Zayira stood in the doorway and watched her aunt show the new students the ins and outs of the dining hall. None of them spoke the Midlands tongue; that much was obvious. But the older two surveyed the students surrounding them with narrowed eyes as if they understood the whispers and backhanded comments flying around the room. "Look at them–they're so thin!" "Their skin is so much darker…" "No darker than yours after harvest season!" "What beautiful hair–I wonder how she keeps it." "Ugh, they reek of poverty." The mumbling infuriated Zayira. Who were they to judge? It smacked of small-minded hypocrisy.

Before she could stop herself Zayira strode into

the room after the Zhedaban students. The older girl in the group blinked at her in surprise, but Len smiled as she approached. "*Do we all get to eat this? What is it? Is there fish in it? I don't like fish, but I'm supposed to say I like whatever I'm given.*" She made a playful face that melted Zayira's anger in an instant.

What word did she use for "fish?" I don't remember that one…ugh, I should have practiced more with my aunt! Out loud, she did her best to answer. "*Not fish; vegetables. Potato.*" Zayira pointed at the steaming pile of mashed tuber set before the girl. "*Summer greens.*" She pointed at the boiled greens next to the potatoes. Len made a face and poked at the substance, sucking on her finger after discovering it was hot. Her fine eyebrows shot upward and she picked up a tiny piece with her thumb and forefinger, blew on it to cool it, then popped it into her mouth.

"*I like these!*" she exclaimed. "*Summer…greens?*" The words came out sounding more like "sah-mah greens," but it was close enough that Zayira had no problem understanding. She nodded and Len trotted off to show the tall boy she'd walked in with what she'd learned.

A stubby hand appeared to Zayira's right. "*Excuse me,*" it said, and her eyes traced the round fingers up a sturdy arm to a round face. "*I'm Bo.*" The boy offered a sign of polite greeting, but his hand shook as his fingers went through the motions. Zayira replied in kind, noticing that he looked either worried or nervous. *Or scared, I suppose, though I can't see why.* She glanced behind her and realized that Jase had walked over to the group to watch.

A tense moment passed as the oldest boy and Jase

sized each other up. Just as the silence grew unbearable Jase made the sign for polite greeting. *"I'm Jase,"* he said in halting Zhedaban.

"Ri." The boy signed an equally polite response, then hesitated before putting forth his hand. Jase took it in his own and shook it firmly, meeting the boy's eye.

Just like that, the dam broke, and the new students were greeted in both Midlander and broken Zhedaban as they crossed the room. Zayira fell back into the press of bodies, then retreated toward the door at the first opportunity. Her aunt caught her eye and nodded, a proud smile lighting her already warm features. Zayira blushed and almost ran into another figure ducking out the door.

"Ouch! Watch where you're going." The boy's tone was rough, but his voice was sweet, almost musical.

"I'm sorry," Zayira answered, then froze. Black eyes glared at her from beneath a fine brow, their depth both drawing her in and repelling her at the same time. The boy's face was drawn in a scowl, but some other emotion she couldn't identify hovered at its edges. It spoke of an internal struggle she couldn't fathom.

"It's fine," he huffed. The boy turned toward the pitch outside the stables.

"It's Hulvai, right?" Zayira wasn't sure what made her try to continue the conversation; her voice worked of its own accord. He stopped and half turned to listen. "Why don't you come sit with us at lunch today? We have room at our table." The world seemed to hold its breath as Zayira awaited an answer. Hulvai shrugged one shoulder and continued toward the pitch and his first class.

Was that a yes? She would have to wait until lunch

to find out. Why had she asked in the first place? She was sure the farm kids would welcome him if she introduced him; they were all curious about the only kid who chose to sit alone at every meal. Most came from households with multiple children, like Zayira, and the concept of choosing to be alone at mealtime made little sense to them.

It was Zayira's turn to shrug. Maybe maths class would hold some of the answers.

CHAPTER 18

Introducing the Zhedaban students to the school schedule at Weatherwatch turned out to be the biggest challenge Glorya had faced as a teacher. The children lacked discipline and manners, even by Zhedaban standards, and were far more interested in satisfying their curiosity about their new surroundings than they were in attempting to learn. She knew they would need to learn Midlander quickly, as it was the language in which classes were taught, but she had no ideas as to how to get them up to speed quickly. Zayira's ploy at breakfast had worked beautifully, but she couldn't spend every moment of every day translating for the children, and not all of their fellow students would be so forthcoming.

Mira volunteered to translate for the Zhedaban students in their first period class–history and geography–so that Glorya could have a break to plan, but for second period she'd have to cover. Selene spoke no Zhedaban, claiming an absolute block when it came to learning languages. Lunch would sort itself out, and after lunch came languages and etiquette, in which Mira

had promised to teach in both Zhedaban and Midlander in hopes of encouraging the class to trade languages
organically. Last period was weatherworking, and
since Glorya taught that herself she could keep the new
sunchasers informed through hand gestures and translation.

Their plan worked beautifully for the first half
hour, up until the oldest boy, Ri, stood in the middle of
Antonus's history lecture during first block and strode
out the door. Len scooted after him, and before anyone
could catch them the rest slipped out the open door of
the squat stone building, their teacher's yelled protesta-
tions trailing behind them.

Glorya happened upon them while crossing the river. *"Shouldn't you be in class?"* she asked, brow furrowed
in confusion.

"It was boring," Ri answered, his gestures flippant.

*"Boring it may be, but necessary. And did you get per-
mission to leave?"* Ri shrugged, and the rest of the children refused to meet her gaze. Glorya sighed. *"Return
to your class. Mira will do her best to help translate, and I'll
see you in your next block."* She herded the group back
into Antonus's building and apologized for their behavior, citing cultural misunderstanding as the cause. He
narrowed his eyes, but let the statement pass without
remark.

By the time Mira delivered the group to Selene for
maths Glorya could tell by the less than placid expression on her face the rest of history had been difficult.
Small pieces of the etiquette teacher's hair had escaped
the confines of her simple coiffure and drifted on the
breath of wind floating through the door as she ushered
them in. Selene practiced the Zhedaban greeting Glorya

taught her one more time; it was the greeting for supe-
riors to subordinates, and Glorya hoped it would better
set the tone for their next class.

Ri led the way, as always, with Len in his wake.
Bo occupied the middle of the group, with Jei peeking
around him and An bringing up the rear. She held her
head high, but her gaze slid often toward the fourth
form table, where Glorya could just see the unruly mop
of sandy hair that marked one of the older boys. *Looks
like I'm going to have to have a conversation with her about
a few things before that gets too far.* Zhedaban society was
much more open about relationships than the Midlands,
and the school had rules against student "fraterniza-
tion," as they called it. Not that it stopped many of them
once they'd surpassed a certain age.

"Good morning, class," began Ms. Selene. She
repeated her greeting in clumsy Zhedaban and the new
students sat up straighter in their seats. Glorya made
a mental note to make that greeting a habit for all the
staff.

Maths required less translation once the younger
Zhedabans learned the Midlander numbering system.
Some of the Midlander students knew enough of the
Zhedaban numerals to assist, and before long Glorya's
translations were obsolete. Len and Bo showed a greater
aptitude than the rest and moved up to the second form
table before the period was over.

Lunch was easier to navigate than breakfast. The
new contingent remembered where to get their food
and where to put their plates when they finished, and
they were welcomed at Zayira's table. It was crowded; some of the merchant kids joined them in order to
speak with their newest classmates. But there was one

addition Glorya hadn't expected: Hulvai. He ate with his usual speed and disregard for proper table manners while pretending to ignore Zayira, who sat beside him on the bench with enough room between them to fit another student. No one dared take the spot despite space being at a premium. Poor Zayira was stuck splitting her attention between the new students and the distant loner beside her. Glorya smiled. *That's my niece; always in the middle of everything, always reaching out. Never lose that, Zayira.*

After lunch came languages, which meant Glorya got another break from her new charges as Mira used them to help teach her Midlander students–and vice versa. In the meantime Glorya went out to the pitch to prepare for weatherworking with the mixed group. The armsmaster had agreed to help her by kindling some clouds for the students to pick apart, both individually and in groups. By the time her students arrived he'd left them clouds of varying sizes and complexities hanging over the pitch, waiting for their assigned groups to demolish them. They wasted no time getting to work; even the Zhedaban students were able to dissipate the clouds they were given without difficulty. Glorya ended with a short lecture in two languages before dismissing the class. She stopped Ri and An on their way back toward the dorms to make sure they knew the school's schedule for the evening–and that certain types of conduct were not allowed. Both looked confused, but nodded and thanked her before running to catch up with their younger friends.

"What a day." She didn't realize she'd said it out loud until Rylen answered from behind her.

"Went that well, did it?"

Glorya turned, shoulders sagging as the day's tension drained from her body. "Better than it could have," she admitted. "It's a good thing Mira's been teaching Zhedaban. I wouldn't have gotten anything done today if I'd had to babysit them the entire time."

Rylen cast a sympathetic eye over her disheveled appearance. "You look like you could use some dinner, a bath, and an early bed," he noted. "Care to join me at the dining hall?" He offered her his arm, which she took gratefully as she joined him on the short trek to the dining hall. They prattled on through the meal like the old friends they were, and the conversation was a balm to Glorya's overworked psyche.

On her way back to her cottage Glorya spied Zayira once again, this time as she headed out to the dock that jutted into the bay. *I can go whole weeks without seeing hide nor hair of her, but today I've seen her twice.* The sunset rivaled their matching red locks as it painted the shifting horizon over the bay a brilliant coppery orange. The now-familiar pang of homesickness settled in Glorya's gut. She set it aside more easily this time, but a part of her knew the day would come when it wouldn't budge. Until that day, she had a job to do.

She turned on her heel and stalked to her cottage to draw an unfulfilling bath and find her bed.

CHAPTER 19

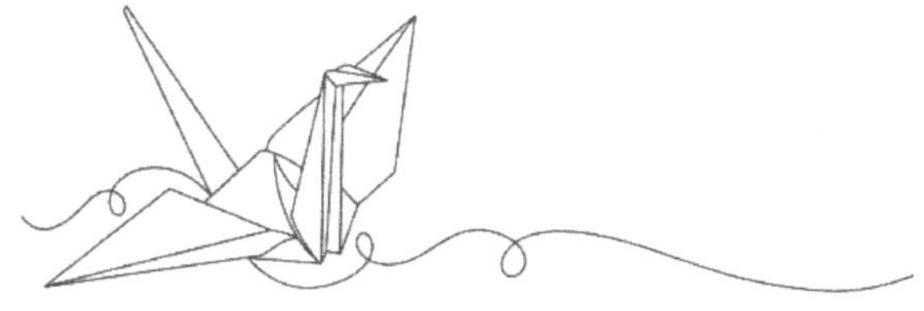

Zayira's shoulders slumped as she walked down the dock toward the figure dangling its feet off the end. She'd spent the whole afternoon trying to think of a way to apologize to Hulvai for not being able to speak to him much at lunch despite inviting him to join them, but had come up empty every time. He was so difficult to figure out! If he just talked a little more, maybe she would know more of what he was like, what he was interested in, or something–anything–useful.

Hulvai lifted his hand and a breeze sprang to life heading out to sea, defying nature's efforts to push the damp sea air inland. A folded sheet of vellum shaped roughly like a bird floated above his hand in the jostling air currents before shooting out to sea. It danced over the swells and around the old lighthouse at the mouth of the bay, then threaded through one of the exposed loops of the giant chain strung across the bay's entrance. Zayira lost sight of it once it crossed the setting sun. The boy's control of the wind fascinated Zayira. She'd never been able to wake a strong wind, only slight breezes, but windwaking was her second weakest talent of the three. Still, she could feel the working as Hulvai pushed his little craft further and further out into the ocean.

"That's a really neat trick," she said as she approached the end of the dock.

Hulvai's head whipped around. His lowered brow and fiery eyes made Zayira feel as if she'd interrupted some private moment. She took a half step back, then lifted her chin and stood her ground. Apologies were more important than whatever it was Hulvai was mad about. "I'm sorry about earlier," she started, unsure of where to go next. Hulvai continued to stare at her. "At lunch, I mean." More glaring. "I invited you to our table, then didn't get to talk to you much because of the new students, and that was rude of me." The glare softened to mere annoyance and he turned back toward the sunset. "Mind if I join you?" she asked warily. When no answer or gesture was forthcoming she shrugged and sat down beside the surly boy. The tide was out and the water rode well below their feet, giving Zayira plenty of room to swing hers without endangering her shoes.

After a few quiet, tense minutes Zayira cleared her throat. "So do you always come out here in the evening?" *Mama always says to start with the weather or something commonplace if I'm not sure what to say. Maybe she's right.* Anyway, it was worth a shot.

Hulvai shrugged. "Sometimes." Zayira wondered how he could still see anything; he hadn't taken his eyes off the setting sun since she'd sat down. Hers burned from a few glances.

"I like your folded bird," she hazarded after enough silence had passed for the sun to dip below the horizon. "Could you teach me how to make one sometime?"

"I guess." Another shrug accompanied the grudging agreement. Despite her opponent's nonchalant answers Zayira decided she'd won some small measure of good grace from Hulvai even in the face of her earlier rudeness. She wasn't sure why it mattered to her beyond the fact that Hulvai didn't seem to have any friends. *I wonder what he's like when he's not mad or upset about something.* The problem was that he was always upset.

"Well, I guess I'd better get back," Zayira announced. She dusted her hands off and stood, taking in the foreboding lighthouse with its bright flame once more. "Want to walk back with me?" She offered Hulvai a hand up.

"No." He didn't even look at her outstretched hand. Zayira deflated and turned to go. "But I'll see you at lunch tomorrow," he added without turning around, his words caught up in the breeze off the ocean. They curled around her ears as if they were meant only for her, and she felt the tips of them burn along with her cheeks.

"Good night," she whispered, unable to raise her voice above her own embarrassment as she fled at a fast walk down the dock toward her room.

CHAPTER 20

Glorya tromped across the grass toward the headmaster's house first thing the next morning. She slammed the knocker into the heavy door twice. It wasn't strictly necessary to use so much force, but it bled the edge off the anger roiling in her gut. Brint answered in short order, an apron covering his front and a towel wrapped around one hand. "Sunchaser!" he exclaimed. "To what do we owe the pleasure?"

"I'm here to see Thayer," she growled. Brint took a step back into the hallway.

"He's just sitting down to breakfast. I can see if he minds if you join him."

"Please do. I'll wait." Glorya crossed her arms and spread her feet shoulder width apart on the stoop. Brint left the door open and disappeared upstairs with a worried expression. He reappeared moments later and beckoned her to follow him up the winding staircase to the second floor. Glorya didn't speak the whole way down the hall and into the headmaster's office, not trusting herself to stay calm and polite. *None of this is Brint's fault. No reason to take it out on him, and even Thayer might be ignorant of what's happened. Keep your cool, woman, and don't assume worst intentions until they're confirmed.*

Brint pointed at a seat across from the headmaster,

who was already halfway through a plate of fried eggs and greasy sausage. "Please don't stand on ceremony," Headmaster Thayer requested through a mouthful of fat-laden proteins. "Have a seat and join me for some breakfast."

Glorya sat, forcing herself to be as objective as possible. She speared a sausage and scooped an egg onto her plate from the tray Brint had brought up. The young man sat at the edge of a chair not far away, ready to bolt at a moment's notice if anything more was required. "I've met our new Zhedaban students," she began, stopping to chew a forkful of meat in order to thwart her desire to accuse him of wrongdoing.

"So they've arrived, then?" the headmaster asked.

"All five arrived safe and sound, despite having no adult escort." The headmaster's bushy eyebrows shot up.

"They came all that way alone?"

"So they say." Glorya stabbed another fried egg and dragged it onto her plate. It was cathartic. "They arrived as the sun set night before last with little to their names but the clothes they wore. Where did you find them?" she inquired in what she hoped was an offhand manner.

"A contact of mine in Joveru told me they wished to send us some of their weatherworkers for training as an act of diplomacy and goodwill." The headmaster's features, usually so self-assured it was irritating, held a hint of uncertainty.

"And who was this contact? What was their name?" Glorya pressed, her egg forgotten.

The headmaster frowned. "A woman named Tija. She seemed knowledgeable as to where to find some children in need of training, and the paperwork looked above board, though I speak and read little Zhedaban."

Rage burned the edges of Glorya's vision. "I know her–at least, I know of her. I would never want to truly know the woman. Did she offer you anything to take them?"

"She did," Headmaster Thayer mused. "Come to think of it, they were supposed to bring some coinage with them to help defray the cost of taking them on. Did they mention anything about it?" He leaned forward in his chair as he took another bite of his sausage.

Glorya shook her head in amazement. "You'll never see that money, if it even existed." She set down her fork, her appetite dulled by the conversation. "Are you aware of most Zhedabans' beliefs surrounding sun-chasers, Headmaster?" He stared at her with his brows drawn down, chewing on his breakfast for all the world like a cow with its cud. "They're considered a curse on their families. Many are forced into hard labor to atone. Children are given up as soon as their abilities are dis-covered, often as young as six or seven, and the lucky ones end up in orphanages; others learn to make their own living in the streets of the cities. Some are left out in the desert." Thinking of the stories she'd heard made Glorya's blood boil anew. The headmaster's horrified expression mollified her and she continued. "Tija is a common huckster. She finds ways to take advantage of anyone and everyone in Joveru while toeing the line of legality. Chances are good these children were chosen to get them out of someone's way–which means we just in-herited a problem we know nothing about." She sighed. *I need to write some letters.*

Headmaster Thayer blinked at her owlishly once,

twice. "So what you're saying is that these children were abandoned, then foisted off on us? And without any help supporting them?" Glorya nodded. "Can we send them back?"

"No!" Glorya exclaimed. "Until we know why they were chosen we should keep them here for their safety. I can make some inquiries–"

"What about the safety of our regular students?" the Headmaster interjected. "I'll not put them in danger over a band of uncivilized foreigners." He crossed his arms over his chest, leaning back in his chair.

Glorya narrowed her eyes. *New tactic.* "You're ignoring the opportunity these children present," she argued. "The school can advertise itself as multicultural, giving it more credibility in well-traveled–and wealthier–circles, where these children's plight will be pitied. It will open new doors for funding and support, maybe allow for expansion in the future." She watched the calculations run through the headmaster's mind and seethed internally. "You could be responsible for making Weatherwatch into the premier weatherworking school in the world." That was the lynchpin; the headmaster's eyes lit up and he relaxed, taking up his fork once again to conquer the rest of his breakfast.

"You're right," he agreed, and he stuffed another forkful of eggs into his mouth. "Besides, we wouldn't want word to get out that we turned away such poor, unfortunate children."

The man can spin anything. "Indeed," Glorya said aloud and pushed her plate away from her, scooting back from the table. The greasy breakfast sat heavily in her gut; their entire conversation nauseated her. "If you'll excuse me, I need to plan my lessons before teaching today." She rose to leave.

"One more thing," Headmaster Thayer called. He hesitated. "Have you found anything…interesting in Sunchaser Keross's things?" He turned his attention back to his breakfast, feigning disinterest.

Glorya schooled her expression to one of boredom. "I'm afraid all he left were some lesson plans and class materials," she lied, hoping the headmaster was a poor judge of misdirection. His deflated response told her he was.

"I suppose that's helpful," he admitted. "If you do find anything, please let me know."

"Should I be looking for anything in particular?" Glorya took a chance asking the question, but hoped it wouldn't give her away. She had found quite a bit of research from her mentor, but she trusted the headmaster as far as she could throw him—and he wasn't a small man.

The headmaster waved dismissively. "You'd know it if you saw it," he said. "Please, don't let me keep you from your duties, Sunchaser."

"Good day." Glorya turned on her heel and waited until she was downstairs to let her anger slip into her expression. Brint appeared from around a corner, took one look at her face, and turned white. "Good morning, Brint," she said a little too brightly.

"Good morrow, Sunchaser," he hazarded. "Is everything well?" He looked like a caged rabbit staring at a wolf.

"Well enough." Glorya took a deep breath. *None of this is his fault.* "Say, you wouldn't happen to know if Sunchaser Keross was working on anything in particular for the headmaster, would you? Some kind of joint project?"

Brint paled, if such was even possible with his complexion. "I–I don't know," he stammered. "I don't think so. He never mentioned anything to me." His eyes darted downward. "If you'll excuse me, I have to clean something." Brint spun on his heel, picked up a dusting rag, and attacked an unsuspecting bust of a prior head-master.

Glorya bid him good day and stormed out. *He knows something, but I won't get it out of him just yet.* She sighed, letting some of her anger go as she exhaled. *At least I know Thayer's intentions weren't evil, just misguided.* His selfishness, while off-putting to her, did benefit the school and its students in the long run, so she decided to let it go. It wasn't likely to change at this point. Besides, she truly did need to prepare for her classes.

CHAPTER 21

The next day

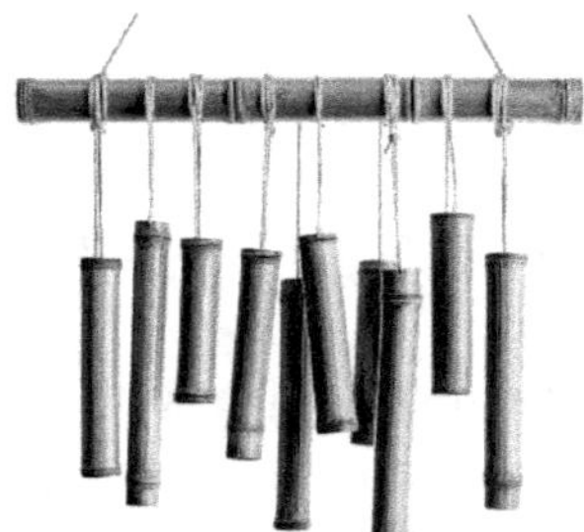

One day a week the students were given a day of rest and relaxation. No studying was required; no classes were taught. Even the teachers took a bit of a break from the routine and wandered the environs, sometimes traveling over the pass for the day to look for an itinerant merchant that frequented the nearest crossroads on such days. Zayira envied their freedom. Students weren't allowed to leave the valley under any circumstances. She understood the reason for it, of course, but it still felt suffocating. Back home she could see for miles around in any direction she chose; here she was ringed in by mountains, confined to an area smaller than her family's largest field. She wasn't sure she could take it for another four and a half years.

"Zayira!" The sound of her name snapped her out of her dark musings. Bo approached, along with Jei and a couple of the farm kids. "Let's play!" His skill at learning the Midlander language made him a favorite among the students who'd accepted their newest classmates by dint of the fact that he made it easier to communicate.

"*What are you doing?*" she asked in Zhedaban, taking the opportunity to practice his own language.

"*Chasing the wind,*" he answered with a grin. "Come! We look for something." He beckoned her toward the stormkindler dormitories. She shrugged, dusted off her bottom from sitting on a hay bale, and followed.

"...noticed it yesterday," Peony was saying to the small gaggle of children at the nearest door. "I was walking out the door and felt the slightest breeze from my right, but there was nothing there but stone." Her brow drew down as she considered possibilities.

"Why don't we go see if it's there today?" Zayira suggested. Peony started at the sound of her friend's voice; she'd been lost in her own thoughts.

"Good idea," Peony announced. "Come on, I'll show you–my room's right by the far door." She pointed at the passage closest to the pass, the door to which stood open in the temperate weather. The nights were cool, but the days remained comfortable, at least for the moment. Zayira fell into step beside her. Curiosity stirred her imagination. Would it be a trick of the wind whistling through the hewn rock of the hallways? Or a restless spirit trying to gain their attention? Maybe there was a secret compartment inside the hallway they didn't know about. What would it contain?

The gaggle of students closed ranks as they entered and approached the end of the hall. Zayira thought she felt a breath of wind on her arm, but chalked it up to the movement of her classmates. She reached out with her senses and found no weatherworking at play. *Maybe Peony is just bored and wants to give us something to do.* "I don't feel anything," she hazarded.

"Hang on," Peony pleaded. "It'll do it again, I know

it will!" She sidled closer to the rock face at the end of the hall with one hand extended.

Zayira considered chancing a use of her meager windwaking to prove or disprove Peony's theory, then discarded the idea. There were too many weatherworkers present and focused on the immediate area for her to be able to sneak her use of it past them. So she waited with the rest, arms folded over her chest. "Should we find a windwaker to help us?" she suggested into the silence. "Maybe they could try to push some air at the wall on the other side so we could see what comes through."

Peony brightened. "Good idea, Zayira! Do you know one who might help?" All heads turned her way.

"Um, maybe," she answered. "I can check if you want." She wasn't sure how he would answer, but it was worth a shot, and if he did agree to help it might make him a few friends.

"Yeah! Let's go ask." Peony turned toward Zayira, waiting for her to lead the way. Zayira shuffled her feet.

"I think I should go by myself," she declared. "He's really shy, and I'm afraid he won't come if all of us show up."

"Who is it?" one of the other students asked. She was a second-year student and knew more children in the other classes than Zayira. "Most of the windwakers want nothing to do with us or the sunchasers."

"Is it one of the other farm kids?" another student asked.

"No," breathed Bo. "Hulvai." He made the gesture for deep friendship as he said the boy's name.

Zayira felt her ears burn. "Yeah, what of it?" she demanded. "He needs friends. Nobody else has been kind to him."

"Ooh, Zayira and Hulvai!" one of the younger boys tittered. "You like him, don't you?"

"He is really cute," one of the girls whispered. The boy's head whipped around to see who had spoken, but no one met his gaze.

Zayira squared her shoulders. "He's really lonely, is what he is. Nobody's even tried to get to know him besides the teachers, and even they haven't been able to talk to him."

"Bet he's not lonely anymore," one of the other kids shot back.

"Good," Peony interjected. "Zayira's right; none of us have even tried to make him feel welcome since he got here. We should be ashamed of ourselves." She lifted her chin and straightened her spine. "Come on, Zayira. I'd like you to introduce me to him so that maybe we can all be friends." And with that she strode back out the door, the stupefied gazes of the other students on her back.

Zayira hurried to catch up with the taller girl's stride. "You didn't have to do that, you know, but I thank you for it."

Peony shrugged. "You were right. We haven't been as kind as we should have been." She slowed as they neared the closest bridge connecting the other half of the valley. It was the second longest, being closer to the shore than the one to the east of it, and gave a better view of the gardens than the beach. "Um, where are we going?" Peony asked.

"Depends," Zayira answered. "Sometimes he's out at the docks, but I don't see him out that way. Maybe he's in his room." The thought of visiting Hulvai's room, even with company, turned her ears pink all over again. *Oh, come on, Zayira. He's not even that cute.* But her cheeks burned all the same, belying her nerves.

"Which one is his?" Peony had turned away to scan the rest of the area and missed Zayira's blush.

"I don't know," Zayira admitted. "We'll have to ask. Do you know any windwakers?"

"Sure do." Peony's face lit up as she spied a gangly boy with mud-brown hair and tanned skin across the bridge. She pointed. "And he's right there! Race you across!" She took off before Zayira could get the message to her feet that they needed to move faster.

The boy turned out to be Peony's cousin, Anders, who'd preceded her to the school by a year. They had more relatives at the school than Zayira could count; each discipline held at least one cousin, with the windwakers most prevalent at three. Peony was the only stormkindler. Anders, at least, seemed just at friendly as his cousin and even more garrulous. He escorted them to the windwaker dorms and pointed them toward the room at the apex of the valley. "That's his," he asserted. "You sure you want to go visit him? I don't think I've ever heard him speak, much less seen him take visitors."

"We're sure," Peony answered. "After all, his door is open." Anders shrugged and left them to it. A hollow musical sound drifted toward them carrying a slow, haunting melody in soft tones. Zayira and Peony shared a look of curiosity, then plowed ahead, Zayira in the lead.

She peeked around the door frame and found Hulvai seated in the middle of his bed, eyes closed. Around the room floated bamboo flutes of various sizes, suspended from various surfaces with twine to allow them to resonate with the air currents winding their way through the space. Zayira chose one such current at random and followed it on its circuitous journey with her senses. It dipped through one flute at a time long enough to sound a note, then danced to the next one, stirring enough of a breeze to lift the small hairs around Zayira's face.

Peony scooted around her to the other side of the doorway, her brown eyes wide with wonder. "Wow," she breathed.

Hulvai's eyes snapped open. Wind tore through the flutes all at once in a dissonant crash of sound, forcing the girls to cover their ears. "What are you doing here?" he asked, his voice carried through the maelstrom on tightly-controlled air currents.

"We came to see if you wanted to help us with something," Zayira shouted, then realized none of her words reached past the door. *Too much wind and noise…I wonder if I can use the wind to throw my voice like he does. He won't notice a small bit of windwaking in the middle of all this.* Peony paid them no attention; she'd ducked behind the door frame to escape the cacophony. *Well, here goes nothing.* Reaching out with her senses, Zayira woke a small breeze, just big enough to fit between the larger currents in the room. It started at her mouth, where she repeated her message, and shot across the space between them. The effort of dodging the larger currents brought on a sweat; she wasn't nearly as strong a windwaker as she was a stormkindler and had far less practice with it. *Please work.*

The discord inside Hulvai's room ceased as abruptly as it started. He met Zayira's tentative gaze with his own sharp regard, like that of a hawk determining whether or not it could eat the animal before it. It was the first time he'd looked at her with anything but anger, and while his expression chilled Zayira, she couldn't help but feel she'd made progress. On what, she still wasn't sure.

"You are not entirely as you seem," he stated, his words soft against the continued roar in her ears. Her blood ran cold as she realized he'd felt her working and she fingered the silver storm cloud pinned to her shirt. *Play it off, Zayira. Maybe he doesn't know.*

"I don't know what you mean." She was proud of the fact that her voice didn't shake as she said the words. Beside her Peony dropped her hands back to her sides and looked around the door frame.

Hulvai held Zayira's gaze long enough for discomfort before continuing. "Why do you want my help?" he asked in his usual disinterested tone.

"We, um, thought you might want to come help us solve a mystery." Peony sounded less sure of herself than she had when they'd left their own dorms. Hulvai hooded his eyes and turned them to where she stood transfixed in the doorway.

"You have other friends who can help, I'm sure."

"Yes, but we thought you might want to join us. You know, to play while the weather's nice." Peony squirmed under the weight of Hulvai's stare. Zayira took pity on her and spoke up to shift his attention.

"Peony and I would like to be friends with you," she explained. "We've noticed you don't seem to have many friends."

"I don't have any friends, and that's fine." It was Hulvai's turn to squirm; he looked away and hunched over a bit further. "I don't need friends." His last statement was almost a whisper, and Zayira felt the despair behind his words.

"Hogwash." The boy's head snapped up and anger flowed into his expression like water filling a dry creek bed. *Good; angry is better than depressed.* "Everyone needs someone. And you have us. Plus the rest of the kids out there want to get to know you; they just don't know where to start."

"I told you, I don't *need* friends," Hulvai insisted. Wind danced along the edges of his hair, making him look even more menacing.

Zayira refused to take the bait. "Yeah, whatever. So do you want to help us find a secret tunnel or not?" She'd been chewing on what might be behind the wall for a few minutes and decided that a tunnel was the most likely option, perhaps something left over from the construction of the school.

"Secret...tunnel?" The wind died and for a second Hulvai looked like a regular eleven-year-old boy who was curious about the world.

"Yeah," Zayira said, grinning. "But we need a good windwaker to find it. You in?"

By the time he slid off the bed and met them at the door Hulvai had re-donned his mask of indifference– but Zayira was certain it was just that: a mask. *He wants to be normal and accepted; he just doesn't know how.* She wondered what kind of life he'd had before coming to the school, then decided it didn't matter. He deserved a chance to be a normal kid for a while. *And I'll do whatever I can to help make that happen.*

CHAPTER 22

On the North Midlands Sea

"Captain Ordulla!" Brizen's rough voice grated over the wind and rain pelting the ship. He clung to a lifeline attached to the mainmast and faced into the teeth of the storm that had ground on them all day.

"What?" the captain demanded from her place behind the ship's wheel. She'd taken over for the helmsman an hour prior to let the man get some rest after fighting the seas all morning.

"I have bad news," Brizen called from amidships.

"All your news is bad. What is it this time?"

"I've hit the end of my strength, ma'am." Brizen dragged his hands across his haggard face to wipe away the rain that lashed at it. "There's nothing more I can do to keep us on course."

The crew jerked as a wave tossed the ship backward. "Yet you still draw breath," the captain replied. "If you cannot keep the ship afloat, what use are you?"

"I can do no more without rest."

"Your rest will be eternal if you do not do more."

A gust of wind jolted the ship sideways and the crew rushed to reorient the sails. The captain could spare no more thought for the exhausted windwaker on his knees on the deck; she had the rest of her crew to think of, to keep safe. Their objective was so close; if they could only keep going a bit longer the way would open before them and their holy purpose could be fulfilled.

Brizen took a deep, shuddering breath and looked to the skies. Their unyielding gray gazed back in confirmation of the captain's statement. Digging deep, he pushed himself to his feet and threw himself at the winds around the ship, finding the smallest ways to redirect them to conserve his energy.

The next time he wiped the rain from his face his hands came away slick with blood. He watched the rain wash it onto the deck to join the storm's lifeblood, sending up a silent prayer to whoever might be listening that they would make it through.

Two hours later the sun shone on the prone figure of Brizen, waist still tied to the mainmast and face down in a shallow pool of blood. One of the crew watched him for signs of life, and upon seeing the uneven rise and fall of the man's chest he lifted the smaller man and carried him to his bunk below.

He washed his hands and asked the blessing of the gods from his captain after touching one so unclean. She gave it freely.

CHAPTER 23

Later that evening

Glorya shifted the position of the maps on her desk for a third time by the light of the guttering candles at each corner. They didn't make sense; none of the trend lines connected across the pieces of the world they showed. *There has to be a pattern here somewhere.* A few came close, but never quite touched. It was maddening.

Over the past few weeks she'd gained an inkling of her predecessor's research goals. She'd run across the germ of his ideas years ago on her first venture across the Great Sea, where she'd studied the weather patterns in the seasonal monsoons. Over time she'd taken into account the cycle of storms that ravaged the coasts across Midlands and Zhedaba and had gained a deeper understanding of the world's rhythms. But what Keross's research seemed to propose was preposterous. *A way to make the inlands habitable?* Everyone knew the deserts in the center of the continents were too vast to cross, much less settle. *There must be something I'm missing.* It didn't help that the only time she could find to study his work was at the end of the day when her eyes were already crossed from handling students.

Glorya stood, stretched, and shuffled the vellum she'd been studying back into its folio. It struck her as she tucked it into one of the drawers in her desk that anyone who could finish Keross's research could become very wealthy–if they were successful. *That's what Thayer is after.* Realization struck like kindled lightning, and she finally understood why it had taken her so long to find the pieces she needed. The ransacked cottage, the headmaster's questions…they all made sense. Sunchaser Keross hadn't wanted the headmaster to get his hands on this research–so he'd intentionally disorganized it and hidden key pieces before his death.

Now it was up to Glorya to carry it forward and protect it from those who would abuse it. She stood taller than she had in days and looked around the cottage, wondering where he might've hidden the final pieces. Her old mentor was always crafty and eccentric; many of the comments he'd made while she was a student hadn't made sense to her until after she left the school for parts unknown. She could almost feel the weight of his gaze as she cast about for a sign–his startling blue eyes boring into her green ones as he willed her to understand, to put the pieces he'd laid down together, as she had so many times over the years.

A flicker of movement across her window shattered the flow state she'd entered. *Who else is up at this hour?* Sometimes Mira or Selene visited her in the evenings, but never so late. The weather had cooled enough to be uncomfortable at night if one was out of doors for too long. She strode to the door of her cottage and cracked it just enough to stick her head out without letting out all the heat from her fire. A small figure flitted between buildings, clinging to the shadows under the waxing moon. *Too small to be a teacher–is that a student breaking curfew?* Glorya sighed and slipped on her boots, wrapping herself in her oiled cloak as she slipped out of her cottage.

The air held the first pricklings of frost, and her breath steamed as she rushed to catch up with the retreating figure. It headed down the north valley wall, flowing from outcropping to bush to boulder seamlessly. Glorya was no stranger to stealth, having grown up stalking deer close to her home. She'd stalked humans, too, to avoid brigands in the forests and deserts between Midlands and Zhedaba on her trips home, so she was confident in her ability to follow without detection. Children were always more observant than adults, though. She'd have to be extra careful.

They reached the beachhead at the northern end of the valley in short order. Glorya chose a large rock and crouched in its shadow to watch her quarry, which did not slow as it approached the chill waters. *Where on earth are they going? There's nothing out there but…the windlass caverns.* She answered her own question as the figure hopped up onto a narrow ledge jutting out from the cliff to its right. *It's a treacherous climb during the day–whyever would anyone attempt it at night?* She started forward to intercept the student, then realized they were already halfway to the gap in the stone that led to the windlass mechanism for the school's boom chain. *Nothing to do but wait.* She shouldn't risk her own neck unless there was clear and present danger the student would fall, and whoever it was looked more sure-footed than she trusted herself to be under the circumstances. So she settled her back against the rock and pulled her cloak tight against the chill of the night.

The sound of the ocean nearby lulled her into a sense of security, and before she knew it she awoke to the cheering of seagulls as they greeted the dawn. *Damn!* She'd fallen asleep on watch for the student who'd snuck out. Worse than that, her toes were numb and she was stiff as a board from sleeping upright under a rock all night. *Been a good bit since you did that. Good to know you still can. Now get moving, woman–you've got classes to teach.* She stomped feeling back into her toes, stretched, and stumbled off toward her cottage.

A ruckus near the headmaster's house caught her attention. "Brint!" a familiar voice shouted from amid a pile of suitcases and chests. "Blast it, where is my breakfast? I'm due to meet the caravan at the head of the pass in an hour and I haven't even left yet!"

"Coming!" answered the higher-pitched voice of his long-suffering assistant as Brint dashed out of the building with a basket. Steam rose from the towel wrapped around its contents. "Here you are, sir." The headmaster snatched the basket from Brint and strode toward the armory and stables.

"Get these things to the stables and saddle my horse," he demanded over his shoulder. As always, Brint scrambled to comply, but the load was too much for one person in a single trip; the headmaster's chest alone filled the small wagon he'd set up outside. On top went the suitcases, which listed drunkenly over the side as he attempted to lift the traces and pull.

Glorya rushed to his side. "May I be of service?" she asked, not waiting for an answer. She took up one of the traces and motioned for Brint to take the other. He deflated and nodded, picking up the other handle and starting forward without a word.

Their combined efforts got the cart across the closest bridge without dumping any luggage into the creek. One suitcase fell off as the wheels landed in a pothole just past the banks, but Brint was able to recover it before it rolled very far. Armsmaster Rylen waited for them with Zinnia, the ornery jennie who had alerted him to Glorya's arrival with Zayira some weeks ago. "Glad to see someone helping him," Rylen whispered as he backed the animal into the traces and hooked her up. "Poor man catches all the headmaster's guff and takes it in stride." He straightened and called to Headmaster Thayer. "I will accompany you to meet the caravan," he announced.

"Very good, very good," the headmaster answered. "Besides, someone must make sure this foul beast is returned to her rightful place." He waved at Zinnia from atop his horse. She brayed her opinion of the headmaster and tossed her head.

"Couldn't do without her," Rylen agreed, winking at Glorya. "I'll be back by lunchtime," he added for her benefit. He took up Zinnia's lead and followed the headmaster to the head of the pass, where they soon disappeared over the hill.

Brint let out a sigh. "Three weeks," he said. "Three weeks to myself. Three weeks of peace and quiet and–" He stopped abruptly, recalling that he had an audience. "I-I mean, however shall I occupy myself?"

Glorya's eyes danced with mirth. "Don't worry; I won't tell anyone, least of all His Majesty," she reassured with a wink of her own. Brint still looked apprehensive. "Come on," she suggested. "Let's get some breakfast–and you don't have to cook it yourself this time." She steered him toward the dining hall and the smell of fresh bread wafting through the doorway. At first he looked as though he'd resist, but the first whiff of toast and jam grabbed him by the nose and lead him through the double doors, Glorya in tow.

Over breakfast she learned that the headmaster would be gone for the next few weeks; he'd received word from a potential patron for the school and decided a personal visit was in order. Glorya was aware the school ran on donations from wealthy benefactors and parents of students, but she'd never thought about how they were acquired. Brint waxed eloquent on the headmaster's methods of securing funding for the school, even going so far as to wonder why there weren't more. "I do the books, you see," he explained. "And I could swear Headmaster Thayer always agrees to more of a contribution than he brings me. Perhaps he's just bad at making deals and always gets shorted."

"Some people do find it difficult to enforce their agreements," Glorya acknowledged. But in her heart she wondered if the headmaster was embezzling some of those contributions before passing them on to the school.

Before long it was time for her to start classes. Brint wandered off toward the house he shared with the headmaster looking lighter and more relaxed than Glorya had seen him. *I need to get him out of that house more often.*

The day had warmed enough for her to be able to doff her heavy cloak, which was still damp from her overnight stay on the beach. She stopped by her cabin long enough to hang up the cloak and check the rest of her clothes for dampness before heading off into the wild unknown of the coming day.

CHAPTER 24

Zayira stretched her neck and straightened her back. Her body was still getting used to hunching over a desk instead of squatting over a garden, and by the end of the day her neck and back hurt in new ways. At least her final class of the day usually didn't involve much writing. Languages and etiquette was her favorite course of study at Weatherwatch–mostly the languages part, if she was honest with herself. But etiquette pulled in cultural understanding as well, which tied it into the spoken and written portions of her study. Her Zhedaban had expanded rapidly with the addition of their new contingent from the south, but she still knew little of their daily customs and life beyond what she'd gleaned from her friends. They didn't speak much about the time before they came to the school, and Zayira could tell it was a painful subject, so she didn't push them on it. Still, she was curious.

Despite the pain in her neck she had one more duty to discharge before meeting up with her friends. She'd been at Weatherwatch a full month and had yet to write a letter to her family. In her defense, she hadn't heard from them, either, but it was harvest time; they were busy in the fields until well after dark. A message from her would lighten their spirits after a long day.

She stared at the top of her small desk. The blank paper before her stared back. Where should she start? Certainly they wouldn't care about every little detail of her life. What would her mother ask about? Or Da? Or Maks and Danil? Her mother would want to be sure she remembered her manners and treated others well. Da would want to know about her schoolwork, and Maks would want to know how she was getting on with weapons training. Danil...well, Danil would probably just ask if she had a boyfriend yet, then want to know all about her friends. So she decided to treat it like a conversation where she couldn't hear the other side, starting with a description of the school itself. She even included a rough sketch of the valley with an X to mark her room.

Three pages later she finished her missive. She folded the vellum into thirds and tied it with a bit of the twine she'd found in the supply closet. *Now what do I do with it?* She hadn't seen mail come or go in the weeks she'd been at the school. It was quite possible she'd just missed it while in class, but she knew who could tell her: the one person who saw everything and everyone who came and went from the valley. The armsmaster.

Her heavy door almost swallowed a timid knock. "Who is it?" she called. It was still early enough for visitors, but she'd told everyone she knew she had a letter to write. She set it down on her desk and went to the door.

Behind it stood Jei, his narrow face scrunched up with anxiety. Zayira noticed he was alone, which was unusual; most days it took three people to pry him away from An, if he'd even cooperate. *"What's wrong?"* Zayira asked.

"I can't find An," he answered. *"I've looked every-where."* The boy hugged himself and shuffled from foot to foot.

"Did you look in her room?" Jei nodded. "The dining hall?" He hesitated at the Midlander words, but nodded. *"By the docks? She likes it there."* Another, more emphatic nod. Zayira put down her letter and pushed herself away from her desk. *"I'll help. Let's go."*

Jei was correct; An occupied none of her usual haunts. The younger boy's anxiety rose the longer it took to find her, and before long he took Zayira's hand, squeezing it for reassurance. He'd never offered to take her hand before, so she took it as a measure of his upset. They'd almost given up looking when a pair of students appeared from around the corner of the history building. The fading light obscured their faces, but Jei gasped and ran forward into the waiting arms of the thinner student, firing off rapid syllables in Zhedaban Zayira could barely follow. She caught something about finding someone, a list of places–presumably the ones they'd visited in their search–and a few choice words one of the merchants' sons had taught them before the Zhedaban students arrived. These last elicited an answering string of speech in shocked tones.

"What's going on? Is everything okay?" As the voice's owner neared, Zayira recognized one of the older sunchaser students, though she couldn't recall his name.

"He missed his sister," Zayira explained while An continued to chide Jei in the background.

The older boy nodded. "I told her he'd get upset if

we snuck off, but she insisted…" He glanced at An, who looked up from her young charge.

"He will learn to go without me," An explained. "I have told him this."

"*I'm scared without her,*" Jei answered, though Zayira wasn't sure of her understanding of his word for "fear;" it was close to one she knew, but not exactly the same.

"Midlander," An scolded with a hiss.

"I'm scared," he repeated. "I need sister." It was true he was younger than most of the other students at the school, even the first formers and newer students, but he was older than Zayira was when she first learned to leave her mother's skirts and work with her family in the fields. She'd learned quickly that it was much more fun to explore on her own without their watchful eyes.

"Do you want to see something fun?" Zayira asked. Inspiration had struck, and she had a theory that might help the boy settle in. His dark eyes rounded with curiosity, but he clung to An just as hard. "It's a secret place," she whispered, trying to think of a gesture in Zhedaban that might help convey her point. She settled on "quiet."

An crouched down and spoke to him in low tones. Most of it was in their native tongue, but she ended in Midlander. "He will go," she assured. Jei sniffled a bit, but nodded and let go of her hand to drift over Zayira. She held out her own hand in case he wanted reassurance. He looked back at An once, then slipped his thin fingers into Zayira's calloused grip.

"What is 'secret?'" he asked as they strode back toward the middle bridge.

Zayira considered her words, shuffling through

what she thought he'd understand to explain as best she could. "It's something you don't want everyone to know." Jei considered this, then nodded.

"Like me," he reasoned. "Mother and Father do not want people to see me. I am a secret." Zayira's heart dropped into her guts. *His parents hid him away? Where are they now? Why is he here? Did they not want him?*

"Why?" she managed to ask around the questions rumbling through her mind.

"I am sunchaser," he answered simply, as if it explained everything.

"So is my aunt, and everyone loves her for it," Zayira pointed out.

"What is 'aunt?'"

"My mother's sister."

They walked in silence the rest of the way to the bridge. Next to the first post sat a trail, barely discernible in the nearly-faded light, which lead underneath the bridge. Zayira grinned and put a finger to her lips. "Secret," she whispered. She checked around, but no one was watching, so they ducked around the corner and into a small alcove beneath the bridge. The support beams that ran the length of the structure sat flush with the bank on this side, creating a small space where the younger children would sit and play or try to avoid classes. It had a dirt floor, but no one cared; the river–a mere creek at this point–could wash away the stains.

The two children tucked themselves up into the alcove, where the wind wouldn't reach them. It was just chilly enough in the evenings to need a sweater, but neither of them had thought to bring one, being in a hurry to find An. "What do you think?" Zayira asked, looking around with a shrug.

Jei considered with a weightier expression than one so young should sport. "Is good place," he decided. "I come here more." Zayira smiled. Her ploy had worked. She'd have to tell An where the alcove was in case she ever needed to find him on short notice, but if it gave her a break and got him better acquainted with the other children, it was well worth sharing Zayira's favorite spot.

"Well, well, if it isn't the farm mouse and the sand flea." A haughty voice floated around the corner of the support beam behind Jei, followed by a pale face framed with dark hair. The fading light of the sunset bruised the boy's features, casting them a mottled blue and purple as he smirked.

"What do you want, Kristus?" Zayira spat with a scowl. She'd grown accustomed to his tampering in her daily life ever since she'd bested him at arms practice her first day.

"Oh, we're just passing through to see what the riff raff do in their spare time," he answered loftily. Two more faces peeked around him, grinning savagely in the fading light.

"Nothing of your concern. 'Sides, everyone knows you have so many sticks shoved up your arse you wouldn't know fun if it hit you in the face, so shove off and let us be."

"You call huddling under a bridge fun?"

"See? No imagination whatsoever." Zayira unfolded from her crouch and emerged into the near-darkness. "But if you want to take your spot as the bridge haunt, we'll leave you to it." Jei, sensing something was amiss, slipped around the other side of the bridge while Zayira held the attention of the rest of the group. She caught a flicker of movement, then he was gone from view. *I really ought to learn how he does that.*

"I wouldn't dare sully myself by sitting on the ground *under a bridge* frequented by the likes of you, especially after it's been used by one of *them*." Kristus gestured toward Jei's now-empty spot. His brow furrowed as he realized half of his quarry had escaped without him noticing. "I bet he's used it as a latrine just like the animal he is," he continued as he cast about in the deepening gloom for Jei.

"You take that back." Zayira could tolerate anything Kristus said as long as it was about her. The moment he spoke ill of her friends a fire lit in her gut, propelling her into a confrontation that could only end poorly. *He's got friends with him. Be smart, Zayira. You just have to make sure they don't get to Jei.*

Kristus danced around, waving his arms like the tiny monkeys in the pictures Professor Antonus had shown them earlier that day. They were studying Temalingar's jungles. "Look at me, I'm a little monkey pretending to be human!"

"You're a twit." Zayira spat in the dirt next to her foot. "I'm going back to my room. This is boring." She knew he only did it to get her riled up, so if she pretended not to be bothered he'd likely leave her alone. At least, that was how it worked with her brothers back home. She recalled the letter she needed to send and turned to leave.

An electric shock zapped into her retreating back, knocking her to the ground. It passed as swiftly as it hit, but in its wake her muscles ached. She stood up without turning around, white-hot rage fueled by the pain throbbing in her shoulders. One of the other kids gasped and murmured behind her. "You shocked me." The words tore from her as she realized what had happened. "You called *lightning* on me." A cloud fumed into existence above Zayira's head. It crackled and glowed as she fed the generation of water droplets so that the cloud charged beyond what would normally be possible. She turned to see Kristus holding a tiny microcosm of what she'd generated in his hand, his eyes wide as he took in the size of the cloud she'd kindled. "You shouldn't bully people," she admonished. "Sometimes people bully back." A flash of light snaked out from her cloud toward Kristus, who watched, powerless, as it approached.

The area near the bridge went dark as all the lightning was snuffed out, leaving the whole group blinking and watching streamers of false light. When they were able to focus again Jei stood in their midst, both hands outstretched from his sides. "Do not fight," he instructed. "Fight is bad." He lowered his arms and stepped over to Zayira's side. "Go home." Taking her by the hand, he led her to the sunchaser dorms and straight to the open door of the room he shared with An. Zayira felt Kristus's eyes on her back until they turned the corner around one of the buildings. Of all the entitled rich kids she'd met, he was the worst. And despite everyone's reassurance it would get better, his treatment of her had just gotten worse. Ever since she bested him at arms practice–before that, even–he'd been awful toward her. She'd done nothing to deserve it.

"Sit," Jei invited, shaking her from her reverie. Zayira sank onto An's bed, which was the only true bed in the room; they'd brought in a small mattress for Jei to sleep on and left it on the floor.

"*Thank you,*" Zayira said, bowing and signing a gesture of humility. "I shouldn't have done that. You were right; fighting is bad." Jei simply nodded and flopped down on his mattress to stare up at the ceiling.

They passed a moment or two in contemplative silence. Then Jei stood and poked his head out of the door. He seemed to be listening for something, one ear turned down the hall as he leaned out of the doorway. Zayira joined him and was just able to make out the sound of Hulvai's wind flutes carried along the breeze from his room. *But he's in the windwaker dorms–they're not even connected to the sunchaser side!* Or were they? She, Peony, and Hulvai had spent days searching for a clue as to whether or not there were any secret tunnels to no avail. She crept out into the corridor and down its length, keeping her footfalls light on the dusty stone floor. Jei ghosted behind her. He tapped her shoulder to get her attention and signed "*Where going?*"

Zayira pointed at the end of the hallway. It was shrouded in shadow, and a chill bled from its depths that spoke of the cooler temperatures outside. Jei shrank behind Zayira, but continued on behind her, one hand clutching the back of her tunic. She patted it.

The sound of the flutes grew stronger as they approached. Zayira reached into the darkness with both her hand and the rest of her senses, feeling for a working at play or currents of air moving across a barrier. At first she felt little. Then she closed her eyes and concentrated on what she felt, and lo and behold, there was a miniscule breeze pushing down through the windwaker dorms into the hallway before her.

Zayira squinted through the thick darkness, straining her eyes to find any speck of light filtering through whatever crack existed. Jei tugged at her tunic, but she shushed him and took his hand once again. She crept along the wall, systematically scanning every inch of the surface for any visible fissure, however small. Jei caught on as they made the second pass and leaned closer to the damp, cold surface in front of them.

There–was that a glimmer of lamplight? If so, it was dim, but something had registered in her sight as she made the third pass. She tugged Jei around in front of her and pointed. He squinted, ducking his head back and forth across the sliver of light. *"I see a hole!"* he exclaimed, using a hand signal usually reserved for outdoor use to show his excitement. He lifted a narrow finger and ran it down the vertical crack they could both now see in the stonework wall.

"Great work!" Zayira replied with a congratulatory gesture. She frowned at the shadowed wall before her. "We need more light. And Peony–we have to tell Peony!" She grabbed Jei's hand and they ran clear across the campus to find their friend. *I can't wait to tell her we've found it!*

CHAPTER 25

On the North Midlands Sea

The seal skins that kept the rain out of the ship's windows flapped in the gusts blowing off the waters. Each day brought colder weather and greater challenges; they had already drifted far enough off course they might miss the next correspondence from their mole inside the school. Cursing, the captain pushed open the door to her quarters and braced her tall frame against the onslaught of wind.

"Ten degrees to port!" she shouted over the wind as she ascended the steps to the poop deck. "We're off course!" The well-muscled man tending the wheel nodded and adjusted their bearing while the crew adjusted the few open sails to compensate for nature's vagaries.

On days like these she could almost understand the need for weatherworkers. It would be so much easier to stay the course if they didn't have to fight the seasonal weather shift all the time…but the teachings ingrained in her from childhood prevented her from continuing her train of thought. Every child knew that to start using weatherworking was to invite evil into one's heart. It was a slippery slope that ended with the wielder's soul trapped in eternal damnation. She'd already sullied her own by using the two damned creatures she employed, but they would be taken care of after they served their purpose. And their purpose was so great she could justify to any priest or scholar the use of small bits of weatherworking to achieve it.

Once the school was gone they would all see how much better the world could be. Her people would roll down the coast like the wind their weatherworkers called, cleansing the world of the scourge the southerners called a blessing. But they needed a jumping-off point, one no one would expect. Not only was the school in a perfect location, it also afforded them the ability to eliminate a concentrated group of damned souls, giving them a clean death and the hope of salvation in the afterlife. The fact that most of them were children was of little consequence.

The captain smiled grimly and ducked back into her quarters, away from the raging wind and her thoughts of victory. It wasn't quite time, but soon their opening would come.

And they would be ready.

Brizen pretended to nod while propped against the bow rail. For weeks after keeping the ship afloat in the last major storm he'd feigned greater illness than he'd felt; it gave him a break from the tender ministrations of the captain. *There's no way that woman is human.* Her entire being revolved around brutality: inflicting pain on others and on herself was her main source of pleasure and gratification. It was as if she had to pay penance for every enjoyable act with her own blood. Brizen had heard of such folk, but had never run across one, much less become one's plaything.

I have to get out of here. The thought ran another circuit in his overactive mind. It was a perennial member of the sad crew that manned the ship of his psyche, along with many questions and a few darker ponderings.

A grunt brought his attention back onto the deck of the ship. One of the mercenaries they'd picked up in Fisherman's Watch leaned on the railing next to him, smoking a fat cigar. "Fair night," he observed, the rolled tobacco waggling in his mouth as he spoke. "Far too fair for a face like that 'un."

"The only fair night I'll see is my first one off this ship." Brizen pushed himself upright with the assistance of the bow rail. "Even if it's pissing rain."

"Mhmm." With a proper angle Brizen could see that the man was older than he, with graying temples and lines around his eyes that weren't from laughter. He took a long drag on his cigar. "Word from the men is we're after some school full of children. You know anything about that?" His tone hadn't changed, but something told Brizen that his chances of continued existence hinged on his answer.

"I've been told not to speak of it." He hesitated, glancing around the deck to see who might be near and lowering his voice. "But they're right."

Smoke billowed past his face. "And you're right

with this?"

"Gods no, but unlike you I'm not being paid to be here. Quite the opposite, in fact." The temperature between the men dropped sharply, but the man simply nodded.

"That's fair, I suppose." Another draw on the cigar, longer this time. "What if I offered you a way out that doesn't involve killing children?"

"Or being reported to the captain?" Brizen chuckled. It would be just his luck if she'd sent the man herself to test his loyalty–or at least the level of his fear.

"Captain can hang for all I care." The man still sounded as if he were discussing the quality of the dinner they'd finished, not considering mutiny. He ashed his cigar and turned to look Brizen dead in the eye. "I've taken money for many things, son, but never that. Never that. If you're with me, be ready as soon as we reach the shore." His piece said, he nodded his goodnight and disappeared below.

CHAPTER 26

An uneventful three weeks passed without Headmaster Thayer looking in on things. He generally took a hands-off approach to managing the school and its everyday workings, but his presence was felt in the person of Brint, whom he required to follow up on his every whim. Glorya had taken to spending the early mornings with the young man to better understand his position and had decided he was gravely underappreciated. He never complained; he could always think of a good reason the headmaster wanted him to count every slate in the valley or inventory all of the supply closets in the dormitories. He just wasn't sure it had to be done at that very moment, as was the usual request.

The more Glorya heard about the man secondhand, the less she liked Headmaster Thayer. He had no compunctions about disrupting the days of everyone around him at the slightest provocation. *I bet no one told him "no" when he was a child.* Selfishly, she considered that he wouldn't be a permanent problem in her life; she was only filling in for Sunchaser Keross, after all, and would gladly cede her position to a better qualified teacher in favor of continuing to build her business. But she knew that Sylene and Mira and Rylen and poor Brint and the rest of the staff would not be so lucky. She resolved to do what she could to make their lives easier before she left.

Classes progressed with less ruffling of feathers as the Zhedaban students adjusted to their new home. They were quick to adapt despite the massive cultural difference between Midlands and their home, and all but Ri picked up the language quickly. Ri was the oldest, Glorya learned, and had spent the longest in the orphanage where they'd been found. She often found him alone by the docks or tucked into a corner of the beach near the sheer cliffs, sketching complex images in the sand and watching them wash away with the tide. On the third such occasion she approached him.

"Hail, Ri." Glorya called ahead as she strolled down the beach, for all the world like she fancied an evening walk and nothing more.

"Hello." His answer in Midlander surprised her; as little as he spoke the language she'd have thought he would wish to speak his own.

"What are you doing?" She peered at the drawing in the sand. Usually his designs were abstract, but this one depicted a large rock outcropping amidst a sea of sand. *I know that place.* It was the only inland Zhedaban settlement of any permanence, a great set of hewn and natural tunnels burrowing beneath the desert sands that provided enough shade and moisture to sustain a population for more than a month. The grand central chamber housed a huge marketplace where one could purchase any piece of worked metal their heart desired–provided they could find the market in the first place. Outsiders were generally not allowed.

Ri shifted his seat on the sand without meeting her eye. "Drawing home." The raw timber of his voice tugged at her heart.

"You are from Garobi?" she asked. He nodded, confirming her suspicion. "Do you have family there?"

"No family." The words cut across the space between them, leaving a chasm of loss. "Only An, Bo, Len, and Jei." Glorya had grown more accustomed to the sadness that floated around the children, but it still raised her ire that they were treated so poorly at such a tender age.

"I have friends in Garobi," she mentioned in what she hoped was an offhand manner. She snuck a few gestures in with her Midlander words to help him interpret any he didn't know.

"You are not Zhedaban." Ri spoke without malice or curiosity; he simply stated a fact.

"I follow the Zhedaban ways when I am at home. Thus, the law protects me. And I have had the opportunity to make friends in many places, Garobi included." Glorya folded herself onto the sand across from Ri. *"I know what it is to be a sunchaser in the desert. I know what it is to hide what I am for fear of censure, but I do not know the pain of rejection by a family who sees my talents as a curse."*

"They did not reject me. They died because of me." Ri swept his hand across his face in the traditional sign of warding and rest for the departed.

Glorya cursed herself mentally for misunderstanding the boy's plight. *"What happened?"* she asked, seating herself across from him. She began to sketch her own home in the sand between them as a way to keep Ri comfortable; he seemed not to enjoy having anyone's full regard directed at him under normal circumstances, which these most definitely were not.

"Our family disowned me," he answered. His long,

thin finger stabbed the earth next to the rock mound and dragged a long line away toward the water. *"They joined me in exile, and the desert took them. I made it to Garobi with no water, no name, and no parents. I've been on my own ever since."* He paused and hung his head. Greasy strands of black hair covered his face, but Glorya could see the tears as they dripped from his nose onto the damp sand.

"They sound like the best of people," she answered. *"You must miss them terribly."*

"They loved me, and they died for it." Silence stretched between them, deep and abiding and filled with years of guilt and self-blame.

"You cannot blame yourself for the skills with which you were born." Glorya ducked her head to peer underneath the curtain of hair. *"It was their choice to support you. If you spend your life feeling guilty for it, you do their memory a great disservice."* Ri hung his head lower. *"They gave up their lives so that you would have a chance to live, not so you would spend all your years grieving for what you cannot change. That is not living; that is existing. Because of their sacrifice you have been brought to a place where you can openly practice your gifts. You are accepted and loved by those around you. This is your chance, Ri–but you must stand up and take it."*

"My chance to what?"

"To live. To grow. To see what you can do and surpass all your expectations for the rest of your life." Glorya dusted off her hands and surveyed her work. Before her sat a passable facsimile of the farm on which she'd grown up, complete with the house, the cow shed, some fenced pastures, and even a few cattle off in the background. It had changed since she left; the first thing her sister had done when their parents left the house to her was add

on a bathroom, and since then the yard and gardens had grown to accommodate their growing family. But parts of it were still–and always would be–home. She unfolded herself and stood, brushing at the sand clinging to her clothing like the shades of her past. "*Think about what we've talked about, and know that if you ever need guidance, my door is always open.*" With that, she left Ri to his thoughts.

Glorya's weary feet took her straight back to her own cottage, where she gazed at the disorganized piles of vellum on her desk with disdain. It was unlike her to leave things so disorderly. Between the pressures of teaching nine days out of the week and conducting her own research in what spare time she had she'd let it get out of hand. "Never let sit what could get done," she muttered, hearing her mother's words escape her own lips.

Half a candle later the piles had migrated to their proper folders and Glorya sat at her desk, staring blankly across the room at the pegs set into the far wall beside the door. All that was left of the sun was a warm glow on the horizon that she couldn't quite see through her southward-facing window. The candle's flame cast dancing shadows across the walls of her cottage each time she moved, but never while she sat still; her teacher had also worked out a method of anchoring his abilities to a single spot, rendering the building impenetrable to all wind and precipitation. She'd written to him for the first time after leaving the school when she'd figured out how to do it herself. Her efforts had permanently becalmed a ship rather than allowing it to catch the vessel she was chartered to protect; his had made his home cozy and snug. The older she got, the more Sunchaser

Keross's efforts seemed the nobler of the two.

The candle flickered as Glorya stood, its light glinting off a piece of metal poking out of the bottom of a basket. She'd stashed it there weeks ago since it looked important, but it had lain there, forgotten, ever since. *Whatever could it open?* She'd scoured the cottage countless times and found nothing–no box, no cupboard, no door it might fit. She stood, huffing in irritation, and took a step toward the bathroom.

The echo of her footstep on the wooden boards caught her attention and she froze. She took a step backward and listened; was there a different tone to the strike of her heel? She couldn't be sure. Another step forward confirmed her suspicion: the board directly beneath her desk shifted when she moved across it. Her bathroom trip forgotten, she dropped to her hands and knees and inspected the floorboards. There–one was loose just at the edge. She pried at it with her fingertips and was rewarded with nothing but a face full of loose dirt as it shifted, but stayed put. Glorya exhaled sharply, unsure of what she'd expected, and rose to answer nature's call.

When she returned she flopped down onto the easy chair to relax before changing for bed. The spavined cushion still held just enough comfort to make it worth keeping despite its disreputable state, though the coverings on arms had long ago given up any pretense of softness. She threw a leg over one of the arms and leaned back, head lolling to stare at the ceiling. A *thunk* beneath the chair drew her attention. *I suppose it's finally broken,* she figured, peeking beneath the seat to see which piece had given up the ghost.

A leather document case covered in dust with

a heavy padlock rolled toward the side of the chair. It stopped as it encountered one of the legs. Glorya reached down and drew it into her lap, blowing the dirt and sand off of the case and drawing a finger down its length to uncover anything that might be etched into the surface. It was plain, but well made, with caps over each end and a strong, fine chain wrapped around it and through the lock. She stared at the lock, dumbfounded, until her mind supplied her with the missing piece to the puzzle and she dove for the basket containing the key.

It was a perfect fit. The lock clicked open and Glorya ever so cautiously removed the caps and unrolled the leather to reveal a wide sheet of vellum. At first the pictures on it made no sense; one looked like Midlands, but Zhedaba seemed too large in comparison, and the ocean too wide between it and Temalingar. Another expanse of land stretched north of Midlands further than she'd imagined. Sprinkled across this unusual map were symbols connected by directional lines that indicated the direction of weather movement around the globe. *All right, it's a weather map. What's so special about it that Keross needed to hide it?* Glorya frowned at the document and tromped over to the desk to weigh down the corners and study it properly. Her candle had burned down to a nub, but her mind had latched onto the problem before her, galvanizing her past her exhaustion and into the midst of its puzzle.

At first the map looked like nothing more than a detailed reference for the overarching weather patterns that drifted across the world, bringing the monsoons and hurricanes and dry spells to each of its countries in turn. But as she studied it she realized it held much more. Alongside the lines for the existing patterns were dotted lines that stretched further inland, toward the uninhabitable deserts on the outskirts of humanity. No one knew how far they extended; none had crossed them and lived to tell. The Zhedaban nomadic tribes ranged across the closest portions, but never passed what they called the Water Line–the point past which it was impossible to find water in time to survive the trip back to civilization. Each year the populations of both Midlands and Zhedaba grew, and each year they pressed closer to the edge of humanity's domain with few options but to crowd closer together in the face of such barren prospects.

Sunchaser Keross had figured out how to redirect the major weather patterns in such a way that over time, the rains would move further and further inland, rendering more of the planet habitable for generations to come. Glorya's hand strayed to her mouth and she felt the pricking of tears in the corners of her eyes. *He did it. He actually came up with a workable plan.* Glorya had figured he was working on it–had corresponded with him to answer questions on the Temalingari monsoons–but he'd given no indication he was even close to finding a solution. With shaking fingers she shifted the paperweights off the corners of the vellum and moved to set it back onto the rolled-out leather of the case for safekeeping.

A smaller piece of vellum set behind the map caught her eye. It was folded into a neat square and bore her name in a familiar, spidery script. Wonder and curiosity overcame her trepidation and Glorya plucked it from the soft backside of the leather, unfolding it with careful precision. Inside she found more of the scrawled handwriting in the shape of a letter.

Glorya, it began, *I hope this note finds you well. I'm sure you're confused and perhaps a bit flustered at receiving this, especially since I've already passed beyond, but I wanted to be sure it made it into the hands of someone who would truly appreciate it. Based on our correspondence and my knowledge of your personality from your student days and beyond, I know you are the exact person to whom I must pass on this knowledge. I will not see my research bear fruit; this I know, as my infirmity progresses faster than I would wish. So I hand it over to you to do with as you see fit, secure in the knowledge that your judgement and motivation are sound and that you will make of it the best you can. All I ask is that you see it through.* It was signed "With hope," with a scrawled signature beneath.

Glorya ran her fingers across the text as if she could conjure its author simply by doing so. Tears flowed from her eyes unrestrained, polite enough to let her finish reading, but unrelenting in their path onto her tunic. *He must've recommended me to the headmaster,* she realized. She'd wondered how the man had gotten her name and address. A second realization followed: that the headmaster knew Sunchaser Keross had found something important and was bent on turning it to his own purpose. It would be easy enough for someone to profit from this project; they would have to play a long game to do so, but the payout would be large if they were patient. *I can't let him find this.* Glorya knew in her bones if she let him see what she'd found he would never let it go. So she rolled back up the map and hid it in the same place Keross had left it, keeping only the letter back for herself.

Between her talk with Ri, her discovery of the

map, and the earlier onset of darkness, Glorya was exhausted. She realized as much the third time her head jerked forward to keep it from falling backward at an uncomfortable angle where she sat in the easy chair. There was nothing for it; her problems would have to wait until the following day for resolution. She tucked the letter into her pillowcase, changed into a clean shift, and crawled into bed with visions of endless farmland scrolling across the fields of her mind.

CHAPTER 27

The stormkindler dormitory vibrated with the anxiety of its older students. Zayira could tell something big was in the offing, but no one outright mentioned it; they all seemed too busy to explain, spending all their time studying or clustered in small groups around the common spaces in the valley. For her part, Zayira kept her head down, studied hard, and took pride in the fact that she'd been chosen to help tend the winter vegetable garden. It was the most challenging time of year to grow food, and despite the fact she'd grown up farming–or perhaps because of it–she found she missed working the land.

Headmaster Thayer had just returned from some kind of trip, which contributed to the tension in the valley. While the students didn't see much of their head administrator, his absence had been an unspoken relief to all. But ever since his return both students and staff had been even more on edge. Just as Zayira felt she could no longer tolerate the anxiety swirling around her she noticed the headmaster's assistant posting flyers around the dorms proclaiming the following week to be a seasonal assessment week. *What's a seasonal assess-*

ment? she wondered. It had to be something to do with their classes, given the recent dedication of the rest of the student body to their studies. Was the assessment how they would move up through the forms in each subject? Or was there more to it?

Zayira entered maths the following firstday and discovered what assessment week meant. Each student was given assignments on their slate, then told to complete them in silence while Ms. Sylene pulled them aside one by one to quiz them on what they'd learned. Many had trouble focusing on their assignments and fidgeted in their seats. Zayira, on the other hand, found the whole process exciting. She'd learned much in her few months of classes and was eager to show her maths teacher what she'd learned.

Her next assessor was Armsmaster Rylen, who met them on the chilly pitch to test their weatherworking abilities. Zayira was confident in what she'd practiced and earned a hearty pat on the back that almost knocked the wind out of her. Most of the other students also did well, and the ones who struggled were met with encouragement and hope by their classmates and teacher.

It wasn't until Zayira entered history and geography that she realized why the other students were nervous. Mr. Antonus–or Mr. Ant-nest, as the students called him behind his back–conducted his assessments in small groups. He expected students to answer questions, some of which he'd never covered in class, and also to debate and challenge each other's answers. Zayira found it difficult to keep up with the rapid topic shifts in her group and was only able to contribute to one discussion. Her interjection sparked a heated debate on the efficacy of tariffs in controlling Midlands trade by sea that lasted the full time allotted. When they'd finished every student trudged out the door, head hanging and eyes glazed over.

Languages and etiquette went as well as weatherworking; Zayira felt she was able to display her progress to the fullest extent, which acted as a nice palate cleanser after her prior grueling examination. Ms. Mira seemed satisfied with the progress of her pupils insofar as she ever seemed satisfied. It was difficult to read the woman's expressions, and times were many that Zayira couldn't tell if she'd done well or put her foot squarely in her own mouth. She chose to take the optimistic angle and hope she'd given a good account of herself.

The dinner conversation that evening revolved around how everyone felt they'd performed. The windwaker students had just left Mr. Antonus's class and looked far worse off than the rest, while the sunchasers–Zhedaban students included–entered the dining hall with smiles. Aunt Glorya–Ms. Glorya while they were at school, Zayira reminded herself–followed them in with a satisfied expression on her face. She made a beeline for the teachers' table. *It looks like she's made some friends, too.* Zayira was glad her aunt had made a place for herself in much the way she herself had.

"What are you smiling about?" Hulvai's rough, angry voice cut through her reverie, demanding her attention as it always did when he felt jealous. She'd noticed he only sounded that way when she paid attention to others.

"Just thinking back on the day," she answered in a non-committal fashion. She didn't meet his eye and knew he'd realize it was a mild falsehood, but hoped he'd refrain from prying.

"It must've gone better than mine." Hulvai pushed his potatoes around on his plate with an unusual lack of appetite. He'd filled out a bit since Zayira first invited him to sit with her and looked healthier than when she'd arrived. The fact that she shared her food with him certainly helped.

"Most of my assessments were good," Zayira admitted, "though I'm not sure anyone did well in Mr. Ant-Nest's class." She shook her head, recalling the looks of horror from all her classmates.

Hulvai made shapes out of his mashed potatoes while he sulked. "It's stupid. He didn't even ask us anything he'd taught us about and just expected us to know things. I've never been to any of the places he talks about! I'd never even been this far south before a few months ago…" He trailed off with effort and Zayira sensed he'd said more than he meant to.

"You're from the north?" she asked, hoping he would take the bait and solve one of the biggest mysteries about him. Very little was known of the northern tribes; they didn't often cross the mountains or ply the seas, instead eking out a living in the tundras. She'd heard they didn't use weatherworking at all.

"What's it to you?" Hulvai's tone modulated from anger to petulance.

Zayira shrugged. "Just wanted to know more about you, seeing as how you know where all of us are from." She glanced at the farm kids chatting with the Zhedaban students down the bench from them. Deen half stood on the bench, telling a story that looked to involve apes and other exotic creatures based on his antics. Bo and Jei cackled at his pantomime while the rest of the group looked on, half in amusement, half in good-natured exasperation.

"What's the point? We're all going to leave in a few years anyway." Hulvai pushed his plate away from him. "See Jase over there? Everyone's sure he'll be asked to test this spring. Four more months at most and he's out." He pointed at the brown-haired girl who had helped Zayira with her sword work on her first day. "And Yulya–she'll be asked to test as well. Both are skilled and will pass, which means they'll leave as soon as it's done." This last statement held a note of resentment Zayira couldn't figure out. Was he jealous that they were leaving? It made little sense, but there was much to Hulvai that didn't add up. *I wish he could trust me to tell me about it.*

"So? That's how school goes," Zayira answered aloud. "You come, you learn, you leave and make a name for yourself." After all, it had worked for her aunt, and she was certain it would work for her.

Hulvai snorted. "I already have a name," he retorted, but she could hear the false bravado in his words.

"Yeah, but not everyone knows it yet." Zayira pointed to her aunt, who sat across the room, chatting with the other teachers. "Take Ms. Glorya over there. You mention her name anywhere on the coast or in Zhedaba or all the way to Temalingar and folk know who you're talking about. Same for Armsmaster Rylen. They've made it so that *other* folk know their names. Don't you want to be known for something?" Her brows drew down in question.

Hulvai slapped the table next to his plate, making it jump and nearly sending the closest farm kids out of their seats. "If I am, it won't be for paper birds and pretty foreign languages." He shoved himself away from the bench, snatched his still-vibrating plate from the table and marched off to return it before stalking out into the cold of the evening. *Don't suppose it much bothers him if he's from the north,* Zayira noted absently. The rest of her mind whirled with the breakneck speed change of their conversation. She'd touched a nerve, she was sure, but which one or why was a complete mystery. Hul-vai had become more and more reticent as the colder weather set in, and it was easy to touch off an argument with him on just about anything. *If all his people are like this I don't know how they survive without killing each other every winter.* Zayira shook her head and decided to join in the farm kids' revelry to take her mind off her erstwhile companion.

CHAPTER 28

Thank all the gods and goddess assessment week is over. Glorya trudged through the early morning snow toward the dining hall. She was still in a mood after reading a letter she'd received the prior day from a contact in Joveru, who had notified her that the woman responsible for finding the students sent to Weather-watch had once again disappeared into the Zhedaban underground. Now the staff planned to spend their tenthday going over the results of their testing, which sounded like a perfectly dreadful way to spend a day off. Based off the results they would select which students would prepare to test for their graduation in the spring. Glorya's mind drifted back to her own test some years back–they'd thrown every weather pattern at her they could think of and she'd dismantled them all. She'd listed all the details she knew about every city she'd studied, read and translated a passage in Old Midlander, and completed complex calculations to determine the maximum load of a ship and its likely velocity while laden. It had taken the better part of half a day to complete all the requested tasks, but she'd passed with flying colors and left the following week with her golden sun.

Zayira appeared from around the corner of a building, arms laden with cloth, and nearly ran into her aunt. "Sorry, Au-Ms. Glorya," she said, fumbling the stack of fabric she was carrying.

"What's all this?" Glorya asked, one eyebrow raised.

Zayira blushed. "Well, seeing as how the Zhedaban students don't have cloaks or anything to keep warm, we took up a collection of extras from the rest of the students–things they'd outgrown, mostly, or replaced. Some of them are really nice," she pointed out, raising one particularly fine cloak within the stack. "I think Len will like that one. Anyway, I was just taking these to them so they could stay warm." Her round face beamed.

"Don't let me keep you, then." Glorya smiled back at her niece, touched by the thoughtful gesture. "Before you go–" she caught Zayira gently by the arm to prevent her running off too soon "–stop by my cottage sometime. We should have a chat soon; we haven't spoken since we got here, and I would love to hear how you're doing." Zayira nodded, then dropped a hurried curtsey on her way across the valley to deliver her gift. Glorya had no doubt it was her niece's idea in the first place. She mentally applauded the girl for following up on it.

Halfway to the dining hall Brint appeared, chugging his way through the snow like a man much larger than he was. As he approached Glorya realized his technique involved blowing the snow out from in front of each foot as he took a step. It generated a cloud of fine powder around him as he approached. "Sunchaser," he called, half out of breath. "A moment, if you would."

"Certainly." She halted her own progress to allow him to catch up. "And I've told you, please call me Glorya."

"Old habits…die hard," Brint panted as he approached. He stopped in front of Glorya, hands resting on his knees as he caught his breath.

"What can I do for you?" Glorya asked to give the man time to compose himself.

"There's something I would like to show you." Brint dusted snow off of his arms, which were covered in a much-darned wool sweater, and indicated the headmaster's house.

"If it won't take long; I'm due in the dining hall to talk about evaluations after breakfast."

"Only a moment, I promise." Glorya shrugged and indicated Brint should lead the way back down his beaten path through the snow. She had to admit it was much easier going than her own path from the cottage.

They stepped inside and hung their damp cloaks on pegs just inside the door, letting them drip onto the stone floor as the snow melted from their surfaces. Brint ducked through the doorway to the downstairs rooms and picked his way across a menagerie of scattered vellum and objects until he reached a roll-top desk at the back of the room. He produced an old, serviceable key from somewhere about his person and unlocked it, opening it just far enough to pull a sheet of vellum from within before closing and locking it in one smooth motion. *He's obviously done that before,* Glorya surmised as Brint shuffled back across the cluttered space. She wondered what else he'd squirreled away in there.

"I found this among some papers the headmaster asked me to file," he explained as he held the sheet out for her to study. "I wasn't sure what it was or where he'd found it, but that looks like your predecessor's handwriting." He was right; before her sat a drawing of a strange pedestal scrawled across with writing and margin notes in Sunchaser Keross's spidery script. At first glance it seemed harmless enough, but paired with what she knew of her mentor's research she had an inkling there was much more to it.

"Can I keep this?" she asked.

Brint nodded "I don't think he even remembers seeing it. He sure hasn't asked for it, but if he does I'll need it back." Glorya nodded, possibilities already running through her mind as to the function of the device before her.

"Thank you," she said in earnest. "I think this is a piece of something I've been researching." Brint beamed, and once again she wondered how often the man actually got praise. "Let me know if you find anything of its like."

"Of course, of course." Brint waved his arms in a vague conciliatory gesture. "Now if you'll excuse me, I have to file some things before the headmaster discovers them loose about his office, exactly where he left them." He rolled his eyes in exasperation and showed Glorya to the door, where she re-donned her cloak and took her leave. She headed straight back to her cottage to stow the precious research before trudging back to the dining hall in hopes the meeting hadn't yet started.

CHAPTER 29

Tell me again why are we spending our tenth-day out here, in the cold, beneath a window," Peony complained in a whisper. She, Zayira, and Deen crouched below one of the dining hall's windows, which were closed against the winter chill. They huddled close together for warmth against the biting wind that sliced past them and through their cloaks.

"Because some of the older students are paying us to do it to find out who's testing this coming spring," Deen explained again. "I've done this all three years I've been here, and the pay is pretty good."

"Won't we all find out in a day or two?" Zayira groused from within the cocoon of her hood.

"Well, yes, but some folk want to know *first* so they know what to expect." Deen cocked one overlarge ear toward the window. "'Sides, does it matter if they're paying?"

"Suppose not, 's long as nobody comes to harm over it." Zayira shrugged and turned her own hearing toward the goings-on inside. She could just make out the voices of Ms. Sylene and Mr. Antonus as they engaged in a heated discussion of classroom standards.

Every now and then a softer voice chimed in, unintelligible to Zayira through the thick walls and glass. *Bet it's Ms. Mira. Aunt Glorya is never that quiet.*

The crunch of heavy boots set off alarm bells in Zayira's head. "Someone's coming," she whispered, her voice pitched to cut through the repetitive sinking of boots through the icy crust forming atop the snow. All three students skittered around the corner of the building furthest from the approaching person. The last of their shoes cleared the corner just before Glorya Sunchaser rounded the opposite corner, headed straight for the dining hall doors. Zayira watched her enter, peeking around the shadowed bottom of the building until the coast was clear. They'd heard the voices of the rest of the staff during their vigil so far; she must be the last to join the discussion. Zayira waved her friends forward. Deen slipped right under the windowsill without a noise, but Peony tripped over a buried stone, stifling a gasp of pain. Zayira helped her back to her feet.

"Are you okay?" she whispered.

"Fine," Peony answered through gritted teeth. "Stubbed my toe, but I can hardly feel it now from the cold. It'll be all right."

They spent the next two hours listening in shifts as their instructors ran through the roster of older students. Many were passed up, but a few elicited lively discussion; these were the few from whom testing candidates were chosen. Deen's hearing was keenest, so it was he who made out the name of the first candidate: Jase. The entire staff agreed to his readiness to make his way in the world. A few more names passed rigorous inspection, but Zayira didn't know any of the rest of them. Peony looked surprised when one was passed over, but hid her reaction almost quickly enough for Zayira to miss it–almost, but not quite. She filed the student's name away for future reference and to ask Peony about later.

By lunchtime the teachers had adjourned and the midday meal was served. Zayira glanced furtively around the room for any sign that the rest of the student body was in the know. Deen slid past her and dropped a few coins in her lap surreptitiously before taking a seat a few spots away. She slipped them into her pocket and continued eating without missing a beat of the conversation going on next to her, where Peony and one of her cousins were having a heated argument about which type of weatherworking was the most powerful. Peony sided with stormkindling, of course, while her cousin took the side of the sunchasers. Zayira didn't see where it mattered, but their points were interesting all the same.

Hulvai's entrance subdued the rest of the table around him. He'd grown even more distant of late, brooding and snapping at anyone who came near, yet still condescending to sit with them at meals. Zayira decided her next priority was to find the cause of his confounded moodiness; she couldn't take another day of walking on eggshells in his presence. So when he stood and returned his dishes she excused herself and followed him out of the dining hall.

She expected him to head for one of his usual haunts, like the docks or his room, but instead was surprised when he turned toward the stormkindler dorms–or, at least, the canyon wall that contained them. Instead of turning to visit someone, he hugged the cliff and turned right, toward the water. Curious, Zayira did her best to catch up with him without getting close enough for him to notice her presence. The wind galloping off the waves hid any sounds of her pursuit better than she could have hoped as they sidled along the valley wall. Only once did Hulvai turn around to look for pursuit, but Zayira was able to duck into a recess in the stone cliff face just in time. They made their way to the shoreline, where he began to climb a staircase that was hewn from the rock itself. It was narrow and slick, and in places the steps had crumbled away, leaving only handholds and footholds over the foaming waves below. Zayira stopped short of the staircase, unsure not of her climbing ability, but of her ability to swim to safety if she fell. She watched as Hulvai disappeared into an opening at the edge of the valley where the rock face turned south.

Zayira raced along the shoreline to the north in an attempt to find an angle that would let her see into the crevice that held her friend. The only clue to its purpose lay in the massive chain hanging from the valley wall that dipped its weather-beaten length into the waters below. It barely registered the motion of the water with its back and forth swing, its seaweed-encrusted links rendered inaudible by both the whistling of the wind and the softness of their natural casing. Before she knew it Zayira found herself at the end of the dock, peering over the edge to see more of the canyon wall in vain. She harrumphed and sat down cross-legged at the end of the structure. It bothered her that Hulvai would sneak off to climb to such unsafe, but interesting places and never mention it to her or anyone else. What if he fell? No one would ever know what happened to him. And what on earth could be interesting enough for him to want to risk his life to go see it? It stung that he would exclude her from such a confidence given her efforts to gain his trust.

She sniffled once, then picked herself up off the dock and ran back to the dining hall to seek out Peony and Deen. Maybe they knew something she didn't.

CHAPTER 30

North Midland Sea, closer to the shore

Captain Ordulla squinted against the reflection of the setting sun on the water. After weeks at sea it was difficult to make out anything very far past the immediate vicinity of the ship, but she tried anyway. They were due an update–overdue, in fact–and she didn't fully trust Brizen to report everything he was passed. He was a foreigner, after all, and could easily be covering for the boy to get both of them out of the straits they were in. But he hadn't been worth much these past few weeks, ever since the storm, and she didn't think him capable of enough complex thought to trick her. So she kept a weather eye herself and trusted to the wisdom of the ancients to keep her safe.

"Note incoming, Captain." Brizen's voice was thin and thready. He sat in a sling seat amidships looking out off the port side of the ship, his green eyes tired. Ordulla pinched her lids closer together in an attempt to see what the windwaker saw, but gave up after a few painful moments.

"Where?" she demanded.

Brizen pointed, and a tiny mote of movement

danced up and away from a swell. He beckoned and it shot toward the boat to land directly in the captain's outstretched hand. *At least he's regained some of his abilities.* The man had been useless for two weeks after his ordeal; she'd considered killing him and having done with it, but held off in case he recovered and there was another storm in the offing. Besides, he made such a good plaything.

The note was folded once again like a paper bird, which she unfolded to peruse its message. *Chain is unlocked. It will drop tonight.* Scrawled beneath in the margin was a hasty note, an afterthought from the author. *Please don't hurt anyone.* Ordulla shook her head, a grim smile playing across her features. He knew what their plans were and how hopeless his plea was, yet he still made it, the poor fool. They must've filled his head with the nonsense southerners believed about their abilities being a blessing and a useful trait. There was no help for it; she'd have to stamp them all out, the boy included.

After tonight his purpose would be fulfilled.

CHAPTER 31

An anxious knock sounded through Glorya's cottage, startling her up from the maps she pored over during most of her free time. She hastily shoved them under some other sheets of paperwork and went to answer the door.

Zayira tumbled in with two of her friends in tow. Glorya knew the girl, but the older boy wasn't familiar to her. All three started talking at the same time and she held up a hand to staunch the flow of words. "Good even to you all," she greeted, and was pleased to see all three bow or curtsey in response. "Now, slow down—what has happened?"

"Hulvai has run off," Zayira explained breathlessly. "He's gone up to the cave in the cliffs past the stormkindler dorm and hasn't come out. He didn't tell any of us why he was going there or how long he'd be, but he never stays gone this long when he disappears."

Glorya's brow knotted. "By the dorms, you say? In the cliffside?" Three heads nodded. "Any idea why? The only thing up there is the boom chain mechanism…" A flash of a recent memory shoved its way to the forefront of her mind—a small figure climbing the perilous cliffs by the sunchaser dormitories. *It was Hulvai. And now he's gone into both of the boom chain chambers. What is he up to?* It took two windwakers to lower the boom chain: one to push each of the great flywheels on the outsides of the cliffs. They turned opposing directions to make it more difficult to lower them, and neither would move unless they were unlocked manually. Drills were done every quarter to practice lowering and raising them, but usually the folk responsible for unlocking the chains arrived at the mechanism by rowboat since the cliffside paths were too worn and dangerous.

A thought occurred to Glorya. "Has Hulvai mentioned anything odd lately? Has he acted strange or mentioned any sort of self-harm?" All three students shook their heads, but then Zayira piped up.

"He's never talked about hurting himself, but he has been *really* testy the past few weeks. More even than usual."

"But he won't talk to us," the other girl, Peony, lamented.

Glorya frowned. "Have you mentioned this to anyone else?" Zayira shook her head. "Come," Glorya announced, grabbing her cloak from its peg. "We need to talk to the armsmaster." Rylen might know another way to get up to the boy without such risk of injury or death.

The group tromped along the most traveled paths through the melting snow until they reached Rylen's door. Glorya knocked twice and waited for a response. When none came she knocked again, then once more before a mumbled "I'm coming" floated through the solid oak. Antonus answered in his nightclothes looking frustrated. His critical gaze swept the group and landed on Glorya, who did her best to look concerned in a most adult manner. "What do you want?" he asked, sounding resigned.

"Is Rylen at home?" Glorya asked. "We are in urgent need of assistance with a student and I'm hoping he can help."

"He's still at the dining hall as best I know," Antonus said with a shrug. "I'm an early sleeper and an early riser, so he sometimes gets bored and sits up talking with the other teachers. Wonder you weren't there yourself." He eyed Glorya, the expression on his long, thin face speaking of mistrust.

"I'll look for him there." Glorya ignored the barb in favor of expedience. "Thank you, and sleep well!" Before he could close the door she'd turned and headed for the dining hall as fast as her feet would go without outright running. The three students behind her were hard pressed to keep up.

Glorya pulled open one door to the dining hall and stuck her head inside. It was vacant except for figures at two tables near the back where the staff liked to sit. There he was–she picked out Rylen's head of dark hair from across the room. "Wait here," she instructed Zayira and her friends, leaving them in the growing gloom of twilight. By the time she crossed the room she had the attention of all four of the staff occupying the back tables simply by dint of her grave expression. Rylen had his back to her at first, but turned before she was halfway across the space and rose from his chair.

"What's wrong?" he asked without preamble.

"Hulvai has climbed out to the southern windlass for the boom chain." Rylen's eyebrows flew upward. "I'm pretty sure I saw him climbing the northern one some time back, but this time he's stayed up there. Some of his friends saw him head up there and came to me out of concern."

Rylen's eyes narrowed in thought. "The only way I know to get up there besides the climb is by boat–how does the harbor look?"

"Tide's high and incoming with rough chop. I wouldn't go out on it in small craft until it's settled or the tide's turned."

Rylen cursed under his breath. "Then if he's stuck he'll have to wait until morning."

"Excuse me," called a small voice from halfway across the hall. "I think I might know another way." Five heads turned to see Zayira tentatively approaching the group.

"I told you to wait outside," Glorya chided, but Rylen cut her off. She bit back her annoyance in case her niece had helpful information. The girl didn't usually speak up without good reason.

"What do you mean?" Rylen demanded.

"Aren't there secret tunnels between the dorms?" Zayira asked. "They're blocked up, but if there's one up to the wind-glass thing we might could clear it and use it to get to him."

"What do you mean?" Glorya asked, looking to Rylen for an explanation. He squeezed his eyes shut and put a hand to his brow.

"There's always one who finds them…" He looked up at Glorya with a long-suffering expression. "Usually it's a third- or fourth-year, but I suppose some of this group is a bit more precocious." He turned to Zayira. "Yes, there were tunnels between the dorms and from the dorms up to the windlass housings, but they've been shut up for years. It might take until morning to break them down."

"Couldn't we call a bit of rain to soften the mortar and mud?" Zayira asked. "Then you could break through it easier. There are already cracks in most of them."

"Well, it isn't exactly easy to fix the cracks without the students noticing, is it?" Rylen asked. "But I suppose you're onto something there. Let's go get some tools and give it a shot." He strode for the doors, Glorya and her charges in tow.

The groundskeeper supplied them with a pickaxe and some shovels without asking questions despite the oddness of the request and the late hour. It wasn't long before the group stood before the wall at the end of Zayira's dormitory closest to her room. *At least she's the only one sleeping down here,* Glorya mused. Rylen rolled up his sleeves, took aim, and rammed the pickaxe into a tiny chink in the wall as Glorya and the children held lanterns and candles to illuminate the work. It took a few tries, but before long a small hole appeared just large enough to see through. Glorya could tell the hallway had been hastily blocked some time ago; the limestone patching they'd used around some piled-up stones and debris crumbled easily. Past the veneer sat rough-hewn rocks large enough to pose difficulty in prying loose despite the weakness of their mortar. Rylen's face set in grim determination as he worked to remove the first of the stones. It was stubborn, and in the end he had to clear the limestone patching around it to free up its edges. After a good quarter hour of work it tumbled free, nearly crushing his toes as it fell. He muffled a curse and jumped back.

As one the group leaned toward the gap in the

wall. It was the size of Glorya's head, but no light shone from within its murky depths. The rasp of waves grew louder in the dormitory hallway. Glorya pushed far enough forward to extend her lantern through the hole and peeked around her arm to see what lay beyond. Ahead of her lantern floated detached spider webs flapping in the salty breeze that cooled her face through the opening. She could see a few paces down the tunnel, but before long it slanted upward, obscuring her view. "It looks clear as far as I can see," she declared, withdrawing her arm, "though the spiders have made it their home." The children shuddered with the exception of Zayira, who looked interested.

"Let me widen the gap," Rylen suggested, reclaiming his pickaxe from where it sat against the wall. Now that some of the larger rocks had shifted it was easier to pull a few more from their resting places, and within a few minutes they stood before a hole large enough to pass a child through. Rylen paused to wipe sweat from his brow and Zayira leaped forward to peer through the opening.

"You weren't kidding, Auntie," she breathed, taking in the waving webs.

"Auntie?" Peony echoed behind her. Glorya chuckled.

"Zayira is my niece, though we've taken care not to advertise it. I would appreciate it if you two did the same." Peony and Deen both nodded solemnly. Glorya hoped their will was as solid as their intentions.

"I can fit through there," Zayira pointed out. Glorya looked at Rylen, who shrugged.

"If anyone has a chance at getting him to come back down, it's her," he said. "He's been more friendly to her than to anyone else since he arrived."

Glorya bent down to look her niece in the eye. "If the ground is at all unstable, or if you are concerned about the safety of the tunnel, come right back," she instructed. Zayira nodded gravely. "Armsmaster Rylen will continue to widen the hole so that we can follow you through. If you need our help, call and we'll hear you. If you can't call, do a working and we'll know something's wrong." Zayira nodded again and turned to go. "Take care," Glorya pleaded, a part of her heart following her niece through the hole and into the dark tunnel beyond. Someone poked another lantern through the gap. It disappeared shortly with Zayira as she strode cautiously around the spider webs and up the rough-hewn steps toward the windlass housing.

Glorya picked up the pickaxe Rylen had discarded and hacked away at the wall, determined not to leave Zayira without hope of aid or recourse for long.

CHAPTER 32

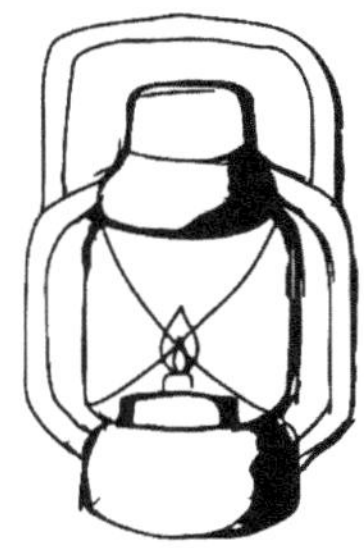

Zayira held the lantern before her as she ascended the old stone steps. The spider webs her aunt had warned her about waved across her face, but she found they lent an air of mystery and disuse to the place that was more a draw than a deterrent. *Maks and Danil always told me I had more bravery than sense, but it hasn't gotten me into trouble yet.* A little voice in the back of her mind told her there was always a first time, but she ignored it and continued on. The steps themselves were in good shape; water had dripped divots into a few of them, and they were slick with moisture from the sea air, but since they were hewn into the living rock there was no wobble or instability to them. Ahead the tunnel continued upward out of reach of the lantern's illumination. Zayira doggedly climbed the steps, her breath quickening and her legs burning enough to chase thoughts of ghosts and banshees from her mind.

Two brief stops later her portable pool of light exposed a flatter area that ended in an opening. Beyond it she could see the winking stars in the heavens and hear the roar of the sea as it crashed upon the cliffs below. No movement caught her eye across the space as she waited and watched; no sound reached her ears but that of the ocean. She scooted forward, uncertain, until she could see more of the room at the top of the stairs. It was a little larger than her dorm room and was bare with the exception of a large mechanism consisting of a huge shaft wrapped in the largest chain she'd ever seen with wheels attached to each side. Each of the chain's links were as tall as she was. One wall of the room was open to the night air with no railing or protection from the elements, and through it she spied long, dark shapes that looked like fan blades under the cover of darkness. They were still for the moment, but looked to be attached to the mechanism.

A metallic screech drew Zayira's attention to the far side of the shaft, where a small figure pushed with all its might on a lever sticking out of one of the wheels. It had rusted from exposure to the elements, but finally moved just as Zayira swung the lantern around far enough to see that it was a brake holding the great wheel in place. It slipped out of its housing, allowing the wheel to move freely. Without the brake set the wheel groaned in its housing and spun with dizzying speed, paying out the giant chain until it was spent. The fan blades outside the small cave kicked up a strong wind as they turned along with the shaft. It jerked to a stop after a few terrifying seconds and the wind died down to a normal seaside zephyr.

The figure on the other side of the windlass–for that was what the mechanism must be, given her aunt's earlier conversation–slid down the wheel and sat heavily on its bottom. She could make out dark hair and a slight figure, confirming her suspicions on who it was. "Hulvai," she called over the wind. Instead of turning to

face her in anger, as he usually did when she interrupted him doing something, he just stared out to sea. She
crept closer, unnerved by his nonchalance while sitting
at the edge of a cliff, and tried again. "Hulvai, I'm here
to help." Still no response. Zayira knew if she used the
wind to carry her voice it would alert her aunt to trouble, so she waited until she'd fully cleared the mechanism to try a third time. "What are you doing up here?"

Hulvai drew his knees up to his chest, looking for
all the world like a scared little boy instead of the angry
young man she thought she knew. He rocked back and
forth a bit before answering. "I did it. I did everything
she asked me to. That means she'll spare me, right? She
has to. I've been *useful.*" None of this seemed directed at
Zayira, so she scooted closer and tried to gain his attention.

"Everything who asked you to?" she asked.

"The captain. The priestess."

"What captain? What priestess? Who are they,
and what did they ask of you?" Her mind raced as she
tried to piece together his words. He'd released the lock
that held the boom chain across the mouth of the bay
that held the school…that meant that ships could go in
and out. Was he trying to run away while the pass was
closed for the winter? If so, why hadn't he stolen a boat?
And why was he still sitting in the cave, barely coherent?

"The captain. The one who brought me here from
the north on her ship. She's a priestess." He finally
looked at Zayira and her lantern illuminated his face
from beneath, giving it a macabre glow. "She told me to
find her a way in. So I found one." There was something
less than sane in the boy's expression, and it chilled

Zayira more than the cold sea air.

"Why does she want to come here?" Zayira asked. She was still missing an important piece of the puzzle. Whatever it would show, she was sure it wasn't good.

"To erase the curse." Zayira felt his whisper in her bones. "She has to cut it out at its core so she can rid the world of our kind."

Every instinct screamed at Zayira to run, to put as much distance as she could between herself and Hulvai and to yell from the rooftops that there was danger. But she remembered the times he'd been kinder to her and tamped down her fear. She set down the lantern and reached toward him slowly so as not to startle him, treating him like she would a wounded animal that needed help. "You mean weatherworkers, don't you?" He flinched as she said the word, but didn't back away. "Who told you we were cursed?"

"My parents, my tribe, the priestess…everyone up north. Weatherworking"–he spat the word out like it tasted horrible–"is a curse that blights the world. It keeps us from the natural order of things and makes my homeland as cold and unforgiving as it is. It gives the pirates that ply our seas unearthly powers so they can catch our fishing and hunting boats and kill our people for their cargo." His voice rose as he finished this explanation, then softened. "And when we find it within the tribe, we stamp it out." With that he turned back to the sea and pulled his knees back into his chest.

Zayira sat at arm's distance, horrified. *He's been told that all his life. No wonder he's so mad all the time.* "So what's going to happen next?" she wondered aloud.

"She's going to come, and she's going to take over the school by force so she can use it as a base of operations," Hulvai answered with a calm he didn't seem to feel given his shaking frame.

"When?" Zayira demanded.

"Tonight." He pointed to the horizon, where she could just make out two dark spots on the horizon in the shape of sails.

Footsteps rang out behind them. It took a moment before Zayira realized her aunt and the armsmaster had joined them; she couldn't take her eyes off the ship on the horizon, as if by staring at it she could make it turn around and leave. Aunt Glorya shook her by the shoulder and said something, but it didn't register. She exchanged words with Armsmaster Rylen, who didn't have an answer, then tried again. This time the words filtered through the haze of fear. "What's wrong, Zayira?" she demanded.

Zayira turned to look at her aunt. The woman's hair was in disarray thanks to the sea winds, but it looked right somehow, as if it was meant to be wind-blown. *She's fought ships before. She'll know what to do.* The fog lifted from her mind and she pointed out to sea. "Hulvai dropped the boom chain so that ship can come attack the school." The words sounded strange and hollow in her own ears. "They think weatherworkers are cursed and that they need to g-get rid of all of us." She couldn't help but stutter; the thought of someone wanting to slice her throat was too much to bear.

Aunt Glorya's head snapped around, located the ship, then rounded on the armsmaster. "Go wake the staff. I'll get these two down and meet you at the armory." Rylen nodded and bounded down the stairs carrying the lantern they'd brought with them. "Zayira, you've done well tonight, but I need you to keep your wits; your friends will need you, and you may need them to keep yourself safe. Can you get Hulvai to come with us?" The boy was now rocking himself back and forth with a glassy-eyed stare.

"I can try," Zayira agreed with more surety than she felt. "Hulvai?" She stood and laid a hand on his arm. It was thin and shaking, and he didn't respond to her touch or her words. "We need to go." She gripped his arm and tugged at him. He got up obediently and followed where she led with no indication of knowing where they were. Aunt Glorya picked up the lantern and ushered the children in front of her back down the stairs and into the hallway. It looked completely normal, unlike the cave they'd just left, and the dichotomy between the two shocked Zayira. Her nerves were already raw from the past few minutes, but seeing Peony and Deen waiting for her gave her morale a boost. They threw their arms around her neck and asked questions as quickly as they could while Aunt Glorya took her hand and slipped her out of their grasp. "I'm sorry," Zayira answered as she ducked out of a hug she didn't want to leave, "but I have to take Hulvai somewhere. Go back to your rooms; I'll see you in a while." She didn't want to panic them unduly, and besides, she couldn't get the entire tale out quickly enough to explain before she was pulled out of the dormitories, Hulvai in tow.

CHAPTER 33

Glorya half dragged Zayira and Hulvai out of the dorm and toward the armory, where she knew Rylen waited. Her mind still reeled with the revelations it had just experienced; the boy was obviously abused and not in his right mind, but he couldn't be trusted not to make matters worse for Weatherwatch if he wasn't secured somewhere. He responded better to Zayira than to anyone else, so she'd have to bring her niece along for at least part of the plan her mind chewed on as she walked. She'd need Rylen's help with the rest.

"Rylen!" The man appeared at the shout of his name, strapping a sword to his hip as he walked. He'd donned armor made from the hardest leather Zayira had ever seen, with a few plates of metal covering his most vulnerable areas.

"I've not yet alerted everyone," he informed Glorya as she half-dragged the catatonic Hulvai in by his collar. He was getting heavy. "Do you need a place to put him? I've a single lockable cell we built in case we ever need-ed it. Seems the time to use it, all things considered."

"You can't lock him up!" Zayira protested. "He's just a boy! And he's not even able to do anything right now. Look at him!"

Rylen crouched down to look Zayira in the eye. "He's a danger to himself right now as much as every-one else, and the truth is we can't spare anyone to watch him." His voice was gentle, but firm. "I wish we had a choice, but for now, we don't." He rose and handed Glorya a key. "It's through my office." With a nod he jogged from the room to raise the alarm.

Glorya looked at the key in her hand. Her stomach churned at locking up a child–one her niece's age, at that–but she agreed: there was no help for it. *Best to get it over with, then.* Hulvai didn't protest as she maneuvered him into the bare single-person cell and shut the door. "We'll return for you as soon as it's safe," she reassured as she locked the door.

"Nowhere is safe." The boy whispered it without caring if anyone heard. It sent a chill up Glorya's spine.

"We'll come back for you," Zayira promised. She reached through the bars toward her friend, but wasn't able to reach him where he sat against the far wall. When he continued to stare through them she withdrew.

"Come," Glorya said. "Let's get you somewhere safe so that I can join the teachers in working on the defenses. We haven't much time." Zayira let herself be herded out the door and back to her dorm.

By the time she returned to the grounds the rest of the staff had emerged from their various evening haunts looking grim. All were armed; even the groundskeeper, ancient though he was, carried a rusted sword of indeterminate age at his belt. Sylene's weapon of choice was a stout staff made of dark wood, while Mira carried a wicked-looking rapier. Antonus surprised her by appearing next to Rylen, armed with a shovel from the gardening shed. It looked sharp along the digging edge.

"All right, everyone," Rylen called from just outside the armory. They'd all gravitated toward it instinctively when they'd sought to help. "We don't have much information on what we're up against. All we know is there isn't time to reset the locks and raise the chain, and even if we raise a wind they're close enough to still tack into the harbor. We'll have to do whatever else we can to repel anyone who might come ashore."

"They're most likely to use the dock if they're on a sea-going vessel," Glorya offered. "Her draft will be too deep to beach, so they'll either have to dock or come ashore in longboats, which makes it hard to press a numbers advantage."

"How do we know they have more fighters than we do?" Everyone turned to look at Antonus, then did a silent headcount of the six people in the room. The withering looks from multiple teachers silenced him.

"Can we set up any defensive points? Maybe funnel them into certain places?" Sylene asked from where she leaned against the wall.

"Our only hope for that is to catch them coming up the dock if they use it to land," Rylen answered. "And that's only if they don't use boats. I think it's our best shot at keeping the kids safe."

"If I may," Mira ventured into the silence that stretched after Rylen's last statement. "You've been teaching the students how to use weapons, have you not, Armsmaster?" A dangerous glint lit his eyes as he nodded. "Can we organize them to help defend the rest of the student body?"

"Absolutely not!"

"They're still just children!"

Multiple voices protested, but Mira held up a hand. "We are in dire straits, gentlefolk. Desperate times call for desperate measures, and if we can enlist the help of the older students in protecting the younger ones, should we not do so? It gives us the best chance of success."

Rylen fumed for a moment before answering. "I can lethally arm only five," he conceded.

"Thus doubling our numbers," Mira pointed out.

"This is madness." Glorya blinked at Antonus; he didn't seem the type to stick up for the students, especially since they categorically loathed the man, and well he knew it. "They're children. We cannot ask this of them."

"You don't have to." Jase stepped out of the shadows between the armory and the stables, startling the entire party. "We volunteer." Behind him stood three more of the older students, all members of the morning defensive training group.

Glorya watched Rylen's expression shift from despair to steely conviction as he clasped arms with the young man. "I wish we had a choice, but damned if we can't use you, son." It broke her heart to watch him don the mantle of a soldier once again, knowing how much it cost him to do so. "Come. We must secure the young ones while there's time. Antonus, you and Yulya are on watch; climb up to the roof and keep an eye out for the approaching ship. When it clears the harbor, give a long whistle and we'll come running." Both nodded and hastened to fetch the ladder. "Mira, you take young Pol–" he indicated a boy of about sixteen with a mop of curly brown hair–"and go secure the windwaker dorms. Sylene, take Hansen with you to the headmaster's house and rouse him and Brint; they'll fight if they know what's good for them. Glorya, you take Fiol and secure the sunchasers. Listen for the signal and meet at the dock when you hear it. Jase, you're with me." The young man nodded and stepped over to the armsmaster's side. "Don't just stand there–get going!"

245

CHAPTER 34

"Land ho, cap'n!" The cry went up from the crow's nest just after the sun sank below the horizon. With the wind at their backs and all the sails full, plus Brizen directing their path, it wouldn't be long before they made it to shore. The boy had provided them with a detailed map of the valley that Captain Ordulla had required the crew and mercenaries to memorize before they landed. They'd have to berth at the dock given the craft's deep keel, which would give the defenders an advantage, but if the water was shallow enough they could abandon the dock and bypass any defense they met to flow across the valley like a cleansing tidal wave.

"Beat to quarters!" Her order rang out across the deck. "Make ready to sally forth as soon as we land!" Sailors and mercenaries alike belted on weapons and scurried about both above and below decks, preparing to drop anchor and begin her war against the weather-workers.

One of the mercenaries caught her eye–the older one, with the silver hair. It was his attitude that made him stand out; he went about his preparations slower than the rest of his men. Ordulla hoped she hadn't made a mistake in hiring him; among her people age was an asset to be respected and revered if it could be achieved. She'd come to understand that some of the lower countries felt differently. Still, his movements weren't stiff or forced and he seemed of sound mind and body, so she put it out of her thoughts to concentrate on directing the crew.

It was full dark before they pulled up alongside the dock. A storm gathered above them, sending lightning into the sea, and she called out to the gathered crew in her own tongue, knowing the mercenaries would not understand. It was best they didn't. "Tonight we begin our crusade!" Her countrymen and women cheered. "We will conquer this den of evil and feed its children to the Father of the Underworld to feast! His belly will be full of cursed souls tonight. Do not stay your blades, brothers and sisters, no matter their pleading! We must cleanse this world, starting with the biggest blight of them all: Weatherwatch!" More cheers went up and her followers worked themselves into a frenzy. The hired swords stood to one side, eyeing the zealotry before them with skepticism. *They'll help us clear the docks. That's all they need to do. The rest is up to us.* Captain Ordulla nodded to the mercenary captain and ordered the gangplank lowered. Beside her, the first mate chewed and spat something out into the water. *And you, my beautiful monster, will be my right hand as I fulfill my holy vow.* With the leaf he'd chewed coursing through him Sental was unstoppable, an impenetrable wall of sacred will made flesh. It was a shame he couldn't father children; he'd have made a perfect husband for her. Unquestioning and loyal, he'd been by her side from the very start.

"Come," she ordered. "Let us break these infidels where they sleep."

Stiven lit his last cigar, the light from the match flaring against the growing dark. He hadn't understood a word of what the captain had said, but he could feel the malevolence behind it. Without looking up from his reverie he gave a nod and watched in his peripheral vision as one of his men turned to take up position across the deck. The rest of his men fanned out between them, closing ranks behind the main body of zealots preparing to debark. Their attention was turned outward, toward the near horizon that held the objects of their hatred; none of them noticed the pincer closing in until it was too late. The captain and her battle-maddened second in command made it down the gangplank with a knot of soldiers pressed around them, but the rest were cut off before they could leave the deck. Stiven took no small pride in personally running the last one through.

By the time they'd finished with the group on deck there was nothing they could do but watch the small group of defenders fight off the ones they'd let slip by. Stiven reminded himself there were too many for his small company to take all at once, but it still ate at his gut that they hadn't done more. He knew this night–like so many others–would play itself out in his dreams for the rest of his days and thanked whatever gods might listen that he had fewer left than he had behind him.

249

CHAPTER 35

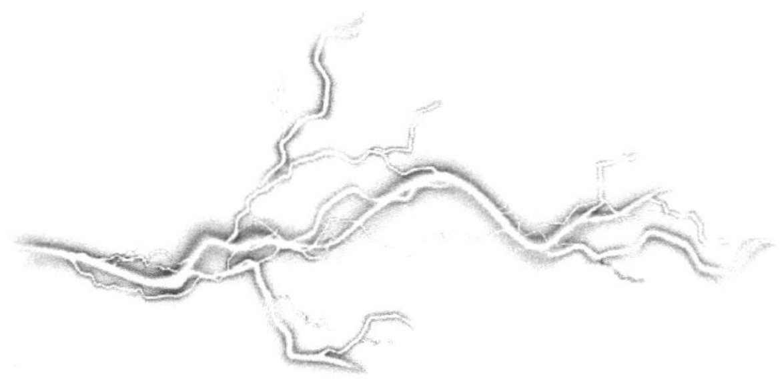

Zayira hated waiting, especially when she knew there must be *something* she could do to help. *I've been training with weapons, learning to use my powers…why can't I be out there with them, helping fight?* Her rational mind told her that sparring with friends her age and size was very different from fighting adults, but still she fought against her own sensibility. *If I can't fight, there must be something I can do to help!*

A knock at the door stopped her pacing. "Meeting in the washroom," someone called from the other side. It sounded like Jase, but she couldn't be sure. She cracked the door and peeked out just in case it was a trick, but Jase's departing figure as he headed to the next door reassured her, and she slipped out to follow.

"What's going on? How can I help? Is there going to be fighting?" The questions spilled out of Zayira until Jase quelled them with as dark a look as she'd ever seen. It was out of character for him and shocked her into silence while he gathered the rest of the students in the dorm.

Armsmaster Rylen met them in the crowded washroom dressed much differently from his everyday garb. Leather armor covered much of his body, and a wicked sword hung from his belt, its hilt twinkling in the lamp light. "Attention, all," he shouted over the din in the tight space. "We find ourselves in a precarious situation tonight. A ship will soon arrive carrying enemy troops set on destroying the school." Gasps and the sound of some of the younger children crying filled the space left after his declaration. "We've brought you in here because there is safety in numbers and you can stay here for an extended period of time comfortably due to the toilets. Please, wherever you do, *do not leave this room* until a staff member comes to get you. It may take all night for us to clear the grounds, so make sure you're comfortable. If you need blankets and pillows from your rooms, you may make one trip as soon as we leave to get such things. After that you must push the bathtub against the door and remain here until summoned. Am I clear?" The armsmaster's hand resting on the hilt of his weapon prompted nods all around. "Good. Stay quiet." With that he and Jase strode back outside and into the darkening night.

Across the room students burst into action all at once, some panicked, some running for their rooms to get their things. A few slumped against a wall, staring vacantly at their classmates. Annalia stood next to the door in a vain attempt to assert order, but was pushed aside by a large boy on his way to grab what he could from his room. Zayira felt a stab of pity for the girl; her intentions were good, even if most of her classmates couldn't stand her. "Oi!" she yelled, using her best Danil-is-across-the-field-and-Pa-is-coming voice. The chaos stopped. "Pay attention–Annalia's trying to say something." All heads turned to the head girl, who stood a bit straighter at the attention.

"Thank you, Zayira. I was simply stating that if we can form an orderly line, everyone can get where they're going quickly." Beside her a line formed and she directed students out on the right side of the door, leaving room for entering students on the left.

Enough tension remained to make everyone uneasy, but it didn't look likely to spill over anytime soon. Zayira, knowing she could never sleep after the evening she'd had, chose not to return to her room, opting instead to find the best place to watch whatever might be happening outside through the small, slitted windows at the back of the room. It was full dark, but the scant moonlight illuminated just enough of the grounds for her to make out the shapes of the teachers flitting between buildings. A shrill whistle split the night and they converged on the dock, weapons in hand. The distance was too great for Zayira to see what each of them carried, but compared to the ship that loomed ever closer they looked dishearteningly insignificant.

"I can't believe my parents sent me here to get killed." The offhand comment piqued Zayira, and she whipped her head around to find Kristus craning his too-long neck to see out the next window. She was sorely tempted to wring it and spare the group his bellyaching.

"So don't get killed." It was the most polite thing Zayira could think to say.

"And how do you propose I do that? By cowering in a bathroom with a bunch of smelly, low-born scum?" Kristus slumped down against the wall.

Zayira ignored the barb. *I don't think he knows how to be nice to folk. Bet his parents aren't nice, either.* The dimming of what little light came through the windows drew her attention back outside, where she could both see and feel clouds forming over the bay. She'd never seen the armsmaster kindle a storm, not a real one, and she found herself in awe of both the size of the storm and the control he exerted over it. In moments the sky was dark and thunder rumbled overhead.

"We have to help them." The words slipped out without her realizing they'd escaped.

"Who?" Peony appeared beside her and craned her neck to see out the window. Zayira slid over far enough for her to see and pointed.

"All our teachers are about to fight whoever's on that boat, and Armsmaster Rylen has called a storm to help out. Who's best with lightning?" she called over the din in the room.

"I always hit the frog I'm aiming at," Deen boasted.

"Think you could help the armsmaster aim his bolts?" Zayira ushered Deen next to Peony as the first flash tore a white streak across their vision. A concussive wave beat against the window immediately after. Deen concentrated, squinting in the aftermath of the strike. The next bolt illuminated figures running from the deck of the ship onto the dock. It struck the water next to the ship, missing it by a hand's width. "Don't let them hit the teachers! Or the water if they're in it!" Deen cursed under his breath, but nodded.

A sliver of moonlight appeared over the water, just bright enough to expose the figures charging down the dock. Metal glinted in their hands. *Aunt Glorya knows what she's doing. She's fought people before and won.* So has the armsmaster. Zayira chanted it to herself, a litany of comfort that held little sway over her worries. The staff held the home ground advantage; tactically they had a good chance of winning, just not without cost given the numbers arrayed against them.

Aunt Glorya knows what she's doing.

CHAPTER 36

In the few winks of moonlight she gave them through the clouds Glorya counted at least ten figures debarking from the ship. Her mind, kicked into overdrive by the adrenaline coursing through her, noted half a dozen odd details; the simplistic animals painted on either side of the ship's prow, its square sails with mismatched patches, and the animal skins their opponents wore as armor registered in the dulled depths of her psyche to be filed away and analyzed later, when there was more time. For now her consciousness was fully in the moment and focused on the first of their assailants. They closed the gap quickly and Glorya braced beside Rylen, ready to break their charge.

A flash of lightning beside the dock caused three of the figures to stumble just as they reached the defenders. Glorya took advantage of their uncertainty and pounced with her light blade, scoring a deep thrust through the man's chest and retracting it in time not to lose it when he fell. *One down. Next.* Her world narrowed until it contained only the fight around her. Beside her Rylen waded past two more and shouted something, but the wind that pushed them forward stole his words. She risked a quick glance around and discovered some of their opponents had jumped off the dock to swim around behind them. A few made it to land in time to engage their flank, but the rest were caught in the water as another blast of lightning rained down beside them. The nearness of it made every hair on Glorya's body stand on end. By the time she was able to look around again she'd felled three more and four floated next to the dock.

Behind her she heard a cry from Fiol, the boy she'd paired up with to secure the dorms. A strangled sound came from deep within Rylen's throat as he backpedaled, leaving Glorya to secure the line on her own. She didn't dare look away; instead she shifted to the center of the dock to face down the last two figures leaving the ship. One looked much the same as the rest, but larger; the other was female, tall and lithe, with coal-black hair pulled back into a tight braid that swayed behind her as she unstrapped two wicked-looking blades from her waist. Aboard the ship another dozen pairs of eyes looked on. *So they do have reinforcements. But with this many lost, how will they sail home?* There was no time for further thought; the man before her charged, and it was all Glorya could do to keep up with his attacks. He wielded a single cutlass with the speed and strength of one born to it with many years of training and practice, and she was unable to capitalize on any of the openings she saw in his guard.

I have to hold them back as long as I can. Glorya had faced her own mortality enough times to know she had no fear of death, but no desire to seek it. Regardless, she felt in that moment that to give her life protecting these students would be the most honorable death she could hope for. She threw everything she had into her swordplay, feinting just inside her opponent's reach, then dancing away only to swing back into it when he least expected it. Her first attempt earned her a glancing slash on the wrist as she barely parried in time, but her second slash scored a deep gash in the man's dominant side. He grunted, but continued as if nothing was amiss. *He must have taken something to dull pain.* It was not an unheard-of practice in many places to chew leaves or eat mushrooms before battle that would dull the senses enough to keep pain from slowing you down. Glorya had seen warriors take death blows and ignore them until their bodies stopped working. She valued the feedback the pain gave her too much to ignore it, choosing instead to put it to the back of her mind until she had time to catalogue it and treat her wounds.

Heavy footsteps behind her prompted her to spin out of the way just as Rylen reappeared. The look on his face was not fully sane as he barreled into the larger man, bringing him down and breaking one of the man's legs with a sickening crunch. "Watch out–he's on the leaf," Glorya yelled as the two tussled.

Another blade flashed past Glorya's face as she dodged instinctively. "Die you cursed scum!" the tall woman screeched as she launched another attack, this time with both blades at once. Glorya parried both and riposted, the tip of her sword grazing the woman's ribs. She could feel herself tiring and knew she had to finish the fight fast. Behind the woman the dock stood empty beneath clouds ripe with rain; none of her other companions had left the ship. Glorya took a chance and used the extra space to circle her opponent. It allowed her to slip inside the woman's reach before she could react and score a good hit on one arm, rendering it useless. One blade clattered to the boards at her feet and the woman laughed, her chuckle a deep, throaty sound. "Your weapons cannot stop me!" She swung at Glorya again, wild and committed, and it was all Glorya could do to get out of the way. "My purpose is pure!" Another swing, this time wider, and Glorya stepped out of the way more easily. Blood dripped freely from the woman's arm, but also from her back beneath the seal skin she wore across her shoulders. Glorya didn't recall scoring a hit there. "You and your spawn will all die by my blade!" Glorya didn't need to step out of the way of the next blow; it went wide all on its own.

Glorya took advantage of the woman's loss of balance and struck, her light blade cleaving into the woman's collarbone. Blood spurted from the wound; she'd caught the right spot. It wouldn't be long now.

The woman looked down in confusion. Her second blade dropped onto the dock as she stared at the point of a dagger protruding from her chest. It twisted as she watched, then disappeared through her back from whence it came. "You don't deserve this quick a death, Captain, but these folk don't deserve one at all." The woman's eyes rolled back into her head and she collapsed, bringing Glorya face to face with a red-haired man about ten years her junior. She raised her blade, but he replaced his dagger on his belt, still bloodied, and held up his hands in supplication. "I mean no harm; please don't run me through." She lowered her blade, but only far enough she could bring it back to bear quickly if necessary. "Seems your friend has taken care of the giant." The man nodded to the pile of something that was once human next to Glorya. It was barely recognizable with the armsmaster still sitting atop it, pummeling what was left of its head.

"Rylen! Stop!" Her voice cut through the haze in the armsmaster's eyes and he shook his head, then climbed off the corpse. "Seems we may have allies aboard the ship." She nodded toward the man still standing on the dock, hands in the air.

"Who are you and what do you have to do with these animals?" Rylen snarled. His face and clenched fists were covered in blood, dark and sticky in the scant light.

"I am–*was*–her prisoner." The red-haired man indicated the now-cooling body of the woman on the dock. He spat on it before continuing. "Seems she comes from a place where us weatherworkers are considered cursed. She forced me to work with some kid she dragged out here to get into this school so she could kill everyone in it. Problem is, she didn't tell any of the mercs she hired she was out to kill children when she hired them." He looked back toward the ship, where a dozen or more heads leaned over the railing to see what was going on at the docks. "Weren't much they could do about it once we were underway, but they found out and planned on double crossing her soon as we landed. You lot took care of the rest of her crew for us."

"At the cost of one of my students!" Rylen roared. He looked as if he might charge the man, so Glorya stepped between him and the interloper even as his words flowed ice through her veins. "He was a *kid!* He shouldn't have even *been here!*" Tears streamed down the burly man's face.

A figure crossed the gangplank and approached slowly, keeping its hands in full view. "Rylen? That you?" A flash of lighting lit up a wrinkled visage with close-cropped, steel-gray hair.

"Stiven? You–how could you?!?" Glorya put both hands on Rylen's chest in an effort to keep him from charging the man in front of them.

"I didn't know she planned this when I signed on, I swear it!"

"But you didn't stop it, either!" The accusation hung heavily between the men, stilling the charged air around them. A lightning bolt went off a hand's breadth from the last bollard on the docks.

The older man leaned forward. "We snuck ten of 'em into the drink dead as doornails before they could make it down to you." He rocked back onto his heels. "I was hoping it'd be enough."

"You always were a coward, Stiven. Now get out of here before I decide you need to pay for your negligence."

Stiven hung his head and returned to the ship in the beginnings of the rainfall from the storm that had been conjured over the dock. "Come on, lad. Let's get out of here." He collected the red-haired man and boarded the ship, pulling up the gangway as he went.

Glorya glanced past Rylen, dreading what she would see, but needing to face it. At the other end of the dock she counted silhouettes; all were present and upright save one. She took Rylen's arm and half dragged the man past the bodies strewn about. They pulled up just short of the ring of people around one more body, this time one of their own.

Jase's face stared, lifeless, from where he lay on the boards, his lifeblood spilled from a wound in his side. "I always told him to watch his parries," Rylen choked out. He fell to his knees and clutched the boy to his chest, wailing his despair to the skies, which had opened up to receive his anguish.

We may not be done yet. "Did anyone get past you?" Glorya demanded of Antonus, who had joined them by the dock.

"I–um–that is…"

She grabbed him by the collar. *"Did anyone get past?"*

"I saw one crawl out of the water and sneak toward the buildings over there." Yulya pointed toward the headmaster's house, which stood silent and dark a short ways off. "And I think there might have been one that charged past us while we were fighting off the others."

"Mira! Sylene! To me!" Glorya barked. The women's heads snapped up at their names. "We need to clear the buildings and secure the dormitories. Grab your partners and keep to the sides of the valley. Sylene, check the stormkindler dorms; Mira, head up the right side with her and go the long way to the windwaker dorms. I'll take the left and the sunchaser dorms and deal with anyone I find along the way."

"You'll need someone to walk the middle." The ancient groundskeeper stood, brandishing his rusty weapon. "If I find anyone's been at my gardens, I'll give 'em what-for." Glorya nodded.

"Let's move out," she ordered. Antonus started toward the group, but she stayed him with a hand on his arm. "Stay with him." They both looked to Rylen, who still wept over the body of his student. "He needs you, and he needs protection." She looked to Yulya, who nodded and took up a vigilant stance next to the pair.

Without a backward glance, Glorya stole off into

the night, young Fiol in silent tow.

CHAPTER 37

"Can you see anything?" Peony craned her neck as if it would boost her sight beyond its normal limits. "I don't see any more movement on the docks. But the ship–the ship is leaving!" A cheer went up from the students in the bathroom.

"I don't know," Zayira hazarded. "It looks like some of the teachers are coming back this way, but I don't think it's safe yet. I could *swear* I just saw someone sneaking around the dining hall." The same worried hush that had pervaded the bathroom fell back over the group as they considered her words.

Zinnia's raucous braying startled Deen. He flailed nervously, hitting Peony on the back of the head. "Ow!" she shouted, then covered her mouth as a figure rounded the stables. She froze, pointing.

"Everyone quiet," Zayira hissed at the rest of the group. Some preservation instinct within them heeded the urgency in her tone and they sat, silent and still, waiting to see if they would be discovered.

Minutes ticked by. The figure disappeared into the shadows near the cliff wall. Zayira held her breath as if it might make a difference in their security, then remembered to breathe before she had to gasp loudly for air. The absolute silence ringing in her ears made it easy to pick out the footsteps coming down the dormitory hall. One of the younger students started to whimper, but was shushed with a hand over their mouth.

Tap, tap, tap. Tap tap. The footsteps stopped right outside the bathroom. Above the shifted bathtub the handle jiggled, gently at first, then with a harsh jangling sound. The lock held, and their would-be assailant backed up across the hall to throw themselves at the wooden door. It vibrated in its frame, but held as the attacker put their shoulder into it once, then twice.

A vibrant cry split the night and more footsteps charged down the hall, followed by a solid wooden *thwack* and a thud. "Take that!" A familiar voice punctured the silence, and Zayira turned to Peony.

"Ms. Sylene," they breathed at the same time.

"Stay in the bathroom," their maths teacher called through the door. "We'll keep watch outside in case there are more." A cheer went up from the students, only to be shushed quickly. "Watch out the windows and tell us if you see anything!"

Peony and Zayira resumed their vigil, energized by the knowledge their deliverers stood in the hallway just outside. Deen squinted alongside them and was the first to point out a second figure scuttling between the buildings further into the valley. He started toward the door to alert their teacher when they heard the ring of flat metal on something hard and the cackling of the groundskeeper. "Guess that one's not a problem," Zayira conjectured, one eyebrow raised.

"I hope the rest of the students are safe," Peony said. Worry etched a furrow in her fine brow.

"They have people checking on them, too," Zayira pointed out. "Just like Ms. Sylene checked on us. I bet my aunt is out there right now checking on the sunchasers."

Deen's head whipped around. "Ms. Glorya is your *aunt?*"

Zayira winced. "Yeah…we didn't want everyone to know from the start so I was less likely to be picked on." She pulled at a loose thread on the hem of her tunic rather than meet her friends' dumbfounded looks head on.

"That's amazing," Deen whispered. "I mean, I won't tell anyone if that's what you want. But what was it like growing up around her? Did she tell you stories about her travels?"

Zayira shrugged. "It was interesting, I suppose. She's told me some stories, but I'm sure there are more; she kept telling me 'I'll tell you when you're older' every time I'd ask about the really dangerous stuff."

"Is it true she fought off a whole company of mercenaries once on the road from Riverbranch?" Peony asked, eyes wide as saucers.

"That's one of the ones she won't tell me." Peony's face fell in disappointment. "But she did tell me about this one time she got caught in a storm off the coast of Zhedaba…"

A small group gathered around Zayira as she told stories of her aunt's adventures to pass the time. In the back of her mind, she hoped her aunt was safe, and that all the rest of her friends would make it through the night.

CHAPTER 38

Glorya and Fiol slid across the sand toward the headmaster's house, following a set of footprints until it disappeared into the expanse of dead, wintry grass between the shore and the building ahead of them. The windows were as dark as the night outside them, giving no indication of movement or occupation.

Fiol bumped Glorya's arm and pointed to an indentation she'd missed in the brittle sward. It led to another, and another, and before they knew it they'd followed their target's trail up to the house proper. The trail didn't enter the house; it skirted around toward the cottages the teachers occupied most nights, so they crept on past the front door to follow. As they tiptoed past the last first floor window a cry went up beside them and a broom handle smacked Glorya firmly across the shoulders. She cursed like the sailor she was and yanked the broom from its wielder, pulling him half out the window in the process.

"Brint, you absolute nincompoop! What do you think you're doing, giving us away like that?" The squirming mass under her arm froze at the familiar sound of her voice.

"Ms. Glorya, I am so sorry!" Brint extricated himself and tucked his body back into the window. Glorya tossed the broomstick in beside him, wincing at the clatter it made.

"What are you doing skulking next to the windows?" Glorya leaned on the sill, casting the occasional glance behind her to be sure no one was coming.

"The headmaster put me on watch downstairs." Brint met her at the sill. "He's upstairs in his bedchamber with the door locked."

"Coward." Fiol spat the word with more venom than Glorya expected.

"Yes, well, he's nothing if not consistent." Brint picked up his broom. "Are you after whoever went skittering by a few moments ago?"

"We are. Did you see which way they went?"

By way of answer Brint climbed out of the window. "This way," he announced, and strode purposefully toward the teachers' cottages. Glorya slowed him with a hand on his shoulder and took the lead, hoping he would take the hint and go more cautiously. The footprints they'd seen earlier faded into the grass between the headmaster's house and the smaller buildings ahead, but Brint pointed with certainty to indicate the gap between the two rows of cottages. No shadows moved; no figures stalked between structures that Glorya could see, but she still trod carefully, sticking to the lee sides of the buildings and using the grass to deaden her footsteps. Fiol made no sound as they moved despite his goodly size. *That one's stalked deer before, I'd wager.* At any rate, he wouldn't have grown to the size he was without eating well, which supported her theory. Brint, on the other hand, had a hard time keeping his broom handle from whacking across every hard surface they passed. She winced each time a loud thunk rang out beside them, but they passed the cottages with no trouble.

Halfway down the row of houses a loud *clang* rang out between the buildings, followed by a geriatric cackle. They froze, listening for further evidence of a scuffle, but the night remained quiet; even the insects had silenced their song in the face of the clouds off the coast. *Sounds like the groundskeeper kept up his end of the bargain.* She continued on without the need for comment.

Glorya stopped the group behind the last row of buildings. "We need to check the sunchaser dorms," she whispered. "Bets are they've gone inside looking for the students." She didn't need to voice the danger they would face heading down a bi-directional hallway against an opponent who might already be entrenched. "I'll take point; Fiol, you take rear. Give a cry if you see anything; tap on the shoulder if you hear something." Both nodded their understanding and fell in behind Glorya.

At the doorway to the dormitories she stopped, listening. For a moment there was no sound beyond the lapping of the waves against the shore behind them, but just as she breathed a sigh of relief a heavy banging echoed through the hall. Without another thought she charged down the hall on light feet, sword still drawn and bloodied, her friends close behind. As they rounded the first gentle curve toward the center of the hall a hulking figure came into view. It drew back from the bathroom door, set its shoulder, and ran toward it at full tilt from across the hallway. Based on the door's condition it wouldn't take another hit without buckling.

Glorya knew she wouldn't make it in time to stop the next impact, so she shouted to gain the figure's attention in hopes of distracting him from his goal. His head snapped to the side to meet her gaze, but his shoulder continued through the door and into the packed restroom.

Screaming broke out from the students behind the door, but not all of them were frightened; five stood on either side of the door, roaring defiance at their assailant. They grabbed, poked, prodded, and beat the man with whatever they had at hand–bars of soap flew toward his head and a towel covered his face, blinding him. Glorya took the opportunity they created and ran him through before he could recover from the unexpected resistance. She regretted having to do it in front of the children, but their opponents and the situation demanded deadly force. *Better that they see the death of their foe than see their friends killed.*

"Is everyone all right?" She had to yell to be heard over the din. At the sound of her voice the yelling abated only to be replaced by the sobbing of younger children. The older ones cheered, the Zhedaban students among them. An still held the towel over the dead man's face as if he might get up and continue his assault. Ri's arm stayed cocked back, another bar of soap loaded and ready to fly. Len, Bo, and Jei huddled behind the bigger kids with more towels and soap to resupply them. *Of course it was them.* Her heart swelled to see the small group standing up for themselves. She reached across the dead man's chest and touched An on the shoulder. *"You can let go now. He's gone."* Without looking up at her An made the traditional gesture of warding against evil and left the towel over the man's face, her arms dropping to her sides.

"I promised Len it would never be her." An stood in one fluid movement. *"And it never will be."* She took the two smaller Zhedaban children in her arms and herded them away from the corpse.

"Do you need help shifting him?" Ri set down the bar of soap he'd clutched to throw.

"I think between Brint, Fiol, and I we can get it, but thank you." Glorya glanced over her shoulder at her two companions. "I'll get the shoulders. Fiol, you grab his feet, and Brint–just try to keep his middle from rolling to one side or the other." She dug her hands under the still-warm shoulders of the brutish man and waited for everyone else to get into place so they could move him. Fiol picked up the man's feet and Brint stood by his oozing midsection, casting furtive glances at the single hole just under the man's rib cage. He looked pale. "You're not one to faint at the sight of blood, are you, Brint?"

"Bit late to ask, but no; I generally get si–" His sentence was cut off as he leaned against the wall and retched. "Sick," he finished lamely.

"Fiol and I can manage him. You step away until we get him across the hall." Glorya counted to three and engaged her legs and back to shift the man alongside her young charge. It took two tries, but soon enough they had him laid out by the far wall. *Good to know I haven't gone completely soft after all those years crewing ships.*

Through the shattered bathroom door and over the hum of students milling about inside came a sharp whistle, followed by two more with different pitch and length. Glorya hurried down the rest of the hall, sword in hand, but met no more resistance. At the northern entrance to the dorm she put two fingers to her lips and blew a piercing whistle. "That's the all clear," she called down the hall to Fiol and Brint. "You can let the students out now, but please, have them keep to the dormitories, and they should travel in groups of three or more until the morning if they must leave their rooms." She didn't wait to see if her orders were followed; her companions were trustworthy, and the students were either too frightened or too eager to help to disobey.

Glorya kept her sword at the ready as she strode through the gardens toward where she'd heard the groundskeeper's laugh. When she arrived he stood over the still form of a large woman wearing the seal skin livery of their enemy, his shovel brandished before him. "Told you I'd give 'em what-for!"

"I believe you did, sir." Glorya sheathed her sword and clasped hands with him. "Were there any more? We found one in the sunchaser dorm, but I heard nothing else."

"This is the only 'un I caught." The elderly man propped one foot on top of the body below him. "Didn't see no more."

Mira materialized out of the darkness to their left. "None made it to the windwaker dormitory." Her needle-thin blade was clean, which was encouraging. Perhaps they'd caught them early enough to do no more harm.

"Let's check on Sylene and get back to the docks, then." A pall settled over the group, and they spent the walk across the pitch outside the armory preparing themselves for the heavy work before them.

Sylene met them at the southern door to the stormkindler dorms. A light rain reached out past the docks and dampened her sturdy form as she dragged something down the short steps with a sickening *thunk* on each one. "Don't worry, he's already dead," she called out when she noticed the approaching group. "Tried to get into the bathrooms. I made certain he'd never do that again." Her light-hearted tone belied the desperate look in her eye. The man she dragged by his boots was smaller than the one Glorya had faced, but looked no less capable. Without a word Glorya picked up his shoulders and helped the maths teacher lug the body around the corner by the cliff wall. Sylene wiped her hands on the hem of her practical dress and turned to Glorya. "The students are fine. Zayira is telling them stories about you." Her features softened and she smiled, a touch of the manic expression slipping away.

"Let's just hope she's telling the good ones." Glorya offered her arm to her colleague–her friend, she corrected herself–and they collected the rest of their exhausted group to go face the aftermath of the invasion.

CHAPTER 39

The next two days went by in a blur. Zayira and the rest of the students were largely confined to their dormitories as the teachers and staff cleaned up after the incident. None of them spoke much about what happened, which left the students free to cook up wild conjectures about what may or may not have occurred. The headmaster made appearances once a day in each dorm, ostensibly to calm the student body, but they weren't fooled. He studiously avoided looking toward the beach whenever he came and went.

Zayira and her friends joined a few other students at the western doorway between breakfast and lunch on the third day after the invasion. A teacher always appeared to escort them to and from mealtimes, but they hadn't seen Armsmaster Rylen except from a distance. Zayira worried about him; aside from her aunt, he was her favorite teacher.

Peony twirled the ends of her hair around one of her fingers. "When do you think we'll start having classes again?" she asked for the fifteenth time in three days. "It's so boring sitting here all day."

"It's better than what they've been up to out at the docks." Zayira regretted snapping at her friend as soon as the words left her mouth, but the girl's repetitiveness got under her skin after so long cooped up. Peony hung her head.

"I know. It's just hard, you know? Stuck in here, unable to help…"

"I know. And Jase…" All the rest of the older students who'd offered their help defending the school had reappeared at some point on the second day except Jase. None of the adults would answer questions about where he was or what went on that night, leaving the student body to assume the worst. They had no illusions about the fact that there had been a fight; every teacher who had chaperoned their mealtimes carried bandages and bruises. Smoke had billowed up from the beach for two days straight. None of the teachers had explained why, but Deen had quietly pointed out that it was a quick and clean way to dispose of bodies before they brought on sickness. They hadn't talked about it any more after that.

"Look, here comes the headmaster again." Deen pointed across the field between their dorm and the dining hall. Sure enough, there was Headmaster Thayer, with Brint trailing along behind. There was something different about Brint's carriage, Zayira thought; he looked more sure of himself and less like the headmaster's shadow. It could just be her imagination, though; it had been overactive the last few days.

The children stepped aside as the headmaster approached. "Please tell the rest of the students to gather outside the armory," he instructed without entering the hallway. "We're having an assembly." He continued on past the doorway toward the windwaker dorms to the east.

Zayira and Peony looked at each other. "I'll take the inside rooms," Zayira volunteered. Peony nodded and they went about gathering the rest of the stormkindling students.

Half an hour later the entire school milled around the pitch outside the armory. The weather had held for three days, but rainclouds threatened off the coast. They were natural, as best Zayira could tell; the only weatherworking at play was the buffer keeping the pitch dry until their meeting was over. It had the feel of her aunt's work.

"Settle down, everyone." Ms. Mira's voice carried across the crowd on a zephyr that traveled across the pitch in a wide sweep from front to back. An expectant hush settled over the student body. Zayira figured the rest of the groups had done just as much guesswork as she and her friends had over the past few days, and they all felt they deserved some answers.

"Thank you, Ms. Mira." The headmaster's pompous voice carried out over the pitch without the assistance of weatherworking. "I'll get straight to the point. I'm sure you all have a lot of questions after the last few days, and while we won't be able to answer all of them, I shall do my best to give you as much information as possible." He paused and took a deep breath. "First and foremost, it is with a heavy heart I must inform you of the death of Jase Stormkindler. He bravely gave his life defending Weatherwatch from the malicious attack of invaders from parts unknown." The headmaster plowed onward despite murmurings and occasional sobs from across the assembly. "We will hold a memorial service for him by the dock in a week's time.

"Of the rest of the events from three nights ago

there isn't much to tell; our brave staff repelled the attempted invasion of a group of armed men and women who used an inside informant to learn about the school and lower the boom chain from across the bay. Before you ask, we will be giving no further information on said informant, as it is not in the best interest of either the student body or the school. Classes will resume tomorrow, but the armsmaster has informed me that it will be another week before he resumes weapons classes in the mornings. As for today, you may spend the rest of it as you would a normal tenthday; you have permission once again to leave your dormitories and roam the grounds. That is all." The headmaster quitted the assembly without a backward glance.

Murmurs broke out across the field. Zayira heard Hulvai's name from a group of windwaker students and realized the last she knew of her friend was that he'd been locked up in the armory. She felt guilty for not thinking of him and resolved to ask her aunt how he was doing at the first chance she got.

"So they're awarding him his pin posthumously." Deen picked at the hem of his tunic.

"Is that why they called him 'Jase Stormkindler?'" Zayira still wasn't sure about the particulars of the graduation system.

"Yep. You get the designation when you earn your gold pin. We knew he was set to test; he was a sure bet to pass. It's kind of them to add it." Deen sniffled, and Zayira realized he was crying. She'd never seen him cry, and she wasn't sure what to do about it. She looked at Peony, whose expression softened with a sad smile. The younger girl wrapped an arm around Deen's shoulder and held him for a moment while he composed himself.

"Do you think anyone else knows who the spy was?" Zayira didn't realize she was woolgathering until Peony nudged her with an elbow to get an answer to her question.

"What? Maybe. I mean, I heard a few people mention…someone we know just now, but there's no telling if they think he's the spy or if they think something happened to him."

"Is he still in the–where he was last time you saw him?"

"I think so." Zayira was tempted to sneak into the armory for the sole purpose of determining whether or not that was the case, but she remembered something that changed her mind. "I'll ask my aunt! She invited me to her cottage for tea sometime. I haven't gotten a chance yet to go, but this is the perfect day for it."

"Let us know what you find out!" Peony took Deen by the arm and steered him toward some of the Zhedaban students. They hadn't been able to socialize in days due to the restrictions, and everyone looked relieved to be able to talk once more with all of their friends.

Nodding to herself, Zayira slipped away to see if her aunt was at home.

CHAPTER 40

Glorya had just sat down for the first time all morning when someone knocked on the door. "Come in," she called from her armchair, where she'd pondered pulling out the chart that hid beneath it. She forewent that pleasure in exchange for the company of her niece, who peeked in the doorway. "Go on, shut the door–it's cold out there!" The girl slid inside and closed the door softly behind her. She shuffled her feet in an awkward gesture of uncertainty. "Come, sit down." Glorya motioned toward the well-worn chair by her desk. It was the only other seating available. Zayira sat on the edge of the seat, her hands on her knees as if she feared to touch anything. "What's bothering you?" Glorya had never pandered to any of her siblings' children; despite the difficulties of the past few days, she wasn't about to start doing so.

"I'm worried about Hulvai." There it was. Of course she wasn't concerned for herself. "We haven't seen him since–since he climbed up into that cave, and the headmaster said he wouldn't tell us anything about the person who helped the bad guys get into the school, and since I was there I know it was him, but not everyone knows that. They're guessing it, though, and talking about the worst things and what that person deserves…" She trailed off and dashed the back of her hand across her eyes. "I know what he did was wrong, but he was so scared, and most of the school was mean to him…"

"And you're worried they'll do something drastic to punish him." Zayira nodded. "Well, I can tell you he hasn't spoken in three days and has barely eaten. He's spent most of his time catatonic on the straw cot in his cell. We've given him enough basics to stay warm, but we're keeping watch over him most times in case he decides to do himself a harm." Glorya punctuated her sentence with a yawn; she'd been on night duty the prior evening. "He cannot go back to class, but I don't think the school plans to punish him as they would a criminal; in fact, I have a few ideas for places we could send him where he might fit in and have a better life, though I'm not sure he'll speak to me even if I offer them." A spark of inspiration hit and she looked at Zayira, who still sat on the edge of her chair looking even more concerned than when she'd entered. "Would you be willing to try to speak to him? You're his friend; he might listen to you."

"Me?" Zayira looked aghast at the idea. "He's never listened to me before. What makes you think he will now?"

"I think he's listened more than you think." Glorya winked at her niece. "Besides, he needs a friend now more than ever. The staff is worried about him, too, and we'd like to see him at least start eating again." That was likely to appeal to the girl's tender heart; indeed, her expression softened to one of resigned concern.

"I'll try if you think it'll help." Zayira squirmed in her chair. Glorya remembered she'd been confined to quarters like the rest of the student body while she and the rest of the teachers took care of the bodies on the beach and elsewhere and took pity on her.

"I'll come get you when we take him his evening meal." She stood, hoping her niece would take it as a welcome dismissal. "Until then, why don't you go outside and spend time with your other friends? You've been cooped up for too long."

Zayira popped out of the chair and curtsied. "I will. Thank you, Aunt!" She started for the door, then shot over to where Glorya stood and wrapped her arms around the woman. "I love you, Aunt Glorya." It was muffled by Glorya's shoulder, but heartfelt.

"And I you, Zay-zay. Now go play!" Glorya all but shoved the girl out the door before her own tears began to flow. They'd been dammed up for the better part of three days while she saw everything tended to, but she knew they'd have their time whether she wished it or not. *Just let me get through this day and I'll have my cry-out.* In the meantime, she had more to do. Leaving the secret charts in their hiding spot, she instead chose to write a letter to her sister outlining the events of the prior days. Word would get out quickly that Weatherwatch had been breached, and she wanted her family to know first-hand what had happened. Rumors tended to blow things out of proportion.

Half an hour and a hand cramp later, the letter was sealed and addressed, ready to go out as soon as the next supply ship came through. During the winter the pass was perpetually buried in snow, so they relied on ships for both dry goods and news of the outside world. It meant news of what had happened would dissem-inate at the same time from multiple sources. Glorya wondered grimly what sort of response the wealthy families would have to the incident. Would they pull their students out or leave them at school and call for blood? She should be safe from blame, which selfishly relieved her, but she feared for the headmaster. He couldn't have foreseen this turn of events. The only negligence for which he was responsible was a lack of vetting of students, as evidenced by both his recruitment of the Zhedaban crew and the absence of questions surrounding Hulvai's origins. She resolved to talk to Brint about it at the next chance she got.

For the moment, she had other concerns. She set the letter in her desk drawer and took up her cloak to go look in on the armsmaster. The snow had washed into slush with the rains three nights ago, and the slush had frozen into a crust of treacherous ice. They'd held off the worst of the weather in favor of burning the bodies over the two days after the fight, but nature could only be held back so long without consequences. So Glorya removed the barrier she'd put up against the storm front moving in and clutched a smaller one around her as the wind picked up to slice through her clothing. If she had to guess, they'd see snow through the night.

The cottage Rylen shared with his husband was only a few doors down from Glorya's in the little cluster of homes the teachers occupied. She knocked on the door and it immediately opened a crack to admit Antonus a peek outside. He deflated as soon as he saw her and drew open the door. "Thank the gods! Maybe you can pull him out of whatever horrible place he's in." He ushered her inside and took her cloak, hanging it on a peg next to the door.

Rylen sat before the fire in a rocking chair, wrapped

up in blankets. His hair was unkempt and unwashed, and he stared into the fire as if it held answers to the questions that burned in his mind. He showed no sign that he'd noticed Glorya's entrance. "He's been like that for two days." Antonus pushed a steaming mug of tea into her hands. "See if you can get him to drink that. I'll make some more for you while you're at it." He shuffled off toward what passed for a kitchen.

Glorya crouched down in front of her childhood friend. His eyes tracked the flames in front of him over her shoulder, flicking around her shoulders and head instead of meeting hers. "Rylen." He didn't respond, but she plowed forward anyway. "I know you're in a dark place right now. You've lost too many people close to you." She set down the mug to lay a hand on the man's knee. He flinched, but didn't look her way. "It's hard, gods know it's rough. But you have to ask yourself: what would all those people you've lost want for you? Would they want you to exist like this? Or would they want you to live your life in their honor?" She let her hand slip from his leg. "If it were me, I'd want you to live. And I know that's what Jase would have wanted." Rylen's eyes closed at the name.

"He was just a kid." Rylen's voice was gravelly after long disuse. "I shouldn't have let him stay."

"He was very nearly a man, and he chose to stand between those he loved and danger. At his age you would have done no less." Glorya shifted in front of the armsmaster and leaned both elbows on his legs. "Look at me, Rylen." His red-rimmed eyes cracked open just enough to meet her own. "You are doing his memory a great disservice wallowing in your own guilt. Remember him for the man–for the stormkindler–he was, and get back to your life. Your husband needs you. Your students need you, now more than ever. Will you continue to deny them?" Rylen's eyes closed once more, squeezed shut against the truth he felt, but could not voice. Wordlessly he stood, letting the blanket fall from his shoulders, and drew himself up to his full height.

A meaty hand landed on Glorya's shoulder while the other one took the tea from her hand. Rylen nodded his thanks and trundled off toward the kitchen, where Antonus watched with a wary gaze. The bigger man set down the mug with exaggerated care and folded his partner into his arms. Glorya could hear sniffles from both of them as she slipped her cloak off its peg and slid out the door.

CHAPTER 41

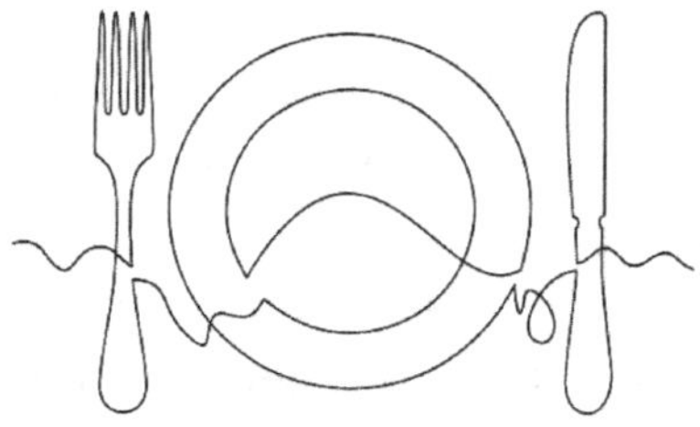

Zayira's stomach flipped itself into knots all afternoon. What would she say to Hulvai? How could she, a *child*, get him to come out of his shell when the adults could not? It struck her that she had answered her own question. They were hoping someone his age could help him where adults had failed. She got the impression that if she couldn't, his situation could become even more dire.

Peony, Deen, and her Zhedaban friends all tried to draw her out with conversation and play to no avail. Eventually they gave up and sat with her in brooding silence until dinnertime, when her aunt appeared with two trays laden with food and beckoned her to follow. Zayira's tray held her usual portion of meat and some winter vegetables; the second tray bore dried fruit, toast, and some kind of well-cooked stew meat that looked soft. They walked in silence to the armory and through the door into the small area with the holding cell. Zayira braced herself, but was still unprepared for how her friend looked after days in captivity. His glossy black hair was matted and stuck to his head in places. Vacant eyes replaced the piercing, dark orbs she was used to, all traces of anger or worry erased from their depths.

The line of his brow followed the flat trajectory of his mouth in a slack expression.

Zayira froze halfway across the room. Her aunt continued on to slide the tray through a short gap at the bottom of the bars before she realized her niece hadn't followed. "Hulvai, there's someone here to see you." Glorya motioned for Zayira to approach. She forced her legs to carry her closer to the apparition in the cage and sat down on a convenient hay bale not far from the door. "She's here to eat dinner with you today. We thought you might like to see someone besides boring adults." Her aunt spoke as if nothing was wrong, carrying both sides of the conversation as naturally as anything. She straightened a few things, then nodded. "I'll leave you two to it. Zayira, if you need anything I'll be right outside." With an encouraging smile she sauntered out the door as if it were a normal winter's day.

Zayira poked at the food on her tray, unsure of what to say. She'd run hundreds of scenarios through her head for hours, but none of them seemed right. So she decided to go the same route as her aunt and act as if nothing was out of the ordinary. "Peony, Deen, and I have been playing in the snow," she began, and her voice strengthened as she spoke. "We've made lovely shapes in it with our feet and rolled it into balls to throw at each other. Some of the windwakers are constantly trying to blow snow onto everyone from crazy places, like over the roof of a building where they won't get caught, but everyone knows where they are. I bet you know all about playing in the snow, though, since you're from the north." Hulvai showed no reaction, so she kept going. "We go back to our studies tomorrow. Nobody's happy about it; we've enjoyed the holiday, but I suppose it's time." She picked up some of the meat on her plate and took a bite. Her appetite was slowly returning, so she paused her soliloquy to eat some of her dinner.

"I...don't actually know much about playing in the snow." Hulvai's sweet voice cracked from lack of use. Zayira stared at him as if he'd grown a third eye.

"But you're from the north." She gesticulated with a piece of a potato before shoving it into her mouth. "You must have gotten tons more of it than we do." This last was barely intelligible around the tuber she chewed.

"That doesn't mean I've played in it." There it was—the belligerent tone Zayira knew.

"Well, why not?"

"I just didn't, okay?" At least he was arguing; maybe it would help his appetite.

"Seems like a wasted opportunity, is all." Zayira pontificated from atop her vaunted hay bale of judgment.

Hulvai lunged at the door to his cage, grabbing the bars and shaking them. "*Nothing* about my life has *ever* been about play! I'm cursed. We're all cursed. We deserve to die." This last statement faded back into hopelessness and he plopped down onto the cell floor, what little energy he had spent.

"Hogwash." Zayira refused to sit idle while he denigrated himself and everyone who had tried to help him. He glared back at her from beneath greasy black locks of hair. "They may say that where you're from, but here we're counted as useful. Windwakers can really make out well aboard ships, for one, and the Zhedabans think they're a blessing from the gods." She picked up a bit of straw and woke the tiniest breeze. Her windwaking was much weaker than her stormkindling, but she had enough control to send the bit of chaff wobbling between the bars and into Hulvai's cell. He caught it in his upturned hand and stared at it. "So you see, it's all a matter of perspective."

Hulvai closed his hand around the piece of straw. "It doesn't matter anyway. Nobody will want me here anymore, now that they know what I've done." He hung his head in renewed misery.

"Peony and Deen and I have been asking about you every day. And the headmaster refused to tell anyone who the sp–the inside helper was. I think some folks have figured it out, but I'm sure Ms. Glorya and the rest can come up with you an excuse of some sort. That's if you want to stay, of course. You could always go back to the frozen north where nobody lets you play in the snow." Zayira watched Hulvai's reaction to her baiting and was rewarded with a narrow-eyed glare.

"They don't want me. I can never go back there. And I can't stay here, either, not after what I've done."

"He's right," agreed Glorya from where she leaned on the doorjamb. She'd snuck closer to eavesdrop as soon as she heard Hulvai's voice. "Weatherwatch is no longer a safe haven for him. But I think I may have a better option, if he's willing to entertain it." Hulvai's sullen silence answered, so she continued. "I have certain contacts in Zhedaba who might be willing to work with a talented windwaker to help him earn his pin. They're well qualified to judge his competence and character." At the mention of Zhedaba the boy's eyes went wide.

"Zhedaba? Where it's hot all year and never

snows?"

"I know it's very different from what you're used to, but–"

"Yes! I accept! Please, Sunchaser, I cannot stay here, and I've always wanted to see Zhedaba and its deserts and the ocean and…and…" Hulvai ran out of descriptors and trailed off.

Glorya chuckled. "You'll have to stay a bit longer, at least until the next ship comes, maybe the one after that. Can you manage to stay out of trouble for that long?" Hulvai nodded warily. "We can only let you out if you promise not to set *one foot* out of line or mention a single thing about your involvement with what's happened. Understood?" He nodded again. "Will you swear to it?"

"I swear on my nameless ancestors I will follow the rules and never speak again of what's happened, especially here at Weatherwatch." It was strange to hear such a solemn vow from one so young. Zayira judged he meant it based on the fervent expression on his face.

"That's good enough for me." Glorya produced a key from one of her many pockets and unlocked the cell door. "Now eat your dinner. I'm sure Zayira here will make off with whatever you don't eat if you're too slow." She winked at her niece, who grinned back up at her.

"I'm already halfway done and still really hungry…" Zayira sized up the contents of Hulvai's tray. "That dried fruit looks good, too." She grinned when he lunged to pick up his dinner, huddling over it like a falcon with its kill.

They spent the rest of the meal sitting on the hay bale inside the armory, talking the way they used to and catching up on the last few days. Zayira's stomach unknotted as they bantered and she relaxed, safe in the knowledge that her friend would be all right.

CHAPTER 42

The next few weeks blew by like leaves before a storm. Hulvai went back to class with the excuse that he was injured in the fighting and needed a few days to recover, which most of the student body accepted, but whispers continued about the strange figure climbing the cliffs that fateful night and how dark its hair was. These he bore with his usual scorn, and before the first week passed the rumors died down. Jase's memorial involved the whole student body and the placing of a marker by the docks so that none would forget his sacrifice for his fellows. His body had been burned the day after the attack and the ashes collected by Ms. Mira to send to his family in accordance with their tradition.

Everything returned to normal, except the things that never would. And even those worked their way into the routine in such a way as to become expected. By the time spring thawed the pass and reopened overland travel into Midlands the school had settled back into the lull of the everyday. So when a group of stern-looking men and women appeared one tenthday morning three days after the spring thaw demanding to see the headmaster, it set many things back into an uproar.

Armsmaster Rylen was the first to greet them, sword in hand, with Glorya by his side. She'd taken to sitting with him and Antonus on their off days to trade stories, and when it looked like they had more than one visitor she followed her friend out to confront the group. Before either she or the armsmaster could speak, a livid, jowled fellow with beady eyes stepped forth. "We demand to see the headmaster at once!" he commanded.

"And who might I ask is demanding this?" The armsmaster's tone was quiet, but deadly. He'd carried an edge to rival his sword since the attack, and the man sensed he was outmatched.

"My name is Parsival, and my son, Kristus, is a student at this school. We are all concerned parents–" he swept his hand to indicate the group at large–"who wish to speak with the man in charge about what will be done to prevent the horrible occurrences this past winter from happening again." He nodded to cries of "Let us see Thayer!" and "Step out of our way!"

Rylen looked at Glorya and shrugged. "This way." The two of them led the mollified herd of parents across the pitch and over the budding grasses to the headmaster's house.

Brint opened the door at the first knock. "Good morn, Rylen, Glorya–what can I do…for…" He trailed off at the sight of the upset throng behind them. "I'll just, um, get the headmaster, will I?" Glorya nodded and set herself in front of the door to wait. She heard it close behind her and footsteps hurry away down the hall. The group of parents milled about uncertainly on the lawn as the wait took the wind out of their sails. Finally, after a few hours-long moments, the door banged open and Headmaster Thayer filled the space between the jambs.

"What's all this, eh?" He reached out toward the group, who recoiled. "Parsival, sir, so good to see you!" The man scowled back and Thayer's genial expression cracked. "Nicola, you look well!" The woman standing behind Parsival shot the headmaster a cold stare and his expression fell further. "What can I do for you all today?"

Parsival, their elected spokesperson, stepped forward and puffed out his ample chest. "We demand reassurance of our children's safety and recompense for last winter's egregious breach!" His face turned a livid pink with the fervor of his speech.

Thayer faltered, his ruddy complexion paling. "I can assure you, sir, we have taken every precaution! You can see–the boom chain is back up, and the ways to its lock rooms have been fixed and secured! And–and we're arranging sleeping quarters for the armsmaster closer to the pass to ensure we're not vulnerable from that direction." Rylen raised an eyebrow at that, but let it pass. Glorya had seen nothing to that effect so far. "As for recompense, I'm afraid we're a poor school reliant on the contributions of such as yourselves to survive; how can we remunerate you?" Thayer spread his arms in a helpless gesture.

"I'm afraid we have no faith in your ability to run this school any longer." Parsival took another step forward and his gut bumped into the headmaster. "We've all spoken, and we're voting you out."

"You–you can't do that!" Thayer sputtered. "You have no power here! The school…I was chosen for my skills with people, my connections–who could possibly take my place?"

"Brint." All eyes turned to Glorya. "He's done the practical running of the school for ages. I see no reason he couldn't take the headmaster's place and do a fine job of it." The crowd turned to Brint, who had shrunk back into the doorway at the first sign of confrontation. He looked around, wild-eyed.

"Me?" Brint squeaked.

Rylen clapped him on the shoulder, half so the man wouldn't run. "Of course! Brilliant plan, Sunchaser. Ol' Brint here will have things back to rights and tighter than ever, you'll see." He winked at the young man and smiled.

"Then it's settled," Parsival agreed. "Thayer, we're stripping you of your position and bringing you with us to face whatever justice we can mete out." He glanced to Brint. "Can you see that his things are packed up and sent to the inn in Market? We make for there today."

"Certainly." Brint still looked queasy, but managed to gather his wits enough to respond.

"We'll make certain to send your stipend along with the next supply caravan, and there'll be a little extra in it for you some presentable clothes. We expect to see you in Riverbranch twice a year for the benefactors' meeting." Parsival nodded and took the erstwhile headmaster by the arm. "As for you, sir, you're coming with us and staying under guard until we get to civilization." And with that, the group frog marched Thayer across the school grounds and through the pass just as the sun hit its zenith.

Brint half collapsed against the door frame as soon as they were out of sight. "I can't believe you just did that!" He sat heavily on the stoop. "I can't run this place on my own! The headmaster…Thayer was much better at the financials, acquiring benefactors, all of that. I'm nobody! How am I supposed to…" He waved vaguely toward the house.

"Brint, you know more about how this place runs than anyone else in the valley." Glorya offered him a hand up, which he took. "In the past few months I've seen you inventory everything we have, run numbers on cost and income, and pay out teacher salaries. The students know who you are and, what's more important, they like you. We like you. The staff supports you, and we'll help you get on your feet." She smiled and was rewarded with a dubious sigh of resignation. "Besides, the kind of person you want in this job is the one who doesn't ask for it." She shooed the new headmaster of Weatherwatch into his house to help him settle in.

CHAPTER 43

The rest of Zayira's first year at Weatherwatch went far more smoothly. She made new friends and watched her older friends test and graduate, including Yulya, who had first made her feel welcome at arms practice. The Zhedaban students grew more and more comfortable in their new home, trading their wildness for manners and warmth and helping the rest of the student body learn more about cultures not their own. Hulvai stayed a few more weeks, but soon was picked up by a supply ship and carried off to learn more about windwaking from a wise man in Zhedaba. Zayira missed her friend, but he promised to write as soon as possible. He'd mellowed in the intervening weeks, and she had hope that he would grow up to become a good man.

Glorya finished out the year busier than ever. The first few weeks of Brint's headmastership were a trial; the man had no idea how to delegate responsibilities and frequently overworked himself to the point of falling asleep in his dinner. He ate with the staff instead of at his own house, which endeared him to the teachers and the cook. Eventually the staff organized a rotation of students to act as assistants and run errands for him. After that things grew much more manageable, and by the time summer arrived in full Glorya finally had time to herself.

She had to admit the short horizon in the valley chafed at her. Her eyes couldn't see half as far as she could sense, and it drove her mad some days to be cooped up in such a limited space for so long. Looking back she hadn't stayed still for more than two to three months in the last fifteen years. Zayira or not, she knew she could never stay at Weatherwatch. So she wrote to a few of her associates and was rewarded with the acceptance of a Zhedaban sunchaser she'd worked with many times who desired a more stable life than the one the sea provided. Headmaster Brint was, of course, quite sad to hear of her intentions, but thanked her profusely for staying on as long as she had. She promised to stay in touch from her home base in Joveru.

Zayira was also disappointed at her aunt's departure, but understood why she needed to go. They promised to write to each other, and Glorya further gave her word that she would look in on Hulvai whenever possible and report back on her findings. One teary-eyed hug later Glorya gathered her things and headed for the pass.

Rylen barred the way. "Thought you'd leave without saying goodbye?" he rumbled, arms crossed over his chest. The twinkle in his eye belied his stern mien.

"You were the first to see me into the valley; it's only fitting you should see me out." Glorya chuckled and opened her arms to embrace her friend. "Thank you. For everything."

"It is I who should thank you." Rylen squeezed her

one last time and let go. "You've helped me through some dark times this year, and while I'll never fully heal from it, I will be able to find some peace." He nodded and stood aside for her to pass. "Now go, and keep us updated on whatever that project is you've been working on for months!" Glorya tried to protest, but he silenced her feeble attempts with a shake of his head. "We all know you're planning something. I'm sure we'll hear about it one day, knowing you."

"One day I may need your help with it, if it all goes as planned." Glorya raised an eyebrow to gauge Rylen's interest.

"I suppose I have to retire eventually," he admitted, and they both laughed. "Now get going, or you won't make it to Market before sundown!" He shoved her gently from behind and sauntered off toward the armory, where Zinnia the jenny sang her a farewell song in her braying tones.

The last time Glorya left Weatherwatch she'd had only the clothes on her back and her sunchaser's pin, newly minted. This time she felt she left behind far more than she had the first time around. But her heart told her she'd made the right choice, and with one foot in front of the other she strode through the pass and out of the valley toward her next adventure, whatever it may be.

EPILOGUE

Zayira straightened her tunic and pinned on her silver stormkindler pin one last time. *I can't believe after today I'll have a gold one.* She'd spent five years at Weatherwatch, working toward earning her gold pin, but it still felt surreal. *I wonder if Ma and Pa will be there, and Danil and Maks. And Aunt Glorya.* She'd said she would attend the graduation ceremony, but Zayira knew she was very busy with the project she'd started as soon as she left Weatherwatch. She had no expectations, only hopes.

A knock on her door broke her out of her reverie. "Zayira? Are you coming? We can't be late!" Peony's voice drifted through her door, still the closest one to the door outside. She'd seen no reason to change rooms, even when more had come available as other students graduated.

"Coming!" With one last check she pulled her copper hair into a quick knot at the base of her neck and opened the door. Peony stood waiting, her tall, dark-haired figure silhouetted against the light pouring in from the end of the hall. She'd grown into good looks and a wonderful personality, and Zayira was sure she'd find a good partner easily. They greeted each other with a warm embrace, almost crushing the small flowers Peony had stuck behind her ear, then trotted off to the armory, where the rest of their classmates waited. A few waved as they entered; there were six of them who'd tested with the spring thaw that year, and all had passed. It galled Kristus to know he would graduate with so many lowborn students, which gave Zayira a certain sadistic pleasure. He was the last of his cronies to leave Weatherwatch, which made it even worse; he wore a scowl darker than any cloud he'd ever kindled as they entered the building. Zayira simply nodded to him, then ignored him. It was best not to feed his self-loathing.

Armsmaster Rylen and Mr. Antonus stood watch by the door to the pitch. They were responsible for making sure the graduates knew when to process out onto the open field to receive their golden pins, a job they took very seriously from year to year. Zayira tried to peek through the doorway to see the assembly there, but her view was blocked by the bulk of the armsmaster, who winked at her. "No peeking," he admonished, shaking a meaty finger at her and turning his attention back to Headmaster Brint, who was giving the commencement speech.

"Can you see anything?" Peony asked. Her voice close to Zayira's ear startled her, but she recovered quickly. Peony had always been light on her feet.

"Nothing," Zayira admitted. "I can hear the headmaster giving his speech, but I couldn't see anyone or anything through the doorway before Armsmaster Rylen blocked my view." She shot him a playful scowl, earning a wink and a grin in response. "Besides, I have no idea what your family looks like to even see if they're there!"

"My mom looks just like me! Or I suppose I look like her." Peony stood on tiptoe and craned her neck to no avail. "Ooh, I hope they made it!"

"I'm sure they did." Despite her reassurance, Zayira shared her friend's fears. What if the roads were still bad from the spring thaw? And the cows would be calving–who would have to stay at the farm to make sure all was well? Certainly they hadn't all come. The thought disappointed her more than she wanted to admit, but she readied herself for the practicality of the more likely happenstance.

The armsmaster started to call students forward. Kristus was first, since they were called alphabetically, and he strutted from the building as if the entire ceremony was held in his honor. "You know, he'd be handsome if he wasn't such a prat," Peony observed.

"I won't even give him that much credit." Zayira plopped down on a hay bale to wait, much to her companion's horror.

"Get up! You'll be covered in chaff!" Peony all but dragged Zayira off of the hay and brushed a few stray pieces off her tunic. "We can't have you getting your golden pin with hay all over you."

Zayira shrugged. "I'm a farm girl at heart. There are far worse things to be covered in." Peony giggled.

Two more students were called before Peony's name came up. She took Zayira's hand, squeezed it once, and walked straight-backed through the armory door to the loud cheering of the crowd.

Zayira was left alone with her thoughts. Who would cheer for her? Would anyone? Would she even be able to make out her family in the crowd? Who

would award her the golden pin? It was usually one
of the teachers, but she was a special case; once it was
safe to share the knowledge of her abilities she'd taken
weatherworking from all three teachers instead of just
one. *I hope it's Armsmaster Rylen.* He'd been like an uncle
to her throughout her tenure, and she valued his opinion above the rest of the staff.

"Zayira." The armsmaster's voice called her as if
summoned by her own thoughts. "It's time." She looked
up from where she stood and saw that he'd stepped
back far enough she could see through the doorway.
She nodded and passed through the portal.

The bright afternoon sun blinded her. Applause
and whoops of encouragement broke through her blind
march forward, only some of which she recognized.
As the crowd came into focus before her she saw her
mother and father sitting up front, looking much as they
always had except for a few more silver hairs. Next to
them were Danil and Maks and a woman she didn't recognize, but assumed must be Maks's new wife, Alina.
Her round face bore dimples as she grinned alongside
her husband. *Not just five of us anymore.* The thought
both warmed and saddened Zayira, but she knew
change was the way of life; after all, hadn't she changed
over the last five years?

She turned toward the short platform to the right of
the doorway, where the teachers stood, waiting. Next to
them stood her aunt, her matching copper hair cut short
and swaying in the breeze. She smiled at her niece's
approach, and Zayira couldn't help but think about
how much she and Zayira's mother, Marya, looked
alike when they smiled. A scant ten steps brought them
together, and before she knew it her aunt removed her

old silver pin and handed it to her. She replaced it with a new one that shone gold in the sunlight and bore not one, but three symbols: a golden storm cloud with a lightning bolt, a golden whirlwind, and a silver sun set behind the others. "Congratulations," her aunt whispered. They turned to face the crowd and Zayira felt her face melt into the biggest smile she'd ever worn. She'd earned this day. She was determined to make the best of it.

Later that evening the student body and visiting families met in the dining hall for a celebratory feast. Zayira and her aunt spent the evening trading stories with the rest of their family to catch up on the goings-on from Joveru to Farmer's Bend to Weatherwatch and beyond. Glorya had heard from Hulvai some months prior; he'd finished his own apprenticeship with a renowned windwaker in Zhedaba and signed on with a new tribe to help establish a new trade route between the city and Garobi. Zayira was happy for him, even though he'd stopped answering her letters. She was sure he was far too busy making a name for himself in the land that had held his curiosity his whole life. Glorya herself had finished setting up a system at each port town across Midlands and Zhedaba for advertising work for weatherworkers by rank and was expanding it to Temalingar in the next year. Ma and Pa still had the farm, but Maks and his wife were set to take over when they decided to retire, leaving Danil to find his own way in the world. He still hadn't settled on a profession.

Zayira took the opportunity to announce her own intention of heading to Riverbranch, where she planned to find work at the great library. A few of her school acquaintances had settled there, and they promised to put in a good word for her with the librarians. The way she saw it, she'd spent her whole life bouncing between farmlands and a secluded valley; some time in the city, learning what life was like for its denizens, sounded fascinating. Everyone agreed it was a wonderful plan.

Finally, after too much food and a late night filled with talking, Zayira retired to her room. She belatedly remembered to find Peony and a few others before turning in; the Zhedaban students would never forgive her if she didn't at least say goodbye before she left. So she made the rounds, earning hugs and teary well-wishes, then turned in for the night.

As always, she was up with the dawn, except this time there would be no arms practice unless she was accosted on the road. Armsmaster Rylen had her teaching the younger students now, so she felt confident in her abilities, but hoped she wouldn't need to use them. She washed her face, dressed, donned her new pin, and reached for the pack containing her clothes and a few belongings–only to realize it was heavier than when she'd packed it. Her brow furrowed. Was this some sort of practical joke? It would be just like Danil to stick rocks in the bottom of her pack just to tire her out. She untied the top and peeked inside.

Atop her clothes sat a shortsword with a leather-wrapped handle. Its well-worn sheath was familiar; she'd practiced with it every day for three years, ever since she'd chosen a weapon. It was blunt when she practiced with it, but as she drew it she could tell the edge had been honed. A hastily-scrawled note beside it just said "Keep it close." *Armsmaster Rylen's handwriting.* The gift touched her more than she could express. Beside it she found a letter postmarked a few days prior

from Joveru in another hand she recognized. *Hulvai.*
She ripped it open and devoured the news inside. He
apologized for the delay in writing, but he'd gone
abroad for some time at the end of his apprenticeship to
help a Zhedaban trade ship navigate the perilous seas
just north of Weatherwatch. It did her heart good to
know he'd faced his fear of his people's retribution. She
resolved to write to him as soon as she was settled at
Riverbranch.

Tucking the letter back into her bag, she took up the
sword and threaded it onto her belt, determined not to
travel alone and unarmed when she had another option. Then she took up her pack, took one more glance
around her room, and strode out the door.

The early sun hadn't yet peeked above the cliff
walls, but the ring of steel from the practice field let
Zayira know that the next generation of students was
up and about to gain an education in self defense. She
waved at the armsmaster as she passed, and he jogged
across the field to see her.

"Thought you could leave without saying goodbye
too, did you?" He wrapped her in a great bear hug.

"Too? Who else tried?" Her voice was muffled
against his chest.

"Why, your aunt, of course!" The armsmaster released her to hold her at arm's length. "She stole away
late last night to camp in the foothills. I think she just
spent too much time with people the last two days and
it got to her." He winked.

"Thank you for the gift." Zayira fingered the hilt
of her familiar weapon. "I have a long journey ahead of
me, and it'll make me feel far more comfortable knowing I have my own protection."

"I think you'll find a little more in that pack of yours, too. Best be sure to keep it close." The twinkle in the armsmaster's eye made her curious, but she didn't want to delay her departure long enough to look. She'd sort through it again the first time she stopped. "Now, get out of here! The day is young and so are you." He turned her around and gave her a gentle shove toward the pass. "Give my best to everyone at Riverbranch!" he called to her back. She waved over her shoulder and walked on, eager to meet whatever fate had in store.

ALSO BY
EMILY BARLOW

SUNCHASER
(BOOK ONE OF THE WEATHERWORKER CHRONICLES)

THE RAVEN'S CHILDREN

INVOLUNTARILY IMMORTAL

Sunchaser

She can bend the weather to her will...but will it help her forge her own path?

A small inland farm and a valley in the mountains are all Glorya has ever known. When she graduates from weatherworking school penniless, she must rely on her ingenuity and determination to make a name for herself. Her resourcefulness earns her a berth on a ship in exchange for protection against the foul weather that runs rampant off the coast.

But the coastal weather–and the people who sail through it–are unlike anything Glorya has ever experienced. Soon she finds herself navigating both extreme weather and new cultures as she struggles to make a place for herself in the world.

Will it be enough? Or will the raw power of nature combine with deadly foes to defeat her before she has a chance to prove herself?

*** Note: Sunchaser is a novella consisting of three short stories that introduce Glorya Sunchaser as she begins her adventures.

The Raven's Children

An ailing king. Three successors to the throne. A kingdom on the brink of turmoil.

Ambjorg, Asbjorn, and Audolf watch as their father, King Hrafn, wastes away before their eyes. Figures lurk in the shadows, waiting for the right moment to strike and steal the crown. And all the while the three siblings and their father share a secret: an affinity with animals they use to keep their homeland safe.

As tragedy strikes the royal family, reports of attacks by aberrant beasts start to trickle in. The siblings are split in many directions, thrust into new responsibilities that test their resolve and their bonds. It will take every skill and ally they have to best whomever--or whatever--is behind all the unrest. But will it be enough?

Or will they lose both their kingdom and the lives of the ones they love?

Involuntarily Immortal

Sable Montgrief wishes her curse would let her die. Unfortunately for her, fate has other plans.

Living alone in a cabin for decades, Sable has done her best to break the spell cast on her that has extended her life for centuries. She never wanted immortality; in fact, she's spent the majority of her long life trying to end it. Her latest attempt has her so close to breaking free she can taste it...until someone breaks down her door to find her.

Adem Ozturk is looking for someone to help his daughter, Ailith, who is plagued with visions of the future she can neither manage nor interpret. They're on the run from an unknown organization with unlimited reach and are up against a wall–until Adem's wife sends a message to Ailith from beyond the grave, sending them to find Sable and recruit her to their cause. If they can convince her to help they may be able to not only save Ailith, but prevent a global cataclysm. The cost: another lifetime of torturous existence for Sable.

If they fail, she'll be trapped in eternal torment; if they succeed, she'll still lose everything she loves.

ABOUT THE AUTHOR

A software architect by day, Emily enjoys reading, writing, knitting, crocheting, sewing, running, and learning martial arts with her family in her spare time. She is supported by her longtime husband and two wonderful children, who endure her eccentricities with enthusiasm.

For more information and to join her mailing list, visit https://emilybarlowwritesthings.com or scan the QR code below!